Chariots of Heaven

R.T. Edwins

DEDICATION

I'd like to dedicate this work to a couple of people. The first is to my late friend, Chris. I wouldn't be the person I am today were it not for your friendship, and the world is less because of your absence.

Second, I'd like to acknowledge my beloved wife. Without her help and dedication, this book would have never been finished and wouldn't be nearly as good as it is. I love you, Sarah.

ACKNOWLEDGMENTS

I'd like to thank the following individuals for their belief in me and this story. Without their contributions and willingness to support my dream, this novel would have never gotten off the ground.

Pablo Altamirano
John Perman
Jeff Peterson
Ron Ruby
Megan Spafford
& My Mom, Terry

R.T. Edwins

PROLOGUE:

The long halls of the Trident were dark and shadowy. There was scarcely enough light for Aeria to see where she was walking, but she knew the way. Every step she took was surefooted, and the white marble under her feet gleamed in the dim blue light as she made her way down the long corridor.

Although she was not particularly tall, Aeria was ever the figure of power and strength. Even the way she walked down the empty corridor in her gleaming silver armor exhibited her unfaltering will. Each step was firm and filled with intent, never wavering from her purpose. By all accounts she was quite beautiful, with piercing blue eyes and short, radiant golden hair. She looked a great deal like her father, although his hair had lost its golden hue centuries earlier.

It was to him that she was walking, and on this day she had the highest purpose. They had finally found the crown jewel of the twelve kingdoms, which had been lost to the heavens over two thousand years before. She, the greatest of Velion's children, had rediscovered it. Great pride swelled in her chest as she marched towards his meditation chamber.

She could finally see the massive, white marble doors at the end of the hall. They were brighter than the rest of the passage, illuminated by lights recessed in the ceiling. As she approached the doors, they began to slide silently apart, disappearing into the walls.

Her drifting thoughts faded as she passed the doors and entered a cavernous room. This room was much brighter than the corridor leading to it, almost too bright. It was circular, with high vaulted ceilings and large, rounded pillars that towered above her.

As she passed the inner row of columns she could see a solitary being sitting in a large chair on a raised platform in the center of the room. The platform was surrounded by floating torches flickering with blue flames and high above it, floating in the air, was a giant rotating gyroscope. The massive brass bands of the gyro revolved gracefully within each other, emitting only a quiet *whooshing* sound as she approached her father. It was no wonder to her that the civilizations they ruled over saw them as gods.

She climbed the shimmering steps to the first tier of the platform, her armor clinking quietly with each step. Bending on one knee, she lowered her eyes to the floor and said, "My lord father."

Velion opened his eyes and peered down at his daughter with irritation. Curtly he asked, "Yes? Why have you interrupted my meditation?"

Aeria had expected this reaction, but she knew her purpose was worthy of the disturbance, and with a grin, she looked up at her father. Standing, she announced, "My lord father, we have finally found it! We have found Earth."

All irritation disappeared from Velion's face and with eagerness he asked, "Are you certain? I will not be amused if you have made a mistake. Show me!"

With her grin widening, Aeria pulled a small metallic cylinder from within the confines of her armor. She pressed one of the buttons on the side, and it was illuminated with a piercing green light. Growing brighter and brighter for a few moments, the light burst forth into a large holographic projection. Spinning silently in the air, a blue-green projection of a planet approximately twenty feet wide hovered above her head. No longer being able to conceal her excitement, Aeria exclaimed, "See father, I told you I would be the one to find it!"

Velion's eyes gleamed in the light of the projection and with great satisfaction, he examined the artifact before him. He knew that she was right. He knew that they had finally found what they were looking for; he only hoped it would not be their undoing...

CHAPTER 1

Kira's hair fluttered gently in the cool breeze, and the light of the full moon shone in her hazel eyes. She began to rub her arms, letting out a shiver as the cold air moved across her smooth skin. Despite the cold, she loved looking up at the night sky. Something about the way the stars floated silently in the heavens seemed to call to her, and although she couldn't explain it, she knew there was more to them.

She was alone in this sentiment, however, as no one else in her village seemed to care about the lights in the sky; except perhaps her sister. No, they rarely seemed to worry about anything besides food or danger or displeasing the spirits. *What a silly thing to worry about*, she thought.

Nothing in her seventeen years of life had convinced her that these so-called spirits existed. Yet her village believed that everything in life was determined by their favor and even claimed that long ago, they had come down from the sky to create her people in their image. *What an irrational idea!* She thought to herself. If these spirits held such power, then why hadn't they healed her father?

Her father was the village elder, and had been taken with a mysterious illness. She had spent the majority of the last week at his bedside, trying to nurse him back to health, but nothing seemed to work. As she stared up at the heavens, she wondered what her mother would do if she was still alive. She would probably comfort her and reassure her that everything would be okay, but sadly, this was not possible.

Breathing in the cool autumn air, Kira remembered back to her mother's passing. She had died several years earlier after being brutally attacked by a sabercat on a night similar to this one. Kira remembered the look of the vile beast as clearly as if it had been yesterday.

Pushing the painful thoughts from her mind, she tried not to cry. Her thoughts drifted back to her father, who despite her care only seemed to be growing sicker. Worst of all, his ability to communicate had left him. When he spoke to her now, his words were nonsense, and his conversation only served to confuse and frighten her.

The village shaman asserted that the spirits were punishing her father, because he had let the last hunting party go without heeding his warnings. She detested the man, but even she had to admit that the last hunting expedition ended dreadfully. They were almost immediately caught in a terrible storm which prevented them from finding any game. What was worse was that her uncle Druin injured his ankle during the trip, and one of the others became deliriously sick, the way her father was now. He had gone to visit the sick hunter, and had become ill the next night, collapsing during the nightly storytelling. When he briefly came around several hours later, he spoke three words to Kira; three words that continued to haunt her days later. "They are coming."

Who was coming? She wondered to herself. *Who had he been speaking of? Was there another village coming to attack?* She dismissed the thought, knowing that wasn't it. Out of fear the elders had sent out scouting parties to check for invaders. There were no invaders... no one was coming.

The other villagers believed it was just his delirium from the fever and had decided to ignore his words, but she couldn't. When he spoke the words to her, he pulled her close and looked her square in the eye with a terrified expression that shook her to her core. He had not been delirious the way he was now. He knew exactly what he was saying and that she needed to hear the words, *but what did they mean?*

Kira shook her head and pushed the thoughts away as her little sister walked up to her. Kaya looked very little like Kira, with long sandy blonde hair and green eyes. She was a tall and lanky girl, standing almost as high as Kira. Only thirteen, Kaya also seemed older than she was; being more mature than Kira had been at that age. Kira suspected that it was the harder living conditions that had made her sister that way. When Kira was a girl, life was relatively easy; it wasn't until Kaya's second year that the droughts began, and the food became less plentiful. What was worse was that their mother died the very next year, adding grief to the starved conditions.

"Why do you stare up at them so much?" Kaya whispered as she stopped next to Kira. "Do they ever do anything different?"

Looking down at her, Kira smiled lovingly, "I stare at them because I believe I am supposed to." Pausing for a moment, she realized she had never said that to anyone before. She didn't really know what it meant, but it was something she always felt. Maybe her father's illness was affecting her more than she thought.

"How do you know?" Kaya seemed confused.

"I don't know, I just... know. It's always been something I've felt. Just like I've always felt that you were supposed to be my sister." With her worry diminishing, Kira gently punched Kaya in the arm.

"Ow!!" It didn't really hurt, but Kaya pretended it did anyways as she rubbed her arm. "What do you mean? Like the spirits decided it?"

Kira took a moment to consider this. Shrugging she said, "Maybe... all I know is there is something really important about those lights up there, and I think that I'm supposed to find out what it is." This time Kira pinched her sister and took off, running back towards their hut. Kaya giggled and chased after her.

* * *

Slightly out of breath, Kira was the first to make it back to their hut. Having almost forgotten about her father's condition, she stopped short at the entry. Her sister, also lost in the moment, nearly ran into her and both of them had to stifle their laughter before they could go inside.

Kira adored her sister. Most of the time, they seemed more like friends than siblings, although this was probably a result of the fact that there weren't many other people in the village around Kira's age.

This was also the reason Kira had not bonded with a man. She was more than old enough for the ritual, but there were no boys her age. This, however, didn't bother her as she'd never really been too concerned with bonding; an effect, most likely, of her mother's untimely death. She never really had an older female to spend time with, except maybe Yamara, her father's cousin and the village wet nurse. At the request of their father, Yamara kept a watchful eye over the girls after their mother's death, but was far from a mother herself.

Once the girls collected themselves, they quietly entered the hut. It was hot and stuffy inside, and seemed to get warmer as they approached their father's bed. He was still sleeping, but his breathing was labored; every few moments letting out a whimper, as if he were in pain. Yamara was sitting next to his bed, holding a damp cloth to his head. By the looks of it, his fever still had not broken, and the concerned look on Yamara's face told them that he was getting worse. Exchanging worried looks, they sat on the floor next to Yamara.

"What can we do?" Kira asked.

"Child, I'm not sure there is anything anyone can do." Yamara replied, shaking her head in disappointment. The sisters exchanged disheartened glances. "I am afraid to say it, but I think your father is only going to get worse. Conran, the sick hunter your father visited, is also getting worse and I'm not sure he will survive the night. All we can do is beg for the spirits to hear our prayers and heal your father." Yamara finished with a grave look.

Tears began to well in Kira's eyes and she could see that her sister was also starting to cry. She knew that she had to be strong for Kaya; strong like she had been when their mother died. Wiping the tears from her own eyes, she put her arm around Kaya and pulled her close. She tried to comfort her by running her fingers through Kaya's long blonde hair, but the young girl's tears turned into labored sobs. The tears started to well in her own eyes again as she wondered to herself, *what would they do? How would they live without their father?* Kira felt angry and helpless.

"I don't want him to die!" Kaya gasped between her sobs. Pushing away from the embrace, she looked to Kira. The tears streaming down her cheeks were almost too much for Kira to bear. She wanted to comfort her, wanted to say he would be okay, but she couldn't find the words.

"Now, you two." Yamara stood up and with a frown said, "Dry your eyes. You know your father wouldn't want you worrying about him, and it's time for bed anyway. There's nothing either of you can do right now besides let him rest. We'll worry again in the morning. Off with you!" pulling both of them to their feet and waving her hands as if she were chasing a chicken out of the yard, Yamara shooed the girls off to their beds.

Neither one said anything as they crawled into their beds. The day had been long and trying for both of them and it didn't take long for either of them to find sleep. Before Yamara left for the night, she made sure each girl was tucked in; covering them with additional furs. Putting out the small fire that had been burning in the hearth, she departed.

As the light diminished inside the hut, soft sounds of sleep could be heard behind her. It would be the last time in a long while that either of the girls would get a decent night's rest.

CHAPTER 2

Falling... spinning... innumerable white lights rotating in all directions. Kira tried to scream but couldn't find any air. Was this the end? Flexing her muscles she found that she had great strength, almost... abnormal strength; more than she could have ever imagined. Gritting her teeth she managed to slow the spin; the blurring lights twisted less quickly and she was able to get some bearings. She could see something below her now, a large blue and green sphere. It floated silently in the ocean of starlit blackness. It seemed familiar to her but she couldn't remember where she had seen it. Straining with all of her might, she was able to stop the spin, but she was still falling, and gaining speed by the second. She knew this wasn't good. She knew that she had failed.

Hopelessness filled her stomach as she watched the large blue-green ball grow larger and larger as she fell towards it. She knew there was no way to survive the fall, so she stopped fighting and let go. There was nothing she could do but accept her demise, so she closed her eyes and whispered a prayer. "Spirits, if you do exist please don't let her kill Kaya. She is just a child..."

Tears welled in her eyes. First she let her father down, and now she was letting her sister down. It wasn't fair! She had done everything she could to protect her, but somehow it hadn't been enough. She looked up. There it was, just floating there; that dreadful monstrosity that brought all the trouble. The sight of it lit a fire within her and she knew she couldn't give up. Anger now replaced the hopeless feeling in the pit of her stomach and rage boiled in every fiber of her being. Finding enough air this time she roared "NO!! Not like this! I will not let you take her!!!!!"

* * *

"Kira!" Yamara was shaking the girl with all of her strength. "Kira, wake up!! WAKE UP! You are dreaming!"

Kira's eyes flew open. She was soaked in sweat, and her heart was racing. Yamara had a startled look on her face.

"Child, it was just a dream. Shhh..." Yamara hugged Kira tightly as she sat in her bed panting. "It was just a dream... you're okay."

"Where's Kaya?!" Pushing Yamara away and looking around the hut wildly, Kira spotted her sister standing by their father's bed, hugging a fur blanket and looking both frightened and confused.

"Child, be still! You were dreaming." Yamara grabbed both of Kira's cheeks and forced her to look into her eyes, in a comforting voice she said, "Your sister is just fine. She is safe and sound, albeit probably a little terrified with all the screaming." Letting go of her cheeks she forced Kira to lay back down.

Feeling disoriented Kira asked, "Screaming? Who was screaming?"

With her face growing more concerned by the moment Yamara replied, "Why, you child. You let out a terrible howl and then started screaming something about having to save Kaya. I think you woke half the village." Yamara explained as she examined the girl, holding her hand against her forehead to check for fever. Finding Kira's head cool to the touch a look of relief spread across Yamara's face and she asked, "Do you remember what you were dreaming about?"

Kira tried to reach for the place she had just been, but like water slipping between her fingers the images faded from her mind. Frustrated, she replied, "I don't… remember. I think I was falling, but I don't know where I was. It was someplace I had never seen before."

Frowning, Yamara tucked Kira back under her fur covers. "Hush now, child. Just rest. It is not yet morning." Yamara turned her head and squinted in the dim light. "Kaya, don't be afraid. Your sister was just having a nightmare. You can come back to bed now."

Hesitant to move, Kaya crawled back into her bed, her teeth chattering as she did so. Kira wasn't certain if she was shivering from the cold morning air, or from having been awakened so suddenly. She wanted to comfort her, but before she could say anything Kaya covered herself and turned on her side, facing away from her. It would have to wait.

Yamara bent over and kissed Kaya on the side of her head, whispering something that Kira couldn't hear. Whatever it was, it seemed to help, as Kaya began to relax under her fur blankets. Yamara stood to leave, but stopped. She looked back at Kira with a worried expression. She opened her mouth to say something, but reconsidered before the words came out. Closing her mouth awkwardly she simply nodded, and turned to leave.

Kira wondered what she was about to say, but decided she could just ask her later that day. She let out a long sigh as her thoughts wandered back to her dream. *What had that place been?* It all seemed so familiar, like she had been there before. But how could that be? She'd only ever lived here, in the village. She supposed it didn't really matter. It was only a dream, even if it had felt real.

Letting out another deep sigh, Kira closed her eyes and started to drift back to sleep. Everything became less pronounced as her breathing steadied and images of her sister's face floated through her mind like reflections in water. She knew she had to protect her, it didn't matter what from; she had to be there for her, no matter what.

* * *

Footsteps. They had a quickened pace. Kira slowly opened her eyes as she heard the steps. The gravel underfoot scraped as they came to a stop outside the hut's entrance. Clearing his throat, a man's raspy voice called out, "Ms. Kira, may I enter? I have important news!"

She knew the voice, and she also knew that she was not fond of the owner. It was the village shaman, the one who blamed her father for his own illness. Wishing she didn't have to answer, she called back, "Yes, Felmar, come in." She sat up in her bed, swinging her feet over the side. As he entered the hut Kaya started to shift and with a sleepy look, she peered at Kira looking for an explanation. Shrugging, Kira wiped the sleep from her eyes and yawned, forgetting to cover her mouth.

Felmar frowned at her, which was not all that unusual; he was always frowning at her. This might have been part of the reason she didn't like the man, but mostly it was because she didn't trust him. Many years earlier, he claimed to have been visited by the spirits, who he insisted had ordained him to be their spokesperson, but Kira was convinced he was as devious as he was mad. He unnerved her, the way he always seemed to scheme and plot, and she didn't like the way he used his "gift" to influence the villagers. She often tried to convince her father to stop listening to this old serpent and make him leave the village, but he never did heed her warnings. He would just roll his eyes, chuckle, and change the subject.

Felmar stood just inside the hut for a long moment. Losing patience, Kira curtly said, "I thought you said you had news. Or did you simply decide you wanted to spend your morning watching me yawn?"

To her amazement, Felmar found a way to frown even more than he already was. Squinting his eyes he replied, "It is a good thing your father isn't awake. I'd hate for him to see his oldest daughter be so *rude* to the man who has come to save him."

Kira wrinkled her brow and with a tone of skepticism asked, "Oh? And how are you going to save my father, Felmar? Did the *spirits* give you healing powers?"

Anger flashed in Felmar's eyes. Kira had hit the nerve she had always wanted to. She felt satisfied, but when she saw the concerned look on her sister's face she decided to let it go. Gritting his teeth Felmar spat back, "Fine! If you don't want to hear what I have to say, then I'll be on my way." He began to move toward the door. Kaya gasped and looked indignantly at her sister.

With a sigh, Kira called after him, "Felmar, wait. Don't leave." He paused in the doorway and looked back at her. He was trying to appear irritated, but she could tell he was enjoying this. His eyes told her that he loved having something to hold over them. Swallowing her pride, Kira asked, "What is your news? How can you save our father?"

Something flickered in his eyes, and with a malicious grin he said, "Ask me nicely, and I might still tell you." Raising his chin he glared down his crooked nose at Kira. She knew that she had to play along. He wouldn't be going to such dramatic measures if it wasn't worth her time.

Straining to sound as genuine as she could, she asked in a polite voice, "Please tell me what news you have, Felmar. I am sorry I was so rude to you." He didn't seem to be buying it.

Squinting his eyes again, he considered Kira for a moment. They both knew she hadn't really meant it, but shrugging he seemed to give in. "Apology accepted. Now, what I have to tell you is not something to be taken lightly, child. Your attitude regarding the spirits is troubling, but you'll have to overcome whatever doubts you have if you're going to save your father."

"Wait. I thought you said *you* were going to save him," Kira reminded him, suddenly confused.

With a wicked grin growing across his face, Felmar said "Oh forgive me, I didn't mean to mislead you." They both knew that had been exactly what he had meant to do. "I meant to say that I have information that *you* could use to save him."

Frustration began to set in as Kira asked, "What does that even mean? What information do you have?"

"The spirits have revealed to me a cure for your

father's sickness, but it won't be easy to obtain. In fact it's an almost impossible journey." Felmar's wide grin indicated that he was enjoying this exchange thoroughly.

Kira was torn between her contempt for this shrewd old bastard and her desire to see her father well again. She looked over at him sleeping quietly in his bed. The color in his face had faded from the night before and she knew it was only a matter of time. Filling with anger her eyes darted back to Felmar.

"Enough games, old man! Just tell me what I have to do." She was so angry, she barely noticed Yamara enter the hut behind Felmar.

"What's happening in here? Why are *you* here?" Yamara interjected with a concerned look. She noticed Kira's irritated expression almost immediately and with an extended, pointy finger, poked Felmar hard in the shoulder. He grimaced in pain and started to rub the spot she had touched. Kira knew from experience that Yamara could poke a person surprisingly hard, especially if she meant it.

With a smug look Felmar replied, "I was just telling this *impolite* child that the spirits visited me last night. They told me of a flower that, if ground up and made into a tea, would cure her father's illness."

Yamara's eyes widened with excitement, "Truly? They came to you and told you this? Where is this flower found? I'll take a group to gather some."

Felmar's beady eyes returned to Kira, and they twinkled as he said, "I'm sorry Yamara, but I don't think you'll be able to find this flower. You see, it can only be found in the Black Wood that grows to the west; where the sun sets." All the air in the room seemed to evaporate as he finished his sentence. Kira, Kaya, and Yamara peered at one another not knowing what to say.

The Black Wood was a terribly dangerous place. Every person who had ever gone there, either did not return, or came back mortally wounded. No one survived the Black Wood; there were too many predators in the dark and overgrown forest. No one ventured there, not for anything.

After a few moments of silence, Kira swallowed hard. She realized this was why he had been so ill-tempered with her. He had never liked her or the way she dismissed his "gift", and she knew he had to be reveling in the idea of her running off into such danger; but there was more to it than that. Felmar had always been a slippery and calculating man. He always kept an eye out for any opportunity to take over the role of village elder, especially since he had become their spiritual leader.

Her heart sank as all the pieces began to fall into place. Felmar hadn't been visited by the spirits, any more than he had been originally. He'd known all along about this flower, but didn't mention anything until Kira and her family were desperate; desperate enough that they would have no other choice but to go on a suicide mission. Kira couldn't just let her father die, but she knew she would be the only one willing to go. The village's people loved her father, but they were already whispering about his coming death, as if it were written in stone.

Felmar planned this, she thought spitefully. He knew she would have no choice but to go by herself; the only other person who would have cared enough to try was her uncle Druin, and he was injured. By the look on Felmar's face, she could tell he fully expected this to be a one way trip. With her out of his way and her father dead from this illness, there would be no one left to stop him from taking over as elder. Even her uncle wouldn't be able to contend with him, and knowing Felmar's manipulative ways, he would just convince the villagers that the spirits ordained him as their new leader. She loved her people, but she knew the fools would believe him, just as they always did.

Kira let out a sigh and asked, "What does this flower look like, Felmar? How would I know it from any other?"

Felmar knew he had won, and with a wicked sneer, he replied, "The flower is called the Night's Widow. It is dark blue, with white dots on the outside petals. It grows most commonly among the mushrooms that feed on fallen trees. You'll know it when you see it. The problem is, they are solitary plants, and each one produces just one blossom at a time. We need the petals from two of them to be sure the tea will work." Kira couldn't tell if he was lying or not. He was not known for outright deception, but he did have a knack for bending the truth when it suited his goals. She suspected he was just trying to guarantee she would fail her task by asking for two, but there was no choice. She would have to find two to be sure.

"You can't be serious, child! You can't go running off to the Black Wood! Have you lost your senses?" Yamara shrieked, giving Kira a scolding look. It was a legitimate question. Something about her father's illness had changed Kira. Even she had to admit that she'd been acting strangely the past few nights. Her hesitation set Yamara off, "I won't let you! Your father certainly wouldn't! What would he say if he was awake?!"

Kira got to her feet, closed her eyes and let out another sigh. She whispered, "but he isn't awake, Yamara. And if I don't go, he will never wake up." In the corner of her eye she could see that Kaya had started to cry.

"You don't know that!" Yamara's anger was evident in her voice.

"Actually..." Felmar interjected, "I went to see the hunter who had the same illness, oh what was his name again... Conran! Yes I went to see him this morning. I'm sorry to report that he is no longer with us. Which means it is very important we find these flowers within the day, otherwise I'm afraid her father will leave us as well." This news silenced everyone. Even Kaya stopped crying for a moment.

There was no other choice. Kira shook her head and said, "Then there is no time to lose. I'll need to leave immediately if I'm going to make it back by tomorrow." Kira turned and started shuffling through her possessions. She knew she would need supplies if she was going to survive this. She expected Yamara to try and stop her, but thankfully, she didn't.

CHAPTER 3

The morning air was cool and humid as the red-orange sun still hung low on the horizon. The dew from the cool night had not yet evaporated and Kira could hear the birds beginning to rustle and chirp in the nearby trees. She pulled the strap of her leather satchel over her head and rested it on her shoulder. Pulling her long brown hair out from under the satchel's strap, she tugged at the sheath on her waist, confirming its presence. Her shale stone knife inside it held fast. The satchel rested comfortably on her opposite hip. Inside the bag, she had packed a skin of water, some fruit and berries, and a small portion of jerky. She knew the journey was long and that there would be no guarantee of dinner, but she couldn't risk weighing herself down if she hoped to make the journey in under a day.

Kira squinted in the low hanging sun as she peered up at her uncle Druin. He had a frown on his face. He didn't think she should go, but knew he wouldn't be able to convince her to stay. He had learned the hard way that Kira was a stubborn and headstrong girl, much like her mother had been. The two were more alike than either would have admitted, and he knew that if his sister was still alive, she'd be quite proud of her daughter.

He had witnessed firsthand Kira's headstrong nature by being the one to teach her how to hunt and fight. At first he had refused to instruct her as it wasn't customary for women to go to war, let alone on the hunt, but eventually he gave in. Since then, she had become exceptionally strong and fast, and was by far the greatest warrior in the village, although he would never admit it in front of the others.

Kira reached out for her spear, but Druin paused a moment before handing it to her. "I wish I could come with you..." he lamented, as he tested his ankle again. He was immediately punished by a sharp, shooting pain. Wincing he asked, "Are you certain that you want to do this?"

"What choice do I have? Just sit here and watch him die?" She shook her head. "I can't let that happen." Looking down at her sister, Kira saw that she had tears in her eyes again.

"Please let me come with!" Kaya pleaded as the tears rolled down her cheeks. "I can help! I promise!"

Kira grabbed her sister's hand, her heart breaking as she shook her head no. "I'm sorry. This time I have to go alone."

"Why?!" Kaya protested.

"It's too dangerous. I shouldn't even be going, but no one else can, or will. You need to stay here with Uncle Druin and Yamara. Take care of them while I'm gone." Kaya tried again to protest but Kira pressed on, "Don't leave father's side either, until I come back. You understand me?"

Crying too hard to speak, Kaya gave in and

nodded her head. Kira let go of her hand and turned back to the others. Wiping the tears that were welling in her own eyes, Kira tried to compose herself. Letting out a long breath she began to walk towards the village gate.

"Good luck," her uncle called.

As she passed through the village's gate she looked back over her shoulder and could see that Druin, Yamara and Kaya were still watching her. She waved and they waved back. *Don't worry about me, I'll be back soon enough,* she thought as she turned back and quickened her pace. She knew she would have to be fast; as there was precious little time.

After a few minutes she reached the top of the first hill and stopped for a moment to survey the path ahead. Rolling hills, strewn with occasional trees, sprawled out before her for miles, but despite how far she could see there was no sign of the Black Wood. She knew it would be a few hours before she'd be able to see it and she wasn't looking forward to that. Checking her satchel and knife one last time, she firmly grasped her spear and began to jog down the hill towards her destination.

* * *

Velion's smile faded for a moment. Seeming to remember something, a dark look passed over his face. Looking away from the projection of the planet, he asked, "Have we conducted a scan of the surface yet?"

Aeria, slightly disappointed by his lack of enthusiasm, replied, "No... not yet father. We won't be within scanning range for about another day. The image on the holoprojection was collected from one of the scouting drones I dispatched a few days ago." She smiled, hoping to hear his praise.

Velion's eyes returned to the projection before him. Still looking grim, he said, "I see. Well then that gives us plenty of time to make preparations. We will need to assemble scouting teams in order to survey the surface for any mineable deposits. We will also need to prepare a fighter squadron to escort the scouting teams." He paused for a moment, thinking to himself. After a several seconds he finished, "I will also travel to the surface myself, so my ship will need to be readied. Do you think you can handle all of that?"

Disappointed by his coldness, she responded, "Of course, Father. Should I also dispatch a messenger back to Tython to report on our success?" This time, her eagerness betrayed her.

Velion scrutinized her and coldly he replied, "Seeking glory again, are you? No, we will not send a messenger. I want to stand before the council myself and tell them when *I* am ready. All in good time, Aeria. Now go; leave me to my meditation."

After kneeling once more, Aeria stood to leave. She marched out of the cavernous room with less confidence than when she'd entered, feeling frustrated at her father's indifference to the news. She felt a surge of anger as she made her way out of the chamber. He hadn't even acknowledged that *she* was the one to find it! Instead he just sent her on another errand, as if she hadn't just discovered the most precious of treasures. They had only been searching for it for *thousands* of years. *And what was that look he had on his face?* She wondered to herself, as the massive doors behind her quietly slid shut. She rarely knew what her father was thinking, but she had never seen him with such a grim look before. Or had she?

As she walked back down the long corridor she

searched her memory. Closing her eyes, a flash of a memory came to her. She remembered running through the courtyard outside of her home on Tython; the Goralia trees were in full bloom and the sweet smell of their blue flowers filled the palace courtyard. She wasn't supposed to be there, but she had skipped out on her lessons with the high priest. He was a boring old man, and a lesser one at that. It was silly that she had to learn from him, considering she was of royal descent and he was part of the lowest caste. Aeria recalled how irritated she had been that day, but could no longer remember the reason why.

She remembered running up the steps and hearing raised voices coming from within her house. Bending to hold her ear against the keyhole, she tried to listen through the door to determine who was inside but she was unable to understand the words or who was saying them. She decided to crawl into the bushes under one of the open windows. From there she peeked into the living area and saw her father arguing with her uncle Hadius.

She remembered overhearing Hadius say, "You know as well as I do that it didn't happen that way! He's meddled with something that could undo us all! We cannot ignore this! What happens if it gets out and the Centuri discover our weakness? It could destroy everything we've worked for!"

"But it can't be true, Hadius. Why would he have lied to us? How do you know this source can be trusted anyway?" Aeria recalled how skeptical her father had looked.

"Forget the damn source! You are missing the point, Velion. We know that he and his men were overpowered. The only way that that could have happened is if they had used the armor and weapons! Think about the consequences of such a scenario."

And there it was: the look on her father's face. There was no mistaking the memory. Aeria knew he had had the same look then as he did a few moments ago. She stopped short in the corridor and pondered aloud, "What does it mean? What were they arguing about? *'They had used the armor and weapons'*? Who had? Not the lesser ones, surely." She let out a snort of derision and started walking again, shaking off the idea. She knew the lesser ones could never use their armor or weapons. It was their genetics that prevented them from integrating with the technology the way she and her family did. In fact it had been countless years since any species outside of her family could use the technology....

Pushing the thoughts from her mind she returned her focus to the tasks ahead of her. She had much to do and not a lot of time to do it. After passing an intersection of four hallways she approached another set of doors, but this time they did not open. Protruding from the left side of the large white marble doors was a round glowing orb that pulsated with a dim green light. Aeria placed her palm around the orb and it lit up brightly. A moment later a low rumble could be heard. Aeria let go of the orb and stepped back. The green ball sank into the wall and like the doors to her father's chamber, these began to silently glide apart. Instead of opening into a cavernous room, however, they opened to a small round room. Aeria stepped inside and turned around. The marble doors closed in front of her with an almost inaudible thud and a panel of lights illuminated to her left. Without looking, she pressed the uppermost symbol and immediately felt the room start to move upwards. After a few moments it stopped moving and a hidden door behind Aeria quietly slid open. Turning around, Aeria stepped into a large and dimly lit room.

The room was wide and had two levels; the door Aeria entered through stood on the edge of the higher of these two levels. This upper platform stretched out approximately thirty feet in front of her and curved forty feet to either side of her, forming a semi-circle. At the center of this upper level was a large throne-like chair, flanked on both sides by two smaller chairs. In front of each stood a short, white pillar that resembled a stalagmite protruding from the floor of a cave. At the top of each of these rounded pillars rested a glowing green orb; similar to the one that Aeria used to open the doors below. On the outside curve of this higher level sat several work stations, each with large holographic screens that hung above rounded control consoles. In front of each console was a small stool. All of these work stations were being operated by individual soldiers wearing black metallic armor.

A set of steps leading to the lower level sat at each end of the semi-circular platform. This lower level was also filled with various control consoles that sat in three parallel rows, the first and third stretching the width of the room. The middle row was interrupted at the center by what looked like a large round table, the top of which consisted of a shimmering crystal surface illuminated from below by a dim blue glow. At the very end of this lower level, opposite to where she had entered, stood a wide flat wall approximately eighty feet wide by forty feet tall. This wall was covered in the same shimmering crystal surface as the round table below it, and was also illuminated by a faint blue glow.

As she entered the room, all of the soldiers on both platforms ceased their work and stood to attention. A tall man, who had been standing next to the large throne-like chair, turned on his heel to look at Aeria. His long silver hair hung gracefully down his shoulders, shimmering in the dim light as he moved to greet her. With a smile the man bowed gracefully at the waist and said, "Mistress Aeria."

With only the slightest of movements, Aeria nodded at the man. At this gesture the soldiers around the room quietly returned to their consoles, and continued their work.

Standing back up, the silver haired man asked with a tone of excitement, "Well, Mistress, what did your father have to say?"

"Never mind that, we have to begin our preparations for landing on the planet," she replied curtly. Immediately the sting of the short answer could be seen on his face and Aeria knew he was as disappointed by her answer as she had been with her father's reaction.

"Of course, Mistress. What would you have me do?"

* * *

The muscles in Kira's legs were beginning to throb and her feet were going numb. She'd been jogging for what seemed like an eternity. By the warmth of the day and the height of the sun in the sky she could tell it was somewhere near midday. Stopping to catch her breath she examined her surroundings. She had just come out of a grove of trees and was standing at the bottom of a steep, grass covered hill. She knew that she was getting close and suspected that when she got to the top of the hill before her, she would finally be able to see her destination.

Dropping her spear to the ground, she opened her satchel. Pulling out her water skin, she decided that this was as good a place as any to take a break.

Nearly collapsing, she threw off her satchel and dropped to the ground exhausted. Unplugging her water skin, she began to frantically gulp down the refreshing liquid. She drank until she started to gasp for air, but not wanting to consume all of the water, she pulled the skin away and let out a long breath. She wanted to drink the rest, but she knew she had to conserve it for the trip back. There was still a long way to go and she would need it before the end. Refitting the plug, she placed the skin back in her satchel. Feeling the pangs of hunter tug at her stomach, she pulled out a large red apple from the bag and began to ravage it. She knew Yamara would have scolded her lack of manners if she could see her now, but she didn't care. No one would know way out here.

The apple was sweet and ripe. She ate it quickly, barely taking time to breath between bites. Nibbling all the flesh from the center, she tossed the core into a nearby bush and laid back in the grass.

Stretching her legs out and placing her hands behind her head, she stared up at the clouds for a moment. Closing her eyes she steadied her breathing and began to let her mind wander. She could have fallen asleep in the warm sunlight were it another day, but she couldn't allow herself that luxury, knowing that there was so much to lose. Opening her eyes she looked up at the passing clouds again. The throbbing in her legs began to fade and her heartbeat finally slowed back to normal. She could feel her toes again and although she knew she should get up and start running again, she just couldn't bring herself to do it. The cool grass felt too good against her back and she knew that she was making good time. *A little break couldn't hurt,* she thought. *I'll make it back in plenty of time.*

In all the time she'd spent running she hadn't

really thought about her father much. All she had been able to focus on was getting to the Black Wood as fast as she could, but as she laid there she couldn't help but think of him now. He had looked so pale when she kissed him goodbye. What would Kaya do if she couldn't get back in time? Assuming of course that she got back at all! The thought of her sister being left all alone was hard to bear. First their mother died, and now maybe their father as well? How would Kaya even handle that? Kira tried to put herself in her sister's position but she couldn't. She remembered what it was like when they lost their mother, but would it be the same? *It couldn't be,* she thought to herself. Their father had been there for them when their mother died. He had taken care of them, had given them the love and attention that they needed to overcome the hardship.

Closing her eyes again, she thought back to those days. Her father was never the same after the loss of his mate and in the years that followed, he had grown quite protective of Kira and Kaya. They spent almost all of their time together; not that the village was large enough to be apart for long. The only time they would separate was when she went with the hunting parties or when she took Kaya to go foraging for fresh fruit. He would join them when he could, but most of the time there were other, more important matters for him to attend to.

Even though the sisters went foraging often and always returned safely, he always had a peculiar look on his face when they left. One time Kira remembered asking him why he looked so worried. To which he had joked, "I just know how much trouble you and your sister can get into! Rarely is there a day where you two haven't gotten into some sort of mischief."

The memory made her smile as she stared up at

the blue sky. His accusation, of course, was quite true, but the look in his eyes told her something different. It was as if he was worried he would lose them the same way he'd lost their mother.

The memory of her death still haunted Kira, but she pushed the painful images from her mind and closed her eyes again. She decided it would be better to just lay there and relax; to not think or worry about anything for a few minutes. Again she felt the soft tug of sleep, but this time the warmth of the sun and the cool grass on her back were too much to resist. She tried to stay awake, but the quiet rustling of the tall grass in the cool breeze was too soothing. After a few minutes, she had peacefully drifted off to sleep.

* * *

Snap! A twig broke in the nearby grove of trees.

Kira shot up and looked around. Without thinking about it, she grabbed her spear and flew to her feet, ready to attack. With her open hand she wiped the sleep from her eyes. How long had she been out? She looked up at the sky. Judging by the position of the sun, she must have been asleep for at least an hour. What had woken her up? She looked around again, and after a few seconds of searching she spotted something moving in the trees. A shadow was darting from tree to tree, heading toward Kira's left. Her heart started to race as she tried to figure out what it was. *Why did I stop? How could I have fallen asleep? I should have kept going!* She scolded herself. Crouching lower to the ground, she started to walk slowly towards the section of trees where the shadow was. She still couldn't tell what it was, but by its movement, the creature didn't seem to have noticed her. She stopped walking, hoping to avoid drawing its attention. Her spear, however, was still at the ready. If she had a clear shot she would take it, as she couldn't risk having a predator following her into the Black Wood.

The shadow stopped moving to the left and paused for a moment. Kira held her breath, trying to remain as quiet as she could. After a few seconds the figure started moving again, this time heading in her direction. She could hear the rustling in the undergrowth grow louder as it moved closer to her.

Kira could feel her lungs desperately crying out for air, but she couldn't risk giving away her presence. Her pupils dilated with fear, as the sounds of the movement grew louder and louder. She gripped her spear even tighter than before, as she knew her opportunity was coming. Once it moved beyond the inner layer of undergrowth she would have an open shot and she knew her only chance was to catch it off guard with a precise throw. If she missed, she would be forced to either flee or to fight with her knife, which would be no match for a sabercat or wolf.

The blood started racing through her veins as her adrenaline kicked in, making everything seem to slow down. She could see the brown fur of the beast through the foliage. It looked like a wolf's pelt. Readying her spear, she calculated the amount of strength she would need to make the throw. She leaned back, starting to propel the spear forward when she heard a strange sound that made her stop.

First a snap, then a heavy thud as the bush shook violently, followed by a muffled grunt. She held the spear mid-throw and, with wide eyes, surveyed the foliage. She couldn't make it out exactly, but it seemed that the creature had fallen or tripped on something. Her heart was racing. Afraid it would leap from the bush at any moment, she pulled her spear back a second time.

"Ow!" a familiar voice yelled out from the undergrowth. "Well, are you just going to stand there staring at me, or are you going to help me out of this bush?"

Kira let out the breath she had been holding, and gasped another one in. The world started to spin for a moment as she tried not to faint from the lack of air. Steadying herself, she dropped her spear on the ground and walked towards the bush. She knew the voice, and with it she knew things had just gotten much more complicated. Walking over to the bush, she could see her sister Kaya tangled in the branches of the large green plant. She reached her hand down to grasp for her sister's outstretched arm. Grabbing her by the wrist she pulled the lanky girl free from her snare and helped her to her feet.

"What are you doing here?!" Kira scolded.

Looking to the ground sheepishly, Kaya replied, "I followed you."

"Well obviously, otherwise you wouldn't be standing here! But that's not what I meant. Why didn't you stay in the village like I told you to?" Kira's fear was turning into anger and was growing by the second.

Surprised by her sister's irritation, Kaya stuttered, "But... but I wanted to help you!"

"Help me? How? By sneaking up on me and scaring me half to death? I thought you were a wolf! I would have killed you had you not tripped and tangled yourself in that bush!" Kira shouted.

Kaya looked at the ground again, this time with look of shame. Tears welled in her eyes. She had not expected this reaction from her older sister, having assumed Kira would be glad to see her. Kaya did not know what to say, so she just stood there, sullen and sniffling.

"You were supposed to stay with Dad. There was a reason for that! I came alone because it was too dangerous for me to bring you along! Now what am I supposed to do?"

Shaking her head, Kira fumed, pacing back and forth in front of her sister. She gaped at the young girl. *How could she be so reckless?* She thought to herself. *Doesn't she know how dangerous it is out here?* She wanted to calm herself, but how could she? It was far too perilous of a journey to have her sister accompany her, but there wasn't nearly enough time to take her back to the village. She didn't know what to do and after her unplanned nap, time was running short. Succumbing to her frustration, Kira stopped pacing and sat on the ground in front of Kaya. She crossed her legs and arms and let out a long sigh. Kaya followed suit and for a few minutes the two girls did nothing but stare at each other. Kira continued to glare at her sister, trying to figure out what to do, while Kaya, still looking sheepish, sniffled and wiped the tears from her eyes.

Kira wanted to scold her more. She wanted to yell and rant and tell her how foolish she had been, but decided not to. What good would it do? She knew that there was no choice but to bring her sister with. She let out another long sigh and shook her head in disappointment. She couldn't just send Kaya back by herself, not with all the predators that would start roaming in the twilight hours. Honestly, it was a wonder that she had made it safely this far on her own.

No, Kira knew that she had to watch over her, even if it meant a slower pace. She had always been responsible for keeping Kaya safe, and this was no different. She hated the idea of bringing her sister into the most dangerous place she could think of, but decided that having the company might not be so bad. Having someone to talk to would make the trip seem shorter and having a second set of eyes would make finding the flowers easier. Letting go of her anger, she decided that if they were going to make it in time they needed to start moving. As Kira went to stand, she noticed something by the trees. She smiled and looked back at her sister.

"You know... you really should try to be less clumsy, little sister," Kira said softly, smirking as she nodded towards the bush Kaya had been tangled in.

Puzzled by the comment, Kaya looked behind her. At first she didn't understand, but after a moment she noticed that towards the bottom of the bush, a small leather satchel was caught on one of the branches. Instinctively she felt at her hip, just then realizing that she was missing her bag. She looked back at Kira, and without a word both girls started to laugh, all animosity between the two fading in that moment.

Still laughing, Kira got to her feet and walked over to her spear. She picked it up and shook her head. "I really did think you were a wolf. You don't know how close I was to throwing this when you tripped." She looked over her shoulder, smiling at her sister.

Kaya giggled and then, pretending to be a wolf, howled, "Ahwwoooo!!" They both laughed again and although Kira still lamented the danger her sister was in, she decided that she was glad Kaya had come.

After collecting their possessions they started up the hill together, still chatting and laughing about Kaya's wolf impression. The hill wasn't steep, but the tall grass made it difficult to climb. After several minutes they crested the top and what they saw when they got there put an immediate end to the lighthearted mood. Kira had been correct in her assumption that they would be able to see the Black Wood from the hill, but she hadn't anticipated the effect it would have. It was still several miles away, across a large valley of grasslands, but it could not be missed or mistaken. Stretching out across the horizon as far as the eye could see it looked like the coast of a black-green ocean engulfing the land from north to south. What she had not expected, however, were the massive dark storm clouds that hung in the distance, directly above their destination. The sisters exchanged worried looks and Kaya asked, "Do you think they will pass?"

Kira tried to gauge which direction the clouds were moving but couldn't as they didn't appear to be moving at all. She was about to say that she didn't know when a cold humid wind, that smelled of rain, blew in from the direction of the storm clouds. Kira realized that they hadn't looked like they were moving because they were coming straight for them. Dismayed at the development, she looked back at her sister and frowned, "I think we might get wet."

Of all the things Kira had prepared for, a storm was not among them, and by the look of these clouds, there was going to be a mighty one. Far off in the distance, she could see violent lighting striking at the heart of the Black Wood. Without saying anything else, she started jogging down the hill towards the valley, Kaya following close behind. Kira knew that if they had any hopes of missing the storm they would have to make excellent time; she just hoped her sister would be able to keep up. The clouds seemed far enough away that they might be able to make it in and out before the storm struck, but even that seemed like a fool's hope. She knew that it would be nearing sunset by time they reached the edge of the forest, so any hopes of finding the flowers rested on the short period of sunlight they still had. Storm clouds would shorten that period dramatically, and would make finding the flowers near impossible in the dark.

The two girls jogged side by side, silently maintaining a slow but steady pace for some time. Kira knew it would do them no good to be exhausted when they arrived. If anything, the run would probably be the easier part of the journey since the terrain would become thick and overgrown with plant life once they entered the woods. They would be forced to fight their way through the underbrush in order to find the flowers, all the while keeping a watchful eye out for predators.

Thinking about the dangers that could be waiting for them seemed to make Kira's already-fatigued muscles burn with renewed vigor. They had been running for nearly an hour and the familiar sting of her legs and numbness in her feet had returned. She knew that if she didn't take her mind off of the pain, there would be no hope to maintain the speed.

In order to distract herself, she looked over at her sister and was surprised to find that the young girl was keeping pace better than expected. Instead of seeing the kid sister she had cared for over the years, she saw a fearless young woman, determined to not fall behind. Kira couldn't explain it, but seeing this hardened determination made her swell with pride. Having been so young when their mother died, Kaya hadn't been able to fend for herself, so Kira had been forced to take care of her; much like a mother would have. In many ways, Kaya was like a daughter to Kira and as a result, Kaya looked up to her more than anyone else.

Kira smiled with pride as she ran, but the pain in her legs was getting worse. She had to try harder to take her mind off of it, so between gasps of air she asked her sister, "So how did you... escape the village... anyways?"

Kaya grinned, and between her own labored breathing responded, "Well... I pretended to go to the food storage... to get stuff for breakfast... and Yamara bought it... so I just snuck out... when no one was watching."

Kira tried to laugh, but was breathing too heavily to manage anything more than a snort. Still trying to distract herself, she tried to ask another question, but was interrupted before she could. Not paying attention to where she had been running her left foot caught on a large piece of wood buried in the tall grass, causing her to fall to the ground. An explosion of pain shot through her left leg as she landed in the grass. Grabbing her ankle with both hands, she cried out in pain. Kaya came to a stop a few yards away and with a worried look ran back to her sister, asking "What happened? Are you all right?"

The pain was blinding as Kira rolled around on the ground moaning. *Damnit!* She screamed in her mind. *How could I have been so careless?* She didn't know what was worse, the pain coursing through her leg, or knowing that an injury would slow them down even more. Tears welled in her eyes as she rubbed her ankle, trying to feel for any broken bones. There were no protrusions and nothing seemed to be permanently damaged, but that was only a slight comfort as the pain continued to shoot up her leg. She finally managed to speak, "I don't think it's broken, but it's definitely sprained."

Kaya didn't respond at first, seemingly unsure of what to do. She sat next to Kira in the grass and stared at her ankle for a moment before something occurred to her. Her eyes lit up as she pulled open her satchel and started to frantically dig through the contents; finally pulling out a long stretch of leather strapping and a small container filled with green paste. Grinning with pride she pulled Kira's hands away from the injured ankle and began to rub the green paste on the swelling skin. Once she had covered the entire area with the strange smelling substance, she started to tightly wrap the ankle in the leather strap until she had used the length of it. With a hard yank and a loud cry from her sister, Kaya tied the strap off as tightly as she could and asked, "Does it feel any better now?"

At first there wasn't much of a change, but after a few moments the pain did begin to recede. Squeezing her ankle, Kira was astonished at her sister's handiwork. "I think... I'll be okay. Where did you learn to do that?"

Kaya smiled. "Yamara showed me. She started teaching me how to mend injuries while you were away, hunting with the others. I also have some other kinds of medicine in case we need it."

Kira was impressed, and felt even more proud of her sister than she had before she tripped. The pain continued to recede as her ankle tingled with numbness, so she decided to test the foot. With a helping hand from Kaya, she got to her feet; placing only a slight amount of weight on her left foot. The moment she did, the pain returned, although not with the same vigor. She took a few steps, leaning on her spear like a cane and wincing the way her uncle had earlier that morning. The pain was manageable, but it would definitely slow her down. Letting out a sigh, she said, "Well, I don't think I'm going to be able to run any more... but I should still be able to walk."

"I can go on alone, if you think I should?" Kaya suggested.

Kira shook her head. "No. I'm not letting you out

of my sight until we are both safely home. I'm coming with you... just more slowly than before. Although, if you are feeling a desire to be helpful, maybe you could carry my bag for me?"

Kaya smiled and nodded, pulling the satchel off of Kira's shoulder. Placing it over her own shoulder, she tried to support Kira's weight for her as they started to walk again, but Kira shook her head. "No, I can do it. I need you to be at the ready in case something sneaks up on us; I don't want you worrying about keeping me on my feet, when you should be running or hiding. Things will be getting much more dangerous shortly." Looking ahead of her, Kira could tell that the Black Wood was only a short distance away and that they would be arriving at its edge soon, even at the slower pace.

The two girls moved as quickly as Kira's ankle would allow, for what seemed like hours; each step hurting a little less than the one before until eventually, her ankle had gone completely numb. What once was shooting pain had now become only a dull throb. Kira tried to keep her spirits up but as the Black Wood grew larger and the storm clouds overhead drew ever closer, she found herself wishing they were back at home.

The humidity in the autumn air rose, and the temperature began to drop. The cold winds became more pronounced, stealing the heat away from the girls, and leaving both of them to shiver in the cold as they trudged onwards. The dark storm clouds hung overhead and were quickly consuming the sky in all directions. It hadn't started raining yet, but it was getting dark and the thunder was getting louder.

When they finally reached the edge of the Black Wood, the sisters exchanged apprehensive glances before stepping into the thick undergrowth. It was difficult to make out anything beyond the first line of trees in the fading grey light; this was going to make things challenging. They couldn't risk starting a fire or bringing torches with them. Their best chance now was to hope to get lucky and quickly find what they were looking for, before anything noticed them.

"Are you ready? Do you remember what we are looking for?" Kira asked Kaya.

"*Night's Widow, a dark blue flower with white dots on the outside petals,*" Kaya repeated, nodding back at her sister.

"And where do they grow?" Kira asked.

"Umm…" Kaya tried to remember what Felmar had said. "Don't they grow next to the mushrooms that feed on fallen trees?" she guessed, unsure of her answer.

"Correct. Now we have to be very quiet in there. No snapping twigs like you did back there and definitely no falling into bushes!" Kira jeered.

Kaya looked abashed and nodded. "I'll be as quiet as a field mouse, I promise," she said with a grin.

"Okay, then let's do this quickly, before it starts to storm. Keep your eyes peeled for the flowers, but also pay attention to anything that moves. If you hear something, or think that you see something, *do not* ignore it. We cannot afford to be caught off guard, okay?"

Kaya nodded again. Both girls started into the trees as lighting struck in the distance, sending out a rolling thunder that echoed across the valley behind them.

CHAPTER 4

Aeria walked over to the three chairs in the center of the control platform, and took a seat in the middle one. As she sat in the chair, the contour of the seat changed almost immediately to fit her figure and armor. The silver-haired man followed her lead and sat in the chair to her left.

Aeria reached out her hand and placed her palm on green orb before her. Immediately the orb lit up and a large holographic display appeared several feet above it, larger than those at the other work stations. As Aeria let go of the orb and sat back in the chair, another holographic display appeared around her waist. Like the cockpit of a plane, it wrapped around her and was filled with glowing controls and levers. She began to work the controls, and after a moment the image of the planet she had shown her father appeared on the display in front of her. Leaning back in her seat and crossing her arms, she considered it for a few minutes, not saying anything.

Seeming to grow impatient, the silver-haired man

asked his question again, "My lady, what would you have me do? What were your father's instructions?"

"Do you know of any reason that would make my father uneasy about finding Earth, Thanatos?" Aeria asked, ignoring his question a second time.

Taken aback by the query, Thanatos stuttered, "I don't... wha... I'm not sure what you could mean, my lady. Did he seem uneasy when you met with him?"

"I wouldn't say that... but there was something *off* about the way he responded to the news. Remind me again, how was Earth lost to begin with?" Aeria inquired, still staring at the projection in front of her.

Becoming more alarmed by the conversation, Thanatos shifted uncomfortably in his seat. "Well, my lady... it was lost by your grandfather, Kronus, many thousands of years ago. If I remember correctly, he claimed that he had stumbled upon the planet while testing the second generation of propulsion engines in this section of the galaxy," he finished, uncertain if his answer would satisfy her.

"Yes, go on," Aeria insisted.

He shifted in his seat again. "Yes, Mistress." He paused, trying to recall the story, "Where was I? Oh yes, after surveying the planet, he claimed to have found a large amount of usable ore; enough to last us hundreds of thousands of years, but before he could chart its exact location, something went wrong with the experimental propulsion core. He claimed that it malfunctioned and caused a tear in space that pulled his ship into it." He stopped again, wondering if he should go on.

Aeria turned to look at him, nodding for him to continue.

"Supposedly, he remained there, trapped in subspace for several months until he was able to repair the core. Once he had, he used the jump drive to re-open the tear in space and found himself, quite strangely, in orbit above Tython; with no explanation of how he had jumped so far or how nearly a decade had gone by." He finished with a wary tone, wondering what this had to do with his orders.

"Do you believe his story?" Aeria asked.

Now completely alarmed by the conversation, Thanatos reluctantly replied, "Why wouldn't I, Mistress?"

"It is a rather fantastic tale, is it not? Almost *too* fantastic, wouldn't you say?" Aeria watched him, her icy blue eyes piercing like daggers.

Thanatos squirmed in his chair. He didn't know what she was playing at, but was reluctant to say the wrong thing. "Well, my lady. I've never heard anything quite like it, if that's what you mean."

Apparently satisfied, Aeria looked back at the display. "I need you to prepare a fighter squadron for when we arrive at the planet. Do you think you can handle that?"

"Yes, Mistress. Although, an *entire* fighter squadron? Is that really necessary? Are we expecting resistance?" Thanatos seemed confused.

"Those are my father's orders. I don't question them and neither should you. While you are preparing the fighters, I'll be assembling prospecting teams to accompany them. He wants to begin charting the mineable deposits immediately." Aeria finished.

Thanatos got to his feet, and bowed again, saying, "As you command, my lady." He turned towards the doors that Aeria had entered through, and began to leave the room. Before he reached the doors, however, Aeria remembered something and called after him.

"Oh, and one more thing... My father and I will be taking his ship down to the planet's surface after the fighters have conducted their security sweep. I expect you to be on board with us, so try to be hasty in your preparations. We will be there within a day."

"Yes, Mistress. Thank you, Mistress," Thanatos replied as the lift doors opened. He stepped in without saying another word and left the room.

Aeria looked back at the display before her, considering the planet again for a moment. She didn't know the answer to his question about there being resistance; by all accounts sending an entire fighter squadron to survey the planet seemed excessive. There weren't any civilized planetary systems within a thousand light-years of where they were, so who could be there? Why the precaution? It seemed absurd to her, unless... unless her grandfather had lied about losing Earth.

The circumstances of his return had been shrouded in mystery, that was easy to see, but why wouldn't he have told the truth? What could he have possibly gained by lying about Earth? If it was filled with as much ore as he claimed, then he would have found the single greatest asset that he or his family could have hoped for. He would have been a fool to hide it, but then there was that strange look on her father's face. She didn't know if it meant anything, but it made her feel uneasy.

Was he hiding something from her? He had always been honest with her before, but there was something amiss about the way he had been acting. Even before their last conversation, his attitude about the expedition had been *peculiar*. He was much more somber than normal, not that he often gave in to levity. What could it be, and why would he keep it from her? The thought of him hiding something made her angry. Hadn't she always been the perfect daughter, ever bowing to his will and command? She frowned at the thought, deciding that she might be overreacting. *If there was something to know, he would have told her*, she assured herself.

Pushing the thoughts away, she began to work with the controls again. Calling out over the room she announced, "Prepare the engines for a sub-space jump. I have entered the jump coordinates into the nav system. Navigation, divert full power to the propulsion system. I want to get there as soon as we can."

"Yes, Mistress!" one of the soldiers called out as he worked frantically at his station.

A moment later the Trident, which had been floating gracefully in the vast ocean of stars seemed to flicker in and out of view until, without a sound, it vanished completely.

* * *

The Black Wood was dark and ominous and the undergrowth was thicker than either girl had anticipated, making it difficult to move without making noise. The storm clouds had not gotten close enough to interrupt their progress, but that seemed to be changing and rather quickly. The once-grey clouds and dim light were now being replaced with nearly black clouds, and increasing darkness. It was going to be next to impossible to find the flowers, Kira was realizing.

A drop of rain landed on Kira's outstretched hand as she was pulling aside a branch to make her way through a clump of particularly dense trees. She stopped walking and examined the droplet.

"What is it?" Kaya whispered from behind, hoping her sister had found a flower.

"Rain…" Kira replied quietly. She looked up towards the canopy of the trees and could see more droplets falling. They were increasing in number by the second and the sound of rain colliding with leaves could be heard all around them. Letting out a sigh, she turned back to her sister and asked, "Do you want to keep searching, or would you rather find a dry spot to see if the rain stops?"

Kaya frowned as she held her hand out, catching a few drops in her palm she shook her head. "I don't want to wander around in the rain, but I don't think we have enough time to sit and wait either." She paused for a moment to consider it again. Deciding, she said, "No, we should keep looking. Dad's not going to get better on his own."

Kira nodded and started walking again. Several missteps on the uneven forest floor had caused her to re-twist her ankle and it was throbbing in pain. Each step made her wince in discomfort but she pressed on. What made things worse was that they hadn't found anything that even *resembled* the flowers; they hadn't even found a fallen tree. The impossibility of the task was starting to nag at Kira's mind, but she wouldn't give up.

The sparse droplets of rain quickly became a fierce downpour and it wasn't long before each girl was completely drenched. The ground beneath their feet became slippery as the dirt turned to mud, forcing them to slow their movement. As bad as the wet conditions were, it was nothing compared to the cold which seemed to drain both girls of their spirit.

After several minutes of slow progress, Kira announced over the dull roar of the rain, "That's it! We're stopping." She looked around and noticed a large rock overhang several yards to their left. She pointed and said, "There! We'll wait there until the rains dies down."

Kaya nodded in agreement, shivering and trying to rub warmth back into her freezing arms. They made their way to the overhang and crawled under it. It was only a few feet above the ground but there was enough space for both of them to sit. Removing their satchels, the two sat as close to each other as possible but there wasn't much warmth to be had. Shivering, Kira whispered, "At least it's dry."

Kaya did not reply but nodded in agreement as her teeth chattered. Together they sat there for a long time as the rain seemed to never end. It was almost an hour before the downpour started to let up and just as one problem was lessening, another was becoming worse. It was now nearly pitch black in the woods and neither girl could see further than a few yards ahead.

"Should we light a fire?" asked Kaya hopefully, still shivering in the wet cold.

"No," Kira replied through chattering teeth. "We can't risk drawing the attention. Not when the most dangerous predators are the ones that come out at night."

"Then what should we do? I can hardly see anything!" Kaya snapped more loudly than she meant to.

"Shh..." Kira hissed back. "We must be quiet!"

"Sorry," Kaya replied as both girls examined their surroundings for any movement or sound. Just when they had decided that nothing was nearby, a bright flash of light erupted, followed almost immediately by a roar of thunder. The sudden sound startled Kira and caused her to jump, smashing the top of her head into the rock overhang. She grimaced with pain and began to softly rub the injured area of her scalp with her right hand. "Ow," she whispered, frowning.

Kaya nearly burst into laughter, but was able to

stifle her outburst before she made any noise. She giggled under her breath and let out a snort, but it wasn't heard because as she did so there was another flash of lighting, followed immediately by roar of thunder. This time neither girl jumped, but Kira shifted her weight in an odd manner. Kaya looked at her; another flash of light and another roar of thunder.

Still nursing her tender scalp, Kira whispered loudly, "We can use the flashes from the lighting to keep searching!" Immediately there was another bright flash and loud roar. Each lightning strike illuminated the entire area around the girls for a few seconds. "Quick! Before the storm moves too far off!"

Kira crawled out from under the overhang and pulled her satchel over her shoulder again. The rush from the idea seemed to drive the cold away and she was able to stop shivering. Gripping her spear tightly in one hand, she used her other to pull Kaya to her feet. It was still raining but the downpour had ended and was now just a slow drizzle of cold rain. Kira stood there for a moment looking around, trying to figure out the best direction to go. She had a decent idea of where they had come from, and decided that it would be best to keep heading towards the center of the wood, rather than risk getting turned around. She pointed to her right and said, "This way."

Both girls set out, walking slowly in the near dark forest, trying their hardest to move as quietly as possible. They slowly but surely made their way through the woods, using the lightning to guide their way. With the lightning only lighting their path every thirty seconds or so, Kira knew that it was a fool's hope that they'd be able to spot the flowers under such conditions, but something inside of her told her to keep moving.

After another thirty minutes of searching, they

finally came across a fallen log, inside of which grew a solitary Night's Widow. Kaya was the first to see it, having nearly tripped over the end of the log it grew in. With excitement and a renewed sense of hope Kira cut the flower from its stem and placed it in her satchel. She looked at her sister and with a smile patted her on the head, saying, "Good going, brat! I guess it's a good thing I brought you along, huh?"

"Oh like it was your idea!" Kaya retorted, giving Kira a gentle shove. She opened her mouth to level another jeer, but, just as she started to speak, something behind Kira caught her eye. "What's that?" she asked, pointing over Kira's shoulder.

Kira turned to look, worried at what she might discover as she did. It took a moment of searching for her eyes to see what her sister was pointing at. It was a small glimmering object, lying in the leaves about twenty feet away; Kira walked over to it and picked it up. It was partially covered in mud, but as she cleaned it off in the drizzling rain she discovered a thick metallic cylinder about the size of her hand. On one side of the cylinder was a row of five small, round protrusions sticking out of the metal.

"What is it?" Kaya asked with a puzzled look on her face. She had never seen anything like it, but was certain it didn't belong in the woods.

"I'm not sure..." Kira replied vaguely, entranced by the object in her hand. The drizzling rain had washed it almost completely clean and in the dim light Kira could see that the five protrusions had symbols on them. She held the object close to her face as she tried to make out the inscriptions, but they were unlike anything she'd seen before. They did not resemble the markings that her village used to account for their grain supplies or livestock numbers. Instead they had a strange, almost otherworldly pattern. Handing the object to her sister, Kira asked, "Have you ever seen markings like these?"

Kaya took the cylinder and examined it. Frowning, she shook her head and replied, "No. What do you think they mean?" She quickly handed the object back to Kira, as something about it made her feel uneasy.

Just as Kira took it, the cylinder started to buzz with a low humming noise. Taken aback by the sudden movement she dropped the object and took a few steps back. *Is it alive*, she thought wildly to herself. *Surely it couldn't be an animal*!

After a moment or two the humming stopped and the object fell silent as it lay in the mud. "Should we bring it back with us? Do you think Felmar knows what it is?" Kaya offered, eyeing the object with renewed suspicion.

"I have serious doubts that Felmar knows much of anything, let alone what this thing is," Kira replied, more harshly than she had meant to. She didn't want to think about that wretched man right now, not when there were more important things to deal with, like this mysterious object.

Confident that it wasn't going to jump to life, Kira approached the object again and tried to pick it up, but the wet metal slipped between her fingers and she dropped it again. This time something strange happened; the humming sound returned and bright green lights started emitting from the symbols on the side.

Neither girl moved as both stared in silent awe at the peculiar object. The grove of trees around them was illuminated by the light coming from the device, and it gave everything a surreal feeling. Kira started towards the object again but stopped when it suddenly went dark. The humming sound stopped and the green lights faded. Blinking rapidly to adjust her eyes to the sudden darkness, Kira tried to feel for the device but couldn't find it in the mud and leaves. "Be careful," Kaya whispered in the dark, also unable to see anything.

After a few moments her sight returned and she could just make out the metallic object a few inches away from her hand. She picked it up a third time, this time dropping her spear and handling the cylinder with both hands. She didn't know what drove her to do it, and in the days that would come she would wonder why she had, but something inside of her told her to press down on one of the symbols. When she did, the object burst to life once again, this time erupting into a large projection in the air. The projection flooded the grove of trees with blinding green light, revealing everything for several yards as if it were daylight.

Kira recognized the projection, or at least she thought she did. She had seen something similar once before, long ago, when the village had been attacked by a raiding party. Felmar had called it a map, only his had been drawn on the hide of a deer and not nearly in such detail as the projection before her.

"What... what is it?" Kaya wondered aloud as she gaped at the image.

"I think it's called a map..." Kira replied slowly, still examining the details of the projection.

"What's a map?" Kaya asked, still unable to take her eyes off of the green spectacle.

"It shows you where things are. Here, look," Kira waved her sister over. Pointing at the projection Kira continued, "You see this marking right here, in the center?" Kaya nodded. "Unless I'm mistaken, I think that's us. All of this stuff around that marking is the land around us. See that blue line there, that's the creek we just passed by. Actually, I wonder..." Kira's voice trailed off as she started to walk in the direction they had been heading. After several yards she stopped and smiled at her sister. "I don't know how, but this map seems to be moving with us. As if it knows exactly where we are and which direction we are heading."

Kaya didn't seem to be as happy about this as Kira was. With a frown she said, "Maybe we should just leave this thing alone. It might be dangerous." But Kira wasn't paying attention, as she had noticed something on the map.

"What do you suppose that is?" she asked, pointing to a triangular object near the edge of the map.

"Didn't you hear me? We shouldn't be playing with this thing. We don't know what it is or how it's making this *map*. We should just forget we found it and keep looking for the flowers," Kaya pleaded.

Frowning, Kira nodded. She knew that her sister was right and that the time for exploring would have to wait, although she supposed there wouldn't be any harm in continuing to look for the flowers in the direction of the triangular object.

"All right, let's keep looking then. Now how do I..." Kira pressed down on the same protrusion that had projected the map. Immediately the device shut down and the woods around them went dark again. They both stood there for a moment, allowing their eyes to adjust to the change before continuing on. Luckily the storm was still near enough that they could continue to use the lightning for guidance.

The drizzling rain continued but was barely noticeable anymore, especially with Kira's mind buzzing over the object they just discovered. *What was it? Where did it come from and how did it emit light? How could it show a map in the air without something for it to draw on?* She wanted to look at it more; wanted to press the other symbols to see what they did, but she knew it would have to wait. Placing the cylinder in her satchel, she walked back to where she had left her spear. Picking it up, she looked at her sister and gestured to her right, "This way. Let's hurry, in case something noticed the light." Kaya nodded in agreement and followed after her.

As the two girls jogged in the dark woods, trying their best not to trip over the undergrowth, Kaya couldn't help but feel like something was watching them. Several times she could have sworn she saw a shadow moving or a person standing off in the distance, but whenever she looked again there would be nothing. She wanted to say something to Kira, but was afraid that her sister would just make fun of her, so she did her best to ignore it.

As before, they scoured the ground for any sign of Night's Widow; stopping occasionally to more closely examine fallen trees and rotting logs. After jogging for quite some time Kaya asked to stop, wishing to rest a minute and catch her breath. Kira couldn't be sure how far they'd run, but she suspected they had to be getting close to the area where the triangular object was. She looked at her sister and said, "Just rest a minute, I'm going to look around a bit. Call out if you see or hear something."

Kaya gave her a reproachful glare, but Kira ignored her and continued to walk away. The dark made it difficult to make anything out and there hadn't been a lightning strike in several minutes. Kira looked up through the canopy of leaves and could see that the cloud cover was thinning out; she could even make out a few stars.

Not paying attention to where she was walking,

Kira stubbed her toe on something hard and fell to the ground, nearly landing on top of a large rock. Rubbing her toe, she looked at the object she had tripped on. It was a long flat stone, protruding a few inches out of the ground, sitting just in front of a large rock. Turning her attention to the rock she realized that it had a very peculiar shape. Instead of being rounded or jagged like most boulders, it was almost perfectly squared off with smooth faces.

In the distance lightning struck, illuminating the woods around Kira. In the flickering light she noticed that the faces of the stone had symbols carved into them, like the ones on the cylinder. She pulled open her satchel and retrieved the cylinder. Holding it up to the stone, she compared the two; they were not identical but there was no mistaking the similarity. Kira knew that whoever or whatever had made the cylinder had also carved this stone.

She stood and made her way back to where Kaya was. Still sitting on the ground, Kaya watched Kira approach, and with a worried look she asked, "What is it? Did you find a flower?"

"No, but I've found something interesting. Come look." Kira said with excitement, pulling Kaya to her feet and dragging her in the direction of the stone. Kaya followed without a word, bemused. When they arrived at the stone Kira pointed to the symbols and said, "Look! They are just like the ones on the cylinder!"

Kaya did not seem amused; if anything she seemed frightened by the discovery. She looked around wondering if there were any other stones like this one and almost immediately noticed another several yards away. Without speaking she pointed towards it.

Kira followed her sister's gaze and immediately

recognized what she was pointing at. Still dragging Kaya along behind her, she jogged over to the other stone. Again it was squared off, forming a large rectangular shape with symbols etched into the flat sides. This time it was Kira who looked around, wondering if there would be a third stone but what she discovered instead took her breath away. Standing in the distance, was what appeared to be a mountain of the rectangular stones, stacked on top of each other, climbing high in the air and disappearing into the canopy. Kira squeezed Kaya's hand and breathlessly pointed at the monument with her spear. Kaya gaped at the massive structure and both her and her sister stood there in awe for a several seconds.

Eventually mustering their senses, the two girls headed towards the huge object, their disbelief growing as they approached it. Most of the bottom was covered in undergrowth, but they could make out enough to see that the structure stretched hundreds of feet to either side of them and rose up above them at least two hundred feet. It was a huge triangular building, larger than anything either of them had seen.

Stunned, Kaya whispered, "What is it?"

Kira didn't know how to respond; it was so unlike anything she had seen. "I don't know. But look at how large it is! I wonder if anyone has ever seen it before."

Kaya's stomach did a flip as the feeling of being watched crept back into her mind. "I don't like it. I think we should leave," she said, pulling hard on Kira's hand. She opened her mouth to explain but froze when a shadow in the distance moved.

Kira looked at her, expecting to have to console her, but instead found her frozen with a terrified look on her face. Realizing that she was staring at something behind her, she turned to see what it was. At first she didn't see anything, but when she did, her heart plummeted into her stomach. There was movement in the underbrush to their right, near the end of the structure. Kira froze and, holding her breath, slowly crouched behind another engraved stone. She pulled Kaya down with her and gestured for her to be quiet. Together they watched as the moving shadow made its way towards them.

Far in the distance lighting struck and dim white light flooded the woods around the girls. It hadn't been bright, but it had been enough for Kira to make out what the shadow was. As her mind processed what she had seen, the air around her seemed to evaporate and all she could hear was the beating of her racing heart. In the distance stood a massive sabercat with long, razor sharp teeth that hung well below its jaw, and spotted grey fur. Its tail swung from side to side in the air as it walked and its bright yellow eyes gazed lazily around while it sniffed the air.

Frantically, Kira tried to think of what to do. If they moved, they would almost guarantee that it would spot them, but if they stood still it might just walk right into them. Kira let go of Kaya's hand, and as quietly as she could, she pulled out her shale knife. There was no time to come up with a plan, which meant there was only one option. If she was going to protect Kaya she would have to fight the cat, knife and spear. Even if it couldn't see them, it would eventually smell them, and then there would be no hiding. Luckily, the cat was upwind from them, meaning there was a chance to surprise it. If Kira could catch it off guard, she might be able to kill it before it had a chance to fight back. Kira gripped her spear and knife tightly, waiting for the right moment as the cat approached.

The sabercat, however, stopped walking and laid down in the undergrowth, letting out a loud groan. A feeling of relief swept over the girls as they realized the cat was unaware of them, but Kira still wasn't sure that they'd be able to escape without drawing attention. She looked around at their surroundings, trying to evaluate the best direction to escape. Ideally, they would flee in the direction that had the highest density of undergrowth between them and the cat, thereby minimizing its ability to sense their movement, but the woods were too dark to really discern what the best route was. Kira looked back at the sabercat, who let out a large yawn and lazily rolled over on its side. In the distance lightning struck again and lit the area with dim white light. That's when she saw them.

Just behind the sabercat, were two Night's Widows, growing out of a rotting log that she hadn't noticed before. Again Kira's heart sank. *What cruel trickery was this?* She wondered to herself. She didn't know what to do; the solution to their father's illness was right there, thirty feet away, but was guarded by one of the most dangerous creatures known to man. Did she dare fight the cat in hopes of winning the flowers? Or did they flee, trying not to draw attention and then hope to come across another one of the flowers? It was possible that they'd *never* find another as they had already been searching for hours and had only by sheer luck come across the one they had. She closed her eyes and shook her head in disbelief. There was no time to hope for more flowers, not when they were already so far behind. She looked at Kaya, who had also noticed the flowers and gave a halfhearted smile. Hoping it wouldn't be her last, she started to move towards the sabercat, readying her weapons.

CHAPTER 5

"Mistress Aeria, we are about to drop out of sub-space. By my calculations we'll be coming out next to the planet's moon," a soldier to Aeria's right announced.

"Very good. Give word to the fighters to prepare for launch. I want them flying attack formation alpha as soon as we drop out of the jump," Aeria ordered.

"Yes, Mistress," a second soldier called out, frantically working at his station.

"Diagnostics, I want long range sensors up and scanning immediately. Give me as much information as you can and link it to my control console," Aeria commanded.

"Yes, Mistress!" yelled a group of soldiers working at consoles on the lower platform.

"Mistress, breaking jump field in 3... 2.... 1..."

In the blink of an eye, the Trident appeared suddenly in high orbit above Earth's moon. Hatches all along the exterior sections opened and small ships poured out of them like a swarm of hornets. Hundreds of these ships flew out and away from the Trident, aligning in formations before heading towards Earth at breakneck speed. Each formation broke off in different directions, spreading out across the backdrop of the planet.

"Mistress Aeria, the fighters are away and are surveying the planet for any hostile contacts. So far there have been none," the second officer reported.

Aeria had both expected this and was surprised by it. From her father's unusual behavior she had expected some sort of resistance or perhaps another civilization she hadn't been aware of, but so far there didn't seem to be anything. She worked at the consoles surrounding her chair and pulled up an image of the planet on her screen. Deciding it was insufficient she pressed a large green button to her right and the projection of her screen disappeared, immediately being redisplayed on the massive screen at the end of the lower platform. Aeria leaned forward, resting her chin on her hand, and stared at the blue-green planet. She didn't care how aloof her father was being about the discovery of Earth; she knew this was a triumphant moment that would be remembered forever.

"Umm... Mistress Aeria..." one of the soldiers from the lower deck called out in a wary voice. "I think there is something you should see..."

Aeria's gaze shot to the soldier below, and with a suspicious glare she asked, "What is it? Put it on the main display!" At once the soldier went back to work and after a moment a small pulsating circle appeared on the display of the planet. Aeria didn't know what to make of it. Losing patience, she asked curtly, "And what exactly am I looking at, Lieutenant?"

"Umm, I'm not sure how to say it, Mistress..." the man looked thoroughly baffled.

"Just spit it out, you fool!" Aeria scolded, a wild

look in her eyes.

"Well, Mistress, it's a transponder beacon from one of the royal holodisk devices. According to its log, it belongs to... Kronus," the soldier seemed to cringe as he said it.

"What? That must be an error. Check it again!" Aeria snapped.

"With respect, Mistress," the soldier closest to the lieutenant chimed in, "I've double checked the readouts, and the lieutenant's assessment is correct."

"That can't be possible. Enhance!" Aeria shouted out. The display at the end of the platform zoomed into a heavily forested section of the planet where the pulsating circle was. There was no mistaking it, there was a holodisk device on the surface of the planet, but how could that be? Aeria's grandfather Kronus was locked in a prison thousands of light-years away. "Can you connect to it? I want to see who activated it!"

"I'm sorry, Mistress; it's a much older version that doesn't have that capability. All we can tell from orbit is that it appears to be moving and that according to its log, the emergency beacon was activated just a few hours ago."

Aeria didn't know what to think. Only a member of the royal family could use one of those devices. How, then, did a holodisk device find its way to the surface? Moreover, who was using it? Obviously her grandfather had been less than truthful about his experiences with Earth, but did her father know this? Based on the way he had been acting, he must have known, but why hadn't he said something? *This was supposed to be a day of triumph, not a day of deception and half-truths!* she fumed to herself.

"Umm... Mistress, there is more," the lieutenant interjected, grimacing as he did. "It seems there is also an indigenous civilization on the planet. Based on initial scans they appear to be a pre-industrial, mostly agricultural species."

"What?" Aeria was growing more alarmed with each report. "Are they lesser ones?"

"Well, that's the strange part. They seem to be similar to the lesser ones, but initial scans indicate genetic variation inconsistent with any known species on record. We would, of course, have to test them directly to know for certain," the lieutenant finished, looking unsure of himself.

Aeria glared at the man. *What kind of circus was this?* she wondered to herself. Before she could ask more questions the image on the massive screen changed, revealing an image of her father's face peering at her and the rest of the soldiers. At once the soldiers stood to attention, but Aeria did not move. Instead she scrutinized the image with a cold stare.

"Has my ship been prepared?" Velion asked, ignoring his daughter's icy stare.

"Yes, Father, it's in the main hangar. I believe Thanatos is awaiting our arrival. Shall we depart?" Aeria asked, anxious to get some answers.

"No, I'll be going alone. Thanatos can come if he wishes, but I need you to stay here," Velion commanded.

"*Stay here?*" Aeria mocked, the anger in her voice evident. "Why can't I come to the surface with you?" she demanded, squinting her eyes in contempt.

"Just do as I've told you!" Velion snapped. Without another word, the screen before Aeria returned to the image of the planet and the pulsating circle. *Stay here,* she thought darkly. Sitting for a moment brooding, her blood boiled with every thought as she wondered, *how could he just dismiss me like that? I was the one to discover the planet! And now I have to stay here? It's not fair!* She slammed her fist down on the control console, the light of the projections flickering in shock as she did. The soldiers around Aeria quietly returned to work, trying to avoid eye contact.

As Aeria stared with fury at the pulsating circle, she remembered something. No one had told him about the holodisk on the surface! Realizing this, she quickly shut the control consoles down and stood to leave. She turned towards the lift doors and started walking briskly towards them. Before entering the lift she called out, "Prepare my ship for departure, I'm leaving immediately!"

"But Mistress, didn't Lord Velion ask you to stay here?" One of the soldiers asked in a startled tone.

"That doesn't concern you, so do as I've ordered!" Aeria shouted, losing her patience.

"Yes, Mistress!"

Aeria stepped into the lift and pressed the lowest symbol on the wall. Immediately the room began to move downwards and after a few moments it came to a stop and the doors slid apart. Aeria walked out of the lift into a large hangar filled with rows of small fighters. At the end of the hangar was a ship that was much larger than the rest. It was made of a gleaming silver metal and was fitted with several large weapon arrays. As she approached the vessel, the platform it was resting on began to rotate, spinning the back of the ship towards her. The door to the vessel started to open, dropping slowly to become a ramp. As Aeria walked up the ramp and into the ship she thought to herself, *if my father doesn't want to tell me what's going on, then so be it, I will just find the answers on my own!*.

The engines on her ship burst to life with a high pitched squeal; green light and hot vapor filling the hangar as it gently lifted off the platform. It hovered for a moment while Aeria configured the consoles. A large door a few yards in front of the ship jolted to life and started to lift up, disappearing into the ceiling. Beyond the door was a long narrow corridor with yellow flashing lights running the length of it on either side. The nose of Aeria's ship dipped down and the vessel slowly hovered forward, stopping just beyond the doorway. Without delay the large bay door began to slide shut again; emitting a loud thud as it sealed itself shut. Aeria punched the accelerator when she heard the door close, and the silver vessel shot forward at an enormous speed, like a bullet racing down the barrel of a gun. The flashing lights became a blur as they sped by and after a few seconds the ship shot out from the corridor into a black ocean of stars, moving at an incredible speed.

Gaining her bearings, Aeria steered the ship towards Earth, racing at full speed towards the signal of the holodisk. It would take a few minutes to traverse the distance, but she would have her answers soon.

* * *

Kira's heart was racing as she ever so slowly moved through the trees towards the sabercat. She could feel panic setting in as her mind caught up with the decision she had made. The air became thin and everything seemed to slow down as she considered the fight ahead. Half of her expected this to be suicide, while the other half was too busy panicking to really think about the odds. Before she had moved, she whispered instructions to her sister, telling her to flee if things went badly. She hoped it wouldn't come to that, but if it did, she would buy Kaya as much time to escape as she could.

Luckily the cat seemed blissfully unaware of her presence, now lying completely on its back, staring up at the night sky while it flipped its tail in the underbrush. If she hadn't known better, she might have thought it looked cute, laying there sprawled out like it wanted someone to rub its belly. She shook the image from her mind; she had to focus. One misstep, one wrong move and that cute *kitten* would turn into a vicious killing machine. She had witnessed firsthand the danger that one of these creatures presented.

Now only about fifteen feet away from the beast, she carefully felt out each step, ensuring that the ground beneath her feet was solid and that she wouldn't snap a twig or branch. She looked to her side and saw her sister still crouched behind the strange rectangular stone, silently watching from the distance. Moving at a snail's pace she refocused on the cat. Now only ten feet away she gripped her spear, readying it for the attack. If she could get close enough, she would lunge from the underbrush and drive the spear down into the cats exposed chest, hopefully driving it through the heart and killing it without a fight. This, of course, was easier said than done as sabercats were renowned for their lightning fast reflexes. Just a few more feet and she would be able to make the leap.

Seven feet; the cat let out a long sigh, still looking away from Kira. Six feet; its tail whipped hard against the ground. Five feet; Kira could smell the stink of the beast's wet fur. She readied her spear above her head, holding her breath as she prepared to leap.

Without warning, there was a loud explosion from above and bright orange light filled the entire area, illuminating everything. Kira looked up and was blinded by a radiant object falling from the heavens. Trying to shield her eyes from the blinding spectacle, she staggered backwards and fell into the underbrush.

64

The sabercat, equally taken aback by the sudden commotion, flipped to its feet with extraordinary agility and let out a loud roar. Distracted by the spectacle, the cat didn't notice Kira, who was trying to divide her attention between the cat and the object falling towards them.

It was like a ball of thunder and lightning hurtling down at them with a long trail of green smoke behind it as it soared across the sky, getting bigger by the second. It wasn't long before Kira realized that it was heading straight for them. Kaya must have had the same realization because she yelled, "Kira, look out!!"

Immediately the attention of the sabercat switched from the ball of light that was hurtling towards them to the girl yelling thirty feet away. Flipping its tail, the cat crouched low to the ground, preparing to take off in Kaya's direction. Kira's heart raced as she scrambled to her feet. There was no time, so without thinking Kira dashed out from the bush and swung her spear as hard as she could, hitting the sabercat in the face right above its nose. The cat let out a loud yelp and recoiled, but only for a moment. Regaining its senses, the cat turned its attention to Kira.

The blow had hurt its pride more than anything, and with a loud roar and fury in its eyes the cat struck back, catching Kira unprepared. As it hit her forearm with its claws, excruciating pain erupted as stripes of the flesh were torn away.

With an overwhelming urge to retch from the agony, Kira staggered back. She tried to keep her balance but the cat pursued, causing her to trip and fall over something behind her, but only just in time. The cat leapt towards her, but not having anticipated her fall, it soared high above her as she hit the ground. Landing a few feet behind her, the cat stopped, confused for a moment. Wasting no time, Kira scrambled to her feet again and with blood trickling down her arm, she readied her spear. With a loud scream she charged the cat with as much speed as her legs would allow.

The cat spun around at the sound of Kira's scream, and growled. Kira sprinted at the beast and took aim at its chest, hoping to drive the spear through, but at the last moment the sabercat shifted to the right. The end of the spear missed the chest and drove hard into the cat's left shoulder, producing a loud *CRACK* as it drove into the bone, shattering it. Again it let out a loud yelp, but the glancing angle caused Kira to drop her spear and lose her footing. She fell headfirst to the cat's left and tumbled through the underbrush while the wounded beast staggered sideways, blood spilling from where her spear had torn the fur.

The broken bone slowed the cat, but blinded by fury it limped towards Kira to attack again, baring its enormous fangs. She tried to get to her feet again but the slippery undergrowth prevented her from gaining any footing. Unable to stand and without her spear, Kira kicked the cat hard in the face, driving her left heel into its nose whenever it came close. This slowed the sabercat but not enough for her to gain any ground. Scrambling backwards, she slid into the base of a tree, halting her movement. Looking up at the massive tree blocking her escape she realized there was no escaping now and that there wouldn't be enough time to stand and run.

As the cat closed in, her heart sank. Accepting that she had failed, she pulled out her knife, and prepared to make her last stand. All she could think about was Kaya and how she hoped that she had bought her enough time to flee. The cat limped closer, baring its teeth for the attack and preparing to lunge. Kira screamed with fury as it jumped, desperately aiming her knife at its throat. If she was going to die, she was going to bring the bastard with her. She closed her eyes, and gritted her teeth, ready for her death. But it did not come. Instead of claws and teeth she was met with a strange sound followed by a heavy thud as the beast fell on her legs, its fur warm and damp as it lay across her body.

Kira opened her eyes. The sabercat was lying still, sprawled out across her legs, its lifeless eyes staring up at her. She blinked, not comprehending what had happened, until she noticed someone standing above her. Standing to her left was a tall blonde woman, covered from head to toe in exquisite silver armor that seemed to radiate a green glow. She had two long blades, one in each hand with the one on the right dripping with blood. Kira looked back at the sprawled out sabercat and noticed that it had a deep wound just below its shoulder, heading straight to its heart.

Kira looked back up at her, confused. The tall woman did not speak, but instead stared at Kira with a puzzled look.

"Thank you," Kira whispered, not knowing what else to say. She wasn't sure what she had expected, but she certainly didn't expect the woman to look even more surprised after she said the words.

"You can speak my language?" the woman demanded in a pressing tone.

Kira didn't know how to answer. Stuttering, she replied, "Your... your language?"

"Yes! My language! Who taught you to speak this language?!" she demanded again.

"My parents," Kira replied, suddenly unsure of her answer.

"Do you mean to tell me that there are others

who speak this language?" The woman seemed agitated.

"Yes, my whole village can." Kira was beginning to think that she had died and that this was some sort of strange afterlife experience.

The woman scowled at her, not saying anything for a few seconds. Seeming to decide something, she sheathed her weapons and reached down to pick up the sabercat. With a single hand she lifted the cat and tossed its lifeless body several yards into the trees. Kira was awestruck. The sabercat had to have weighed four times as much as she did, but this woman seemed to toss it aside like it was a ragdoll. "Get up," the woman ordered. Kira, not wanting to anger the strange woman, slowly rose to her feet. "Where is it?" the blonde woman demanded.

Baffled and wide eyed, Kira replied, "Where is what?"

Growing impatient, the woman growled, "The holodisk!"

Kira had no idea what she was talking about. Who was this woman? Where had she come from? She tried to decide how to best answer the question, but before she could respond, a familiar voice called out from the dark, "Do you mean this?"

Barely discernible in the green glow that the strange woman was emanating, Kaya was standing several yards away, holding a metallic object in the air.

In what seemed like half a heartbeat, the blonde woman unsheathed her weapons and dashed like green lightning across the distance between her and Kaya. In the blink of an eye, she had moved nearly fifty feet with blinding speed. Kira gaped in awe, unable to comprehend what had just occurred. In the distance she could see the armored woman standing firmly in front of Kaya, holding an outstretched blade to the girl's throat.

"Where did you get this?" the woman demanded wildly.

Kaya, dumbstruck by the shocking speed and sudden appearance of the woman, couldn't find any words to respond. She just stood there, frozen in awe and fear, staring up at the woman.

"Where did you get this device? Answer me!" she shouted, driving the edge of her blade harder into Kaya's skin. Blood started to trickle down her throat as the sword cut into her skin.

Kira, finally able to shake off her shock, got to her feet and ran towards the blonde woman. She yelled out, "Don't hurt her! I'm the one who found it!"

The woman peered back over her shoulder, giving Kira a dark look in the faint green glow. Seeming to ease up, she lowered her blade and stepped sideways as Kira ran up to them. The two girls embraced in front of her in a desperate hug.

Letting go of her sister, Kira turned to face the mysterious woman, who did not look altogether pleased, and repeated, "I'm the one who found it."

The blonde woman scowled at her and asked, "Where?"

"In the forest, just a little while ago. It was lying on the ground," Kira finished, wondering why she was looking for the object. "Is it yours?" she asked before the woman could respond, but she did not reply. She just stood there, examining the two girls closely, seeming to be lost in thought.

Nervous and unsure of what to do, Kira continued, "When I picked it up, it started to make a strange humming sound. I pressed one of the symbols on the side and it lit up with what I think was a map."

A look of deep concern passed over the face of the blonde woman. Quietly she asked, "So you mean to tell me, that you just *happened* across this device by accident, and that when you found it, it worked for you?"

Kira nodded, uncertain if this information would make things better or worse. She looked over to Kaya and nodded, indicating that she wanted her to press one of the symbols on the side. Without a word Kaya pressed the first symbol, and again the device came to life, emitting a green glow for a few seconds before the large projection of a map burst forth.

The look of concern disappeared from the blonde woman, and was immediately replaced by a look of alarm. "You mean to tell me she can use the device as well?!" she demanded as she looked back and forth between the girls. "Are you related?"

Kira wanted to laugh, but wasn't sure how that would go over with the strange woman, so instead she merely nodded her head and replied, "She is my sister."

"This is most strange indeed! First I find what appears to be a ruined transport building buried this forest and at the foot of it, I come across two girls who can use our royal technology? How can this be?" the blonde woman questioned, more to herself than to the girls.

Kira was about to ask what the woman meant by, "a ruined transport building" when she remembered something. What had happened to the ball of light in the sky? Had it landed? She had been certain that it was heading straight for them, but she couldn't recall hearing or seeing anything crash. She peered around at her surroundings, but found no evidence that anything had crashed nearby. She looked back to the blonde woman standing before her and an impossible idea went through her mind. *Had it been her in the sky*? It was absurd to think, but something about this woman was very peculiar. She was dressed in clothing unlike anything Kira had ever dreamed of, let alone seen, and she moved with such immense speed. She seemed different in some way, almost like she wasn't human.

Kira decided it was time for answers. They had been more than forthcoming about the object they found but knew almost nothing about this stranger. Straining her voice to hide her frustration Kira asked, "I don't wish to be rude, especially after you've just saved my life, but who are you? Where did you come from?"

As she spoke the words, Kira noticed several shadows shifting in the dark around them, each with a pair of yellow eyes, glinting from the light of the projection. He heart sank again as she realized what was happening. It must have been the sound of the fighting that had drawn them, or maybe it had been the talking; but whatever it was didn't matter because they were already surrounded. Kira reached over to Kaya and pulled her close. Without her spear there would be no way to fight them off.

"Wolves," Kira whispered to her sister, but her words weren't necessary. The pack of wolves began to growl in the dark as they edged closer to them. Kira could feel Kaya begin to tremble with fear as she looked around at the menacing figures. The wolves became more discernible in the light of the projection as they approached and by Kira's count, there were five of them, each as big as the sabercat had been. They were low to the ground, creeping in slowly with their hackles raised, seemingly wary of the projection, but not so concerned as to forfeit what was shaping up to be a tasty dinner. Kira didn't know what to do, but her panic was interrupted when she heard the blonde woman laugh.

"Are you afraid? Perhaps I've overestimated your worth after all," the blonde woman jeered. She turned on her heel to face the wolf nearest to her and, readying her weapons again, shot off in a blur of green light. Her right blade caught the wolf under the throat and as the woman drove the blade upwards, it sliced through its flesh like she was cutting through water.

Decapitated, the wolf's body fell to the ground, lifeless. The woman paused and looked back at the girls with a wide grin. "Child's play," she said in an ominous tone as the other four wolves stopped short, taken aback by her blinding speed. With another chuckle she bolted towards the next wolf, a few yards to her right.

Kira snatched the object from Kaya's hand and pressed hard on the first symbol. Immediately, the projection disappeared and the grove of trees went dark again, the only light now coming from the woman's armor. She shoved the object into Kaya's satchel and grabbed her hand, pulling hard as she began to flee, dragging her confused sister behind her. "Hurry!" Kira cried out as she ran blindly through the impossibly dark forest. Looking back over her shoulder, she saw the glowing woman still fighting with the four remaining wolves; one of them hanging from her arm by its teeth while the others circled around her. The image seemed surreal, like some dream that Kira couldn't wake from. Or maybe it was a nightmare? There was no way to tell now. All Kira knew for certain was that they had to get out of there as quickly as they could.

After a few minutes of running they could no longer see the strange blonde woman and as far as Kira could tell, she hadn't followed them.

* * *

The last wolf let out a loud yelp as Aeria drove her blade into its heart. "Too easy," she mused, removing her blade as the foul-smelling creature fell to the ground lifeless. She looked around at the scattered remains of the wolf pack and grinned. This planet was turning out to be much more interesting than she had expected. She looked off in the direction that the two girls had fled and snorted derisively. "So they think they can run and hide, do they? So be it. So long as they keep that holodisk I'll know exactly where they've gone," she said aloud to herself.

Sheathing her weapons again, she turned back towards the large building behind her and began to walk. As she approached the large stone structure she stopped to gaze upon it. There was no mistaking the design, it had to be a transport building; but who had built it? And when?

She pressed her hand against the cold damp stone and felt the texture under her fingertips. The structure seemed to be half finished, not quite taking the shape of a pyramid like the ones on Tython. The stone was not nearly as smooth and the outside covering that would normally give it a sleek, flat angle had not been put in place. Instead it appeared to have steps, as each layer of stone blocks made up a smaller and smaller square grid. The top of the structure was also flat and incomplete, missing several layers of the stone blocks.

Aeria wondered if the building was functional, despite its incomplete form. She knew that the pyramids didn't have to be complete to still work, so long as enough of the underlying structure had been finished. She began to walk along the base of the building, dragging her hand along the stone as she went. Somewhere along the side there would be a hidden entrance that would illuminate as she passed it if the building was operational.

She'd walked about a third of the length before a small panel of symbols illuminated on one of the stone surfaces. Smiling to herself, she pressed her thumb to the uppermost symbol. Immediately a low rumble could be heard and the stone block in front of her slid to the side, revealing a dark passage leading towards the heart of the structure.

As she stepped into the passageway the stone door behind her slid closed with a soft thud. The air inside was warm and stale, having been sealed in the structure for countless years. She made her way down the long corridor until it came to a junction where she could either continue her descent down or begin to make her way upwards. She knew that if this structure was like the ones on Tython, the lower path would lead to an ancillary control room that would be of no use to her right now; although she did plan to investigate it on her way out. Her destination would be upwards, towards the heart of the structure. The path was steep, but she climbed it effortlessly.

After climbing about a hundred feet, the passageway came to another junction as the incline leveled into a wide platform. This time there were three directions she could go: one straight ahead, one continuing upwards, and another to her side that would lead to a maintenance conduit above her. She continued her ascent and after a short while she entered a large gallery. It was much wider and taller than the passageway had been, extending several feet to either side of her and angling upwards in a semi-triangular shape. As she entered this room, lights hidden behind the large stone reliefs hanging from the walls illuminated, casting green light across the floor and ceiling of the gallery. Aeria smiled at this, as it indicated that the structure seemed to be functioning at regular capacity. The lighting systems were always the first to be shut down, in order to conserve energy should the building be left in a dormant state. If they were still functioning, then there was probably enough energy stored for regular use and transport.

She made her way up the gallery and came to a large stone step approximately six feet wide by three feet high. This step formed a platform extending about eight feet, where it came to another horizontal passage leading to an antechamber with a massive stone door. Aeria stepped up on to the platform and made her way into the antechamber. Once inside, she put her hand up to the wall beside the large stone door. Immediately a hidden symbol illuminated with green light and the massive stone door rotated inwards, revealing a large chamber.

The room was a large rectangle, nearly twenty feet tall, cut straight out of the stone. Stepping into the room, Aeria could make out a large stone coffer covered in symbols similar to the one that had opened the stone door. As she approached the stone coffer it burst to life, illuminating a large projection of controls, similar to the ones she used to fly the Trident.

Aeria frowned at the controls before her, noting that they were different than what she was used to. They had an older, less organized layout but seemed similar enough that she wasn't concerned. She began to work at the controls and after a few minutes was able to pull up a screen that projected against the stone wall at the far end of the chamber. A listing of information projected on the wall and after squinting at the words for some time, Aeria began to grasp what had occurred on the planet. It seemed that the commissioning of the building had been authorized by her grandfather Kronus thousands of years earlier, but for some reason was never completed before his departure from the planet. The last record indicated that even though the building was fully functional, it would be abandoned and sealed shut in order to, "protect the local inhabitants."

She wasn't sure what to make of the information as it didn't provide any clues to what had driven them from the planet, or why they had felt the need to protect its inhabitants. They wouldn't be able to interact with the technology so what harm could they do? It was true that the structure had a self-destruct mechanism that would initiate a nuclear reaction if activated, but who would use such a thing? No one in her family had ever used that function, as these buildings were far too valuable to destroy on a whim. If one of them was ever abandoned on a planet it would just stand as an unusable stone monument that no one outside of her family would be able to operate.

She wondered if the two girls had anything to do with it. They had been able to use the holodisk, so it stood to reason that unless it had been malfunctioning, they would have been able to interact with the structure's controls, but how could that be? How was it possible that they could use the holodisk at all? Could all of the inhabitants of this planet use their technology?

Aeria shook her head. It was an absurd idea, but then again nothing else was adding up. If they were to be believed that they had just found the holodisk, then what were they doing at the structure? Were they trying to break into the building? If so, to what end?

Aeria felt frustrated. Nothing was making any sense and the more she learned the less she seemed to understand. Closing her eyes she tried to focus; tried to fit the pieces of the puzzle together. But as she stood there contemplating, the sound of footsteps could be heard coming from the direction of the antechamber. Her eyes flew open and she whirled around, unsheathing her weapons. Who could be coming? Maybe the two girls had decided to return after all. She dashed out of the room with blazing speed and entered the antechamber, ready to kill whomever she found. She was stopped short, however, as she came across a familiar figure at the edge of the large platform.

With a look of surprise on his face, Thanatos stood up with his hands in the air, blinking at Aeria. Stuttering, he said, "Mis... Mistress Aeria! I *thought* that ship on top of this building looked familiar, but aren't you supposed to be up on the Trident?"

Aeria glared at the man for a moment but couldn't hold the look. Breaking into a grin she replied, "You fool, I nearly ran you through! You should try to be more careful." Walking over to him she clapped her hand on his shoulder, nearly knocking him backwards off the edge of the platform. Chuckling, she asked, "In all the years that we have known each other, how many times have I listened to my father when he's asked me to stay behind? You should know better."

Regaining his balance, Thanatos grinned back at her. "It's true that you rarely do what you're told, but I doubt your father will be so forgiving this time. This planet seems to be filled with mystery and I suspect he had good reason to ask you to stay."

"Well if he did have a reason, then he's kept it to himself," she snapped, her grin fading into a scowl. "Regardless, I've discovered some interesting things in the short time that I've been here, this structure being one of them, but hardly the most intriguing. Speaking of, why are you here?" Aeria measured him with a piercing gaze, wondering if he had discovered the holodisk beacon.

"Well, the scouting ships discovered several structures on the planet's surface that are inconsistent with the technology levels of the indigenous species. I was sent *here* because this building registered an energy spike shortly after our arrival. But it seems you might be to blame for that energy spike?" Thanatos asked.

Aeria paused for a moment, wondering if anything she had done could have been detected by the sensors. It seemed unlikely, but there was no other explanation. Remembering the girls, she tried to decide how much to reveal to him. He had been a loyal soldier and a decent friend for all the years that she had known him (he was even a distant cousin, of royal descent like her) but despite their long history she wasn't sure how much she could trust him. She doubted he would knowingly betray her, but she decided it would be better to keep some of her discoveries to herself, at least for the time being. She still wanted to find out the truth for herself without the interference of her father. "You probably registered my ship as I descended through the atmosphere. Either that or you might have picked up on the energy stores of this building which, as you can see, seem to be fully functional," Aeria pointed to towards the lights in the gallery.

"I can see that, yes. It's intriguing that a building like this would exist on this planet, isn't it?" Thanatos wondered aloud, looking around at his surroundings.

"Yes, although it's not completely finished. I was just looking through the logs before I heard you coming. They indicate that my grandfather commissioned the construction some time ago, but was forced to leave it dormant before it was completed," Aeria replied.

"So it seems your suspicions might have been

right. There *was* more to Kronus's story, after all. Was there any indication as to why the building was left unfinished?" Thanatos asked.

"No. The logs didn't say anything; only that it was to be sealed shut," Aeria lied. She wasn't sure what to make of the information about protecting the locals, but she suspected it might be important.

Thanatos gave Aeria a skeptical look and after a moment asked, "Forgive me for prying, Mistress, but why have you come to the surface? What are you doing in this building?"

Aeria forced a fake grin and with as jovial of a tone as she could muster she said, "My friend, I thought we already discussed this! You know I can never resist a chance at adventure! Especially when my father forbids me!" She lied again, but Thanatos didn't seem to be buying it this time. Seeing his skeptical look she pressed on, "I saw the initial scans of the surface, and this building seemed to be most curious. I wanted to see what it was and find out why my father had told me to stay." This time Thanatos seemed convinced. Maybe it was the hint at truth that had sold the deception, or maybe she was just getting better at lying; either way she was anxious to change the subject. "I noticed a settlement of the indigenous species nearby. I was planning on exploring it after I finished here. Would you like to come with me?" she asked, hoping he wouldn't notice the uneasy tone in her voice. He didn't, but his response didn't make her feel much better either.

"With all due respect, Mistress, I was sent here on orders from your father to investigate the building and to discover the source of the energy readings. As I've done both of those things I think I should be reporting back. Perhaps you ought to come with me? Your father will eventually figure out that you've come to the surface and it would be better for both of us if he discovers it sooner rather than later," Thanatos suggested with a wary tone.

Aeria frowned at the man. She didn't like the idea, but decided it might serve her purpose best to go with him. If her suspicions were correct, the two girls were heading for the nearby settlement, but wouldn't arrive there for a while. Going to see her father would buy some time. He would undoubtedly be angry with her, but unlikely to send her back up to the Trident. If she sent Thanatos back alone, he would ultimately have to report that he had seen her and that she was heading to the settlement, which would undoubtedly lead to questions as to why she had gone there. This would not serve her goal, not if she was going to be the first to solve the puzzle. Aeria shrugged and said, "Perhaps you're right. Let's go."

Thanatos seemed relieved by her answer. "Good! I have a few other stops to make before we head back to your father's encampment and having you with me will make things easier."

The two of them prepared to leave. Aeria was glad he hadn't insisted on seeing the logs for himself. If she played her cards right she would be able to get what she wanted without anyone getting in her way. She would discover the planet's secrets and be the hero of the day if it was the last thing she did. The time had come for the history books to forever remember the name of Aeria, goddess of wisdom and strength! Her chest filled with pride as the green lights of the gallery faded behind them.

CHAPTER 6

Out of breath, Kira stopped and collapsed in the tall grass just outside of the tree line. They had finally made their way out of the Black Wood, but she was too exhausted to feel any relief. The sun was beginning to come up and the piercing dark of the night was fading away. Only the brightest of the stars could be seen through the blue glow of the sunrise.

She was exhausted, and confused and angry; angry that after everything, they had failed their objective. She had tried to look as much as she could while they ran, but there had been no sign of any more Night's Widows. What would they do? They hadn't collected enough flowers to save their father and there was no time to go back in, not without her spear to protect them. She peered over at her sister in the dim morning light. Kaya had also collapsed to the ground, her chest heaving as she desperately gasped for air.

Tears began to roll down Kira's cheek. She didn't know why exactly she was crying. Everything was so awful that it was hard to pinpoint any unique source of her misery. Her whole body ached, the gashes on her arm screamed in pain, and her ankle throbbed incessantly. She could barely remember everything that had happened; it was such a blur. *Who was that strange woman they'd met? Was she some sort of spirit of the forest?* She certainly didn't appear to be human; not with the way she had glowed or the way she moved.

Kira lay back in the grass, catching her breath and crying while she stared up at the fading lights in the sky. She was glad the sun was returning but it did little to raise her spirits, as it meant they were running far behind schedule. She wanted so badly to just fall asleep, but that wasn't an option. The only hope their father had was for them to return as soon as they could. But even if they rushed home now, they were still a flower short. She closed her eyes and just let the misery and pain wash over her. The tears rolled down her cheek and fell into the grass with greater frequency. Rolling on to her side she curled up into a ball and began to sob uncontrollably. It had all been for nothing and her father would die because of her failure.

Kira was so angry and disappointed in herself. She had known it was a near-impossible task when she started, but the thought of failure had never crossed her mind. What would they do? Should they rush home and hope that one flower was enough? Or should they risk staying and looking again for more flowers, burning the precious time they had? Was it better to go home with their mission only half-accomplished only to have him die from not enough medicine, or to collect enough just to arrive too late? Either way it was her failure.

Kaya must have noticed her sister crying because

she got up and walked over to Kira. Sitting next to her in the grass she gently rubbed Kira's shoulder, trying to comfort her. In a quiet voice she asked, "Why are you crying? We made it out of the woods…"

It took a moment for Kira to control her sobs enough to speak coherently. Between gasps of air she replied, "But we failed. We didn't find enough flowers…"

Kaya's face brightened, despite her apparent exhaustion. "Don't be silly, we haven't failed. Look!" Pulling open her satchel Kaya pulled out two flowers and showed them to Kira.

Kira blinked, unable to believe what she was seeing. She looked up at Kaya uncomprehendingly and asked, "How?"

Kaya grinned. "While you were fighting the sabercat. I knew we wouldn't find any more, so while it was distracted I ran over to the flowers and grabbed them."

Kira was speechless. She couldn't have expressed the love she had for her sister in that moment if she had ten lifetimes to do it. She wanted to hug Kaya, but found she was too exhausted to move.

"I would have told you earlier, but with that strange woman showing up and us running like crazy to get out of that dreadful place, there just wasn't a chance. Speaking of, who was that woman?" Kaya asked.

Kira's tears faded as the knowledge of the additional flowers sunk in. Everything seemed suddenly better, and even the pain she was in seemed to subside. She stared at Kaya for a moment, not saying anything. She had set out to protect Kaya, to take care of her and yet, in the end it seemed more like her sister had been there to protect her. Without her, the whole trip would have been a failure. Wiping the tears from her cheeks she responded truthfully, "I don't know who that woman was, or where she came from, but I don't think she was human."

Kaya nodded, "Well whoever, or whatever she was, without her help we wouldn't have made it out of there. Do you think she followed us?"

Kira shook her head. "No, I don't think so. She would have caught up to us long ago if she had. I doubt we will ever see her again." Starting to feel better, she sat up and examined her arm. The gashes were deep, but had finally stopped bleeding.

"Let me see," Kaya said, reaching out to examine Kira's arm. Looking at it for a moment she opened her satchel and pulled out a small clay bowl wrapped in leather. She unwrapped it, revealing a dark brown paste. Dabbing her fingers in the bowl, she gather the brown paste and began to rub it into the gashes on Kira's arm.

The substance instantly caused the gashes to burn with renewed pain. Kira wanted to cry out, but they were still too close to the Black Wood to make that much sound, so she clenched her teeth in agony instead.

After a few moments of tending to her wounds, Kaya rewrapped the clay bowl in the leather covering and placed it back in her bag. She frowned and said, "I'm no expert, but I think you're going to need more than that to keep it from getting infected. We need to hurry; can you walk?"

Kira nodded, and with extreme effort and some help from Kaya she climbed to her feet. Her ankle had gone far beyond being sprained and was now purple and swollen. Without her spear she didn't have anything to help her walk besides her sister, and so for a long while that is how they moved, the two girls walking side by side as Kaya helped support her weight. They went on like that for some time until they came across a fallen tree branch that was just long and sturdy enough to serve as a sort of walking stick for Kira.

They walked silently for hours, too exhausted to carry on any meaningful conversation. They did share a laugh when they passed the grove of trees where they had met up the day before, but that was the extent of their talking. Both just wanted one thing and one thing only: to be home. Around midday they stopped to eat and drink what was left of their supplies but other than that, they did not stop to rest.

As the hours dragged on, the two girls moved more slowly as their fatigue began taking its toll and the lack of sleep started to weigh heavily on both of them. Finally cresting the last hill, they could see the valley of farms and fields of crops between them and their home. They looked at each other and smiled, but only half-heartedly as they knew that their expedition had taken longer than expected and there was a chance their father was already gone.

They began their slow descent down the hill into the valley, almost stumbling their way down the hillside. A few of the laborers in a nearby field stopped working and stood to watch them. Realizing who the girls were, they dropped their tools and ran over to give Kira and Kaya their assistance. Kira was only familiar with one of them and he looked quite concerned as he and the other men approached. Kira, barely able to stand and beginning to feel faint in the warm sunlight, sleepily asked, "Is my father still alive?"

The farmer tried to answer but before he could, Kira collapsed. Reaching out his arms he caught her before she hit the ground, and with the help of the other laborers they were able to stand her back up. Kira's head swam as the world seemed to rock back and forth. She knew she had to get the flowers to Felmar but she couldn't feel her legs anymore. The exhaustion of the trip had finally taken its toll on her and before she could hear his answer, everything went black.

* * *

Humid. Hot. Suffocating heat and vapor. The smell of sulfur and fire. Kira looked around at her surroundings. Her heart sank. How would she ever find what she was looking for in this place? All around her was a dark, burnt, jagged landscape with no light except for the orange glow of molten rock far below her. The heat was unbearable and the smoke stung her eyes. She looked down into the crevasse to her right. A hundred feet below her, she could see a wide river of lava splashing and gushing slowly down the mountainside. The heat rising from it was enough to make her eyes water. She looked away towards her left. Her eyes followed the rock wall up and up until she had to crane her neck to see the peak of the mountain she stood on. The top of it was hollow and was emitting an ominous red glow. All along the face of the mountain she could see more molten rock spewing out and running down conduits like rivers of fire.

She felt afraid. She'd never been to a place like this, never even imagined such a place could exist. It was no wonder the others were so afraid of it; but she had no choice. Something very precious was here and she needed to reclaim it... but what was it? She tried to remember but the thick, choking air and unbearable heat clouded her mind. She felt lost and alone. Everything began to spin, the burnt black landscape blurring together with the orange glow. The ground beneath her feet began to rumble and the next thing she knew she was falling, screaming as she careened towards the river of lava below her.

* * *

"Child! Wake up!" Kira's eyes opened slowly. Her head was still clouded and she felt hot. She looked up at the person hovering above her. It was Yamara.

"Are you all right, child? You were having another nightmare," Yamara said with a worried look.

Kira looked around. She was in her hut, lying in her bed. There were bandages on her arm and her foot was elevated, resting on a stack of furs. It was still purple, but seemed to be less swollen than before. Suddenly remembering the purpose of her journey, she blurted out, "How is my father?"

Yamara smiled, "Shhh child, don't worry. Your father is doing just fine. Felmar just gave him a second dose of the medicine and he seems to be getting better. Frankly, I'm more worried about you!"

"Me? Why?"

Yamara's smile faded. She looked over at Kira's arm and said, "I'm afraid your wound is infected. You've been battling a fever ever since they carried you through the gates."

Kira looked at her arm again. She tried to move it but was immediately punished with excruciating pain.

"No. Don't move it; that will only make it worse."

Seeing Yamara's worry, she reached out with her good arm and grabbed her hand, squeezing it affectionately. Yamara looked at her with a smiled. As she did, the door to the hut opened and Kaya walked in.

"You're awake!" Kaya cried out, rushing over to the bed and dropping to her knees.

Kira smiled drowsily, "You sound like you missed me."

Kaya nodded, "After you fainted in the fields I wasn't sure you'd wake up again."

"Nor was I," chimed in a familiar voice. Felmar, who had been sitting quietly next to her father's bed, stood up and walked over to them. Peering down with a look of what could only be described as bemused disdain he asked, "How are you feeling?"

Kira hated the sight of the man. Even just looking at him made her feel worse. She wanted to come back with something smart to say, but she was too weary. "I feel... awful. Hot and tired."

"As one might suspect after such a journey," Felmar replied curtly. "But before you doze off to sleep again, I have a few questions I'd like to ask the two of you."

"Questions? What kind of questions?" Kaya asked, exchanging a knowing look with Kira. Yamara didn't speak, but seemed to tense up.

"The kind that require both of you to answer. Specifically, how did you come to find so many flowers? And how did you manage to survive whatever creature did that to your arm?" Felmar asked in a cold voice, pointing at Kira's wounded arm.

"What? Didn't you expect us to return, Felmar?" Kira asked spitefully.

Felmar didn't say a word, merely scowling at Kira. Her words had hit a nerve and whether he'd say it or not, that had been precisely what he had hoped would happen.

Before he replied, Kira interjected, "Well too bad for you, my sister came with me. If it hadn't been for her quick thinking we wouldn't have gotten as many flowers as we did." She smiled at Kaya, who blushed at the compliment.

Shifting his weight uncomfortably, Felmar asked again, "But what of the creature who attacked you? How did you survive that?"

Kira hesitated. She wondered if he would believe her if she told him what really happened. She wasn't sure she even believed it herself. "Well... someone helped us."

Felmar's eyes squinted until they were the tiniest of slits; making his face appear snakelike in the dim light. "*Someone helped you*?" he asked incredulously.

Kira shook her head. "I don't have enough energy to tell this story more than once. Yamara, I want you to call the village elders and my uncle. They should hear it firsthand. I don't want this *serpent* twisting my words for his own benefit," Kira said, glaring up at Felmar. Yamara looked back and forth between them. Unsure of what to say, she stood and left the hut.

After several minutes their home was filled with murmuring people, exchanging confused looks. More than just the elders had come, but Kira didn't mind; the more people that heard this story, the better. Heruncle Druin was standing at the foot of her bed, looking quite worried as he eyed her wounded arm. She smiled at him, trying to console him without words.

When everyone was settled in and the murmuring died down, Kira whispered to Kaya, "Do you still have the thing we found? Will you bring it to me?"

Kaya nodded and moved towards her satchel. She pulled the metallic cylinder from the bag and handed it to Kira. Everyone in the hut seemed quite astonished by the device and a few of them gasped and whispered to each other.

"While we were searching in the Black Wood, we found this." Kira told them the entire story: meeting up with Kaya, the storm, finding the object, and the strange building. She told them of the sabercat and finally, the woman who had come to their rescue. She told them of how they had fled when the wolves attacked. When she finished her story no one said anything for several minutes. The hut was silent as everyone seemed to be in awe.

"Ludicrous!" Felmar broke the silence. "This whole story is absurd! She is clearly deranged from her fever." The group of people began to murmur again, some nodding in agreement while others looked skeptical. Druin didn't move or say anything; he stood still, watching Kira closely.

"She's telling the truth! I was there! I saw all of it, and I'm perfectly healthy!" Kaya protested. The murmuring came to a stop for a moment.

"Of course the younger one will back up the older sister's fantasy. Why is her word any more trustworthy?" Felmar spat indignantly. The murmuring began again. Most of them seemed to be agreeing with Felmar, making Kira angry.

"Fine! I'll prove it!" Kira shouted. Everyone hushed, wide eyed. Kira grasped the object and pressed the first symbol with her thumb. Immediately the device began to hum and glow green. After a few seconds the large projection of a map burst forth and hovered in the air. The hut was filled with gasps of awe. No one spoke, not even Felmar. In fact he seemed to be more shocked by the development than anyone else.

"Do you believe us now? We aren't lying. We really saw the stone building and the glowing woman in the forest."

"It must be the spirits!" Yamara cried out, having remained silent up to then. "What else could it be?" Her words seemed to break the spell of the projection, and everyone began talking to each other loudly.

Kira's head swam again as the room seemed to be collapsing in on her. She didn't feel well and all the arguing was making it worse. She just wanted to close her eyes and rest. Druin must have read her mind, because immediately he bellowed, "Everyone out!!" The hut went quiet, but no one moved. They all stood awestruck, staring at Druin, who continued, "She needs rest. We can argue about this in the main hall. Perhaps my other niece would care to join us to help answer these questions?" He glanced at Kaya and she nodded sheepishly.

Without any more fuss everyone poured out of the hut, except Yamara and Felmar. Yamara gently patted Kira on the shoulder and went to leave. Felmar didn't move. Pointing at the metallic cylinder he whispered, "Give me that object, child."

Yamara stopped and turned back, glaring at Felmar. She walked over to Kira and put out her hand. "I'll take it, child. I'll keep it safe, I promise." Kira nodded and handed it to her. Felmar seethed with anger and stormed out of the hut. "Now you rest. I'm sure they'll have more questions later," Yamara whispered.

As Yamara left, Kira looked over at her father. He looked better than she remembered. His face had more color and he didn't appear to be in pain. Kira smiled to herself and, closing her eyes, drifted back to sleep.

* * *

Aeria lowered the throttle as her ship gently landed on a large stone structure; another complex constructed by her grandfather. From the looks of it, Aeria guessed it was part of the groundwork for what would have been a large city center or palace. It was connected to a large square grid that stretched out across the land. From the ground it looked like nothing more than an odd assortment of stone platforms and lines, but from the air it was clear that it was meant to serve as the foundation for one of Kronus's settlements. Like the pyramid they'd just left, it was unfinished; abandoned to stand the test of time and nature. It hadn't fared well as most of the structure was either crumbled or buried.

Aeria looked out through the glass of her cockpit to examine her surroundings. The unfinished compound was now covered by dozens of parked fighters and hundreds of soldiers building military encampments. All around her, men and women clad in polished black armor busied themselves with setting up tents and unloading cargo containers. It wouldn't be long before the abandoned foundation would stand as a city again, if only a temporary one. At the center of the commotion stood Velion's enormous black vessel, dwarfing all those that surrounded it. The outside of the ship was protected by thick black shielding and all along the side were covered ports for the vessel's weapons array. In a fight they would open and reveal a dozen devastating plasma cannons on either side of the ship. There wasn't a vessel in existence that could out last this battle cruiser, except perhaps the Trident.

Aeria had no doubt that her father had noticed her arrival and would be waiting for her aboard the monstrous ship. She wasn't looking forward to the encounter. For all of her bravado in front of Thanatos, she knew that the consequences of her disobedience would be severe. Shutting down the controls of her ship, she pushed her chair back and prepared to disembark. Opening the rear hatch of the vessel she tried to ready herself for what was to come. If she was going to be the hero of the day, then it was up to her to play her cards wisely and in a timely fashion. There were a great many secrets hidden on the planet, and as far as she could tell, she was the closest to discovering them. If her father wouldn't give her the credit she deserved, then she would take it for her own.

As the rear hatch lowered to the ground Aeria saw Thanatos approaching, a smug look on his face. He always got a sort of enjoyment out of watching Aeria get in trouble with her father, and the heavens knew that he'd witnessed it often. She might have been the favorite child of Velion, but she was far from the most obedient. "Are you ready?" he asked, his smug grin growing.

"Always," she replied coldly. Thanatos didn't seem to notice the tone because he kept the same grin on his face. Together they made their way through the bustling encampment towards the royal ship, each step bringing more apprehension. They stopped short, just under the port side of the ship. A few feet above them a hatch opened and an unsuspended platform lowered to the ground. Aeria took a deep breath as they stepped onto the platform.

Thanatos looked over at her and grinned again. He patted her hard on the shoulder and said, "What's the worst that could happen? He'll probably just banish you to live with your uncle Hadius in the underworld."

"Hilarious," Aeria responded coolly. She knew he was trying to make her feel better but there was honestly no telling what her father would do. The unsuspended platform levitated up, lifting them quietly into the bowels of the battle cruiser.

Once the platform stopped moving each of them

stepped off and started down a dim corridor running along the inside of the ship. After walking approximately a hundred feet they came to short metal staircase. Climbing it, Aeria could see the door to the bridge of the ship. Like the Trident, as they approached the door, a panel of green lights illuminated. Thanatos gave her one last look and pressed the uppermost symbol. The door slid open revealing a room identical to the control room of the Trident, only on a smaller scale. In the center of the lower platform three men stood around a large round table talking to each other.

As Aeria and Thanatos made their way down to the bottom platform the three men ceased their conversation. The two men standing next to her father immediately tensed and stood to attention, both calling out, "Mistress!"

Velion gave an almost imperceptible nod and both men stood down, although neither seemed to relax. "Father," Aeria said, lowering her head in a bow. Velion didn't move as he silently examined his daughter with a cold stare. She raised her head and looked him in the eye. No one said anything for almost a minute. Growing visibly uneasy, Thanatos shifted his weight and opened his mouth to say something, but before he could Velion raised a solitary finger to silence him.

"Explain yourself, Aeria," Velion commanded.

Thanatos and the other two men stepped back warily, but Aeria stood her ground. Boldly, she replied, "Why should I? You certainly haven't." The shock that went across the room could be felt as easily as a gust of cold air. Even Thanatos was taken aback by what he was hearing. The look of horror that was frozen on his face nearly made Aeria laugh, but she knew better. The fury in her father's eyes was enough to stifle any humor she might find in the situation.

"What did you just say to me?" Velion hissed, his voice filled with anger.

"I think you heard me," Aeria responded. She could feel the anger growing in her stomach. She couldn't believe his nerve, demanding explanations when he had given none.

Velion's eyes widened with rage and his whole body shook with fury. Aeria knew that if she hadn't been his daughter, he would have killed her then and there, on the spot. No one dared defy him like this, but today was different. She would no longer tolerate his lack of respect. Feeling bold she pressed on, "Tell me, *Father,* how long have you known about Grandfather's secrets on this planet?"

Clearly trying to restrain himself, Velion spoke through gritted teeth, "That is none of your concern!"

"Isn't it? I *am* one of the ruling Council of Twelve, am I not? Charged with finding the most precious of heavenly jewels! Why wasn't I told we'd been here before?!" Aeria demanded, her anger growing by the second.

"How dare you take this tone with me! Have you forgotten your place, *child*? I do not answer to you!" Velion shouted. The three men watching were all horrorstruck. Clearly they had not expected Aeria's defiance.

"No, Father. You don't answer to me alone, but you answer to the council, and by keeping us in the dark you have betrayed us!" Aeria spat before she could think about what she was saying. At once, she knew she had crossed the line.

"*Betrayed you*?!" Velion bellowed. With lightning fast speed he reached over the table and slapped Aeria across the face.

The blow hurt her pride more than anything. She

could taste blood in her mouth from where her tooth had torn into the cheek, but it was nothing. She'd taken far worse before, but never from the hand of her father. Not wanting to appear weak in front of the soldiers, she glared back at her father and spat the blood on the floor. Velion also seemed rattled. He had never struck her before and clearly he hadn't meant to. Quietly he whispered, "All of you, get out."

Not wishing to excite their ruler's wrath again, everyone poured out of the control room. Aeria turned to leave but was stopped when her father shook his head and said, "Not you."

After the door closed behind Thanatos, Velion fixed his gaze on his daughter once more. In a voice that was straining to be calm he said, "You have every right to be angry with me. It is true that I have kept you and the rest of the council in the dark about Earth's history. But that does not give you the right to be insubordinate in front of the soldiers." He glared at her. Aeria nodded. Despite her anger with him she knew that she had been out of line. "Now, I understand it must appear as though I have deliberately kept you in the dark, but that is not the case. I didn't tell anyone about Earth's hidden history because I didn't know for certain that it was true. For all I knew, your grandfather was telling the truth. It wasn't until many years after he'd been imprisoned that I discovered there might be more to the story."

"But why wouldn't you at least tell me when we found it? Did I not have a right to know?" Aeria asked, trying to remain calm as her cheek tingled with pain.

"I realize now my error in not telling you, but in my defense I didn't know *what* to tell you. I had no more information about what we would find here than you did. For all I knew, there could have been an army, ready for battle the moment we landed. This is why I asked you to stay on the Trident. If a battle broke out, there was no one I'd rather have commanding the ship than you," Velion finished.

Aeria blushed a little at the compliment. Perhaps she had been too hard on her father. Looking back at it now, his actions and motives made perfect sense. If she hadn't been so bullheaded, she might have seen it earlier.

"At the same time, I didn't want to start a panic. A lesson you would be wise to learn is that an army that panics, is an army that falters. If I had shown my uncertainty to our soldiers, they might have lost faith in my ability to command. You must remember that much of our power lies in the perceptions of those that follow us. One isn't revered as a god by showing hesitation or uncertainty," Velion continued, eyeing his daughter thoughtfully.

Aeria nodded and looked to the floor in shame. "I'm sorry, Father. I acted impulsively and showed you disrespect."

Velion sighed and gave a small smile, his anger fading from his face. "I should have known better than to expect you to just do as you were told. You've never been one to sit idly by when there was action to be had." Velion walked around the table and put his arm over Aeria's shoulder and kissed her head. "Now that we know there is no danger here, I can commend you on a job well done." He looked down at Aeria. As he was almost a foot taller than her, she had to look up to meet his gaze.

"A job well done?" Aeria asked, suddenly confused.

"Why yes, you did find Earth, after all. Don't think that this will go unrecognized. Once we set up a more permanent settlement, I'll be sending a messenger back to Tython to tell the others of your discovery,"

Velion grinned at her, knowing this would make her happy.

Aeria's heart sank, despite the good news. She had been so disobedient and yet, her father had repaid her actions with kindness. She could feel a tear welling in her eye, but wiped it away before it could fall. Velion smiled again and hugged her. This made her happy, and the fact that the others weren't there to witness her soft side, made it even better.

"Oh, wait, Father, I have news." Aeria pulled away from the hug and looked up at Velion. "I wasn't going to tell you because I was mad at you, but I suppose I should." Velion smile faded and a look of worry passed over his face. The same look of worry he'd had on the Trident and in her memory.

Aeria paused for a moment, wondering how he would take the news. She hoped he wouldn't be angry with her again. "You asked that I explain myself, so I will. The reason I came to the surface was because the Trident's long range sensors picked up an emergency beacon coming from a royal holodisk." The worried look on Velion's face grew more severe. Aeria pressed on, "The sensors indicated the device belonged to Kronus, and had been activated a few hours prior to our arrival."

"How is that possible?" Velion interjected.

"That's exactly what I went to find out. But what I discovered doesn't quite make sense." Aeria stopped, unsure of how to tell her father what had transpired.

"Well, spit it out! What doesn't make sense?" Velion demanded.

Frowning, Aeria went on, "I found two of the locals in possession of the device; two girls to be exact."

"But you said the device had been activated," Velion murmured, confused.

"That's the part that doesn't make sense. Both girls were able to use the holodisk," Aeria finished, watching her father's reaction closely. Velion did not speak. Moving to the nearest chair he sat down in it, looking defeated and somewhat sad.

Confused by his reaction, Aeria asked, "What is it, Father?"

Velion covered his face with his hands, and through them he quietly said, "It is as I feared."

Aeria shook her head, dumbfounded. *What did he mean? Had he expected this?*

"You grandfather's sins seem to have no end. If he were not already imprisoned for eternity, I would lock him away again." Velion dropped his hand and shook his head in despair.

"I don't understand? What do you mean, his *sins*?" Aeria sat in the chair closest to her father.

"It is important we bring this news to the Council of Twelve immediately. What happened to the two girls? Do you have the holodisk?" Velion asked urgently.

Aeria shook her head. "No, they fled into the woods while I was fighting off a group of wolves that attacked us."

"Wait, I don't understand. Start from the beginning."

Aeria regaled her father with the tale, explaining that she had landed on an unfinished transport building just in time to see the older of the two girls fighting a large predator. She explained that after watching the fight for a few minutes she had decided to intervene and save the girl's life. He gave her a very worried look when she told him of the girl's ability to speak their language and seemed unconvinced that the girls found the device by accident. She explained how the pack of wolves attacked and how she had let the girls flee with the device.

"You should have followed them; why didn't you?" Velion asked, disapprovingly.

"I was more worried about the unfinished building than the girls. I found it odd that they were at the foot of it when I arrived, so I wanted to see what they were after. I knew that if they fled with the device we'd be able to follow the beacon," Aeria replied.

Frowning, Velion said, "Unless they learn how to turn it off. Do you have any idea where they went?"

"My sensors picked up a settlement a few miles from where I found them. I'm guessing that's where they were headed." Aeria shifted, realizing how foolish the assumption sounded.

"Then let's hope you're correct. We need to find them and that holodisk as soon as possible. I believe what you've told me, but I must see them for myself. Go summon Thanatos, but only him. We can't risk bringing someone we can't trust. Not even my personal guard."

Surprised by the urgency, Aeria nodded her head and did as her father commanded. After collecting Thanatos, the three of them met back in the control room of the royal ship. Velion took the center seat on the upper platform and started the ships engines. With a roar, the enormous black vessel lifted off the ground. Looking below as they ascended, Aeria could see the confused looks being exchanged by their soldiers. Only the royal guard had been alerted to their departure, but even they weren't given details of their destination.

Aeria walked over to one of the control consoles and began working with the projected screen. After a moment she smiled. It was still there. The beacon was still broadcasting and as she expected, it was nestled in the center of the settlement she discovered.

Working the controls again she called out to her father, "I've entered the coordinates of the beacon. It was right where I thought it would be."

* * *

Kaya followed her uncle as he made his way towards the main hall. All of the elders followed behind them in a long line, discussing her sister's story. With each step Kaya took, her body reminded her of the exhaustion she felt from the long and arduous trip. She wasn't excited to entertain the doubts and questions of these stuffy old villagers. She wanted nothing more than to return to her home and go to sleep, but it would have to wait.

She was worried about Kira. Despite all of Kaya's efforts to help out on the journey, she hadn't been able to keep Kira from harm. When they finally returned from the extraordinary trip, only to have Kira collapse in a fever, it was almost too much to handle. It was hard enough to see her father on what might be his deathbed, but having to watch her sister be carried to their home unconscious was almost unbearable. Kaya had seen death before, even at a young age, but she hardly knew what to do without Kira there to comfort her. She looked up at her uncle and smiled. At least she still had him.

Druin looked down and met her gaze. He gave a half-hearted smile that told Kaya that he was as worried as she was. Bending over as they walked, he whispered, "They will be okay, don't you worry. Your sister is the most stubborn person I've ever met, and the medicine already seems to be helping your dad."

As usual, his words made her feel better. He was always kind and gentle with her, despite his ragged exterior. She nodded and replied, "I know. I just wish I could have done more..."

Druin grabbed her wrist and stopped short, causing several of the elders following them to stumble and knock in to each other. The old men gave him an affronted look and stepped around the two of them, shaking their heads and grumbling to each other.

Ignoring them, he bent over and looked her dead in the eye, "Don't ever doubt what you've done. Maybe we weren't happy that you disobeyed and went after Kira, but what you did was admirable. You showed that you were braver than any of these people here. They all had the opportunity to go with your sister, and they chose not to out of fear, but not you. You went without a thought for yourself and had you not gone, she might not have survived. Do you understand?" He looked firmly from one eye to the other. Kaya nodded and blushed a little. He always knew how to cheer her up.

Looking satisfied, he stood up and patted her on the head. "Now let's go in there and answer the questions of these old codgers. I'm sure they will have many, as they don't normally take the stories of children at face value."

"You believe us, don't you?" Kaya asked sheepishly.

Bending over again and looking her in the eye he said, "Of course I do. I'd swear my life on your word, child." He grinned at her and poked her in the rib, making her squirm and giggle. "Now let's get this over with and get you to bed before you pass out like your sister."

They turned back towards the main hall, but as they began to walk again an odd sound started to grow in the distance. Kaya was the first to notice it. After a few steps, she stopped and surveyed the horizon, trying to determine the source of the sound. After a few moments of searching, she was able to make out a dark object, flying high in the air and rapidly growing in size. Blinking, she tried to determine what it was, but the shape was wholly unfamiliar to her.

"Uncle Druin," she called out, pointing towards the sky.

He stopped walking and followed her gaze. Squinting in the bright autumn sunlight, his eyes found the black object and a look of confusion passed over his face. "What is it?" he asked.

Kaya shrugged and shook her head. By now, the sound was loud enough that the entire entourage of elders also stopped. The group of men and women exchanged startled looks as they stared at the black object.

An uneasy feeling started to grow in Kaya's stomach as she noticed the object in the sky seemed to be slowing down as it approached. The sound it was making kept growing and growing, until it became a deafening roar. The ground began to shake as it slowed to a stop just outside of the village walls. As it hovered there, Kaya was able to get a good look at the flying monstrosity. Truly, there was no better word to describe the large, black triangular object floating high above her. It was enormous, stretching hundreds of feet.

The bad feeling in her stomach twisted into a knot, as she noticed that the large object was giving off a faint green glow; the same green glow that the mysterious woman from the woods had been emitting. There was no mistaking the color. Just as the enormity of the situation was washing over her, Kaya noticed Yamara walking towards her. She held the gleaming metal cylinder in her hand and in that instant, Kaya knew what had happened. Somehow the mysterious woman knew where the device had gone and she was coming for it, just as she had come for it in the woods.

"Uncle! It's her!" Kaya screamed, but Druin, who was standing several feet away, couldn't hear her over the roaring sound. She ran over to him and yanked on his arm. He looked down at her, bewildered, as she yelled, "It's her! It's the woman from the woods!" This time, he heard her. His eyes grew large and without saying anything he ran off towards his hut, limping as he went.

Kaya wasn't sure what he was doing, but there was no time to ask. She knew that she had to get the object as far away as she could, so she turned and ran over to Yamara. Yamara, like everyone else, was staring up at the strange monstrosity, and was so distracted that she didn't even notice Kaya pull the metal cylinder from her hands.

Holding the cylinder tightly against her chest, Kaya sprinted down the hill, making her way towards the eastern gate. She had to get it away from the village. There was no telling what the woman from the woods would do if she found the device in the hands of the elders. Whatever it was, it had only brought trouble so far and she knew it would only bring more if it stayed there.

She ran as fast as her exhausted muscles would allow; passing through the gates unnoticed by the sentries, who were busy watching the sky. She moved as quickly as she could through the tall grass outside the walls, but all of her effort was for naught. For as she made her way further from the village, the object above descended ahead of her, blocking her path. She stopped, watching it lower until it was right in front of her. The rumble from the vessel was so loud that she was forced to drop the cylinder and cover her ears. As it approached the ground, the air surrounding her started to move rapidly, making it difficult to breathe.

There were no words to express her dismay as the vessel extended three long support struts, landing a few yards in front of her. All thought disappeared as she stood in awe of the vessel before her. Nothing in all her life could have prepared her for this.

How could something so large move through the air, she wondered. *How was it possible to even lift such an enormous object*? It stood nearly forty feet above her and stretched for a hundred feet to either side of her. It was unlike anything she had seen before. Made out of black metallic material that was as smooth as ice, it gleamed in the autumn sunlight.

The winds calmed and the loud rumble coming from within the vessel died down as it came to a rest in the tall grass. The green glow that had been emanating from it faded as Kaya stood there, frozen, not knowing what to expect.

Behind her, she could hear the villagers approaching, murmuring to each other about the enormous object before them. She didn't need to hear their words to know that none of them knew what to make of it. As they came up behind her, she could hear some of them praising the spirits, having interpreted the object as some sort of blessing. She, however, was not so optimistic. Regaining her senses, she reached down and picked up the cylinder. If she was right, the mysterious woman would emerge any moment to reclaim the device.

A hush moved through the crowd as the vessel made a loud hissing sound before a section of the exterior started to move. They watched in astonishment as a large platform lowered from the belly of the vessel, revealing three humanlike figures, all of whom were clad in glowing silver armor. To the left stood the mysterious woman from the woods, who had a look of deep satisfaction on her face. At the center, stood an enormous man with white hair and a white beard, who was flanked by a smaller silver haired man. As the platform lowered, the woman whispered something to the others and pointed at Kaya.

The man in the center nodded and fixed his gaze on her. He was the tallest of the three, standing several feet taller than Kaya. He was covered in thick chiseled muscle, his chest as huge as a buffalo's, and his shoulders stretching almost as wide as Kaya was tall. He had long flowing white hair and a shimmering white beard that hung down to his chest. Strapped to his back was a long spear, although it was unlike the one Kira used. It was made out of metal that curved and twisted, forming razor sharp edges all along the length. More peculiar was that it seemed to be glowing with energy, as it was emitting a faint blue light.

As the man stared at Kaya, a chill ran down her spine. She couldn't be sure, but he did not look pleased to see her; in fact he looked rather unhappy at the sight of her. The platform they were standing on came to a stop, and all three stepped off of it.

All around her, the people of the village were dropping to their knees and praying before the three strangers. She looked around and was surprised to find that she was the only one still standing; even Felmar and Yamara, who were at the front of the group, were bowing.

Were these really the spirits she'd heard so much about? Kaya wondered to herself. She looked back at the approaching figures and frowned. The only thing she could be sure of was that they weren't quite human. Sure they looked enough like her, but something about them seemed *different*, almost ancient. The way they carried themselves was as if they were experiencing time differently than she was, like there was no rush, no urgency that was so common among her people. No, these couldn't be the spirits, Kaya decided. They were something entirely different.

She could feel her stomach tighten again as the three strangers came to a stop in front of her. She didn't know what to expect from the other two, but the woman had shown such blinding speed and strength in the woods that there was no chance of escape. The only hope she had was to willingly give the device back to them. Gritting her teeth, she held the cylinder out towards the enormous man at the center.

He peered down at Kaya with a strange look on his face, and examined her with an icy stare for a few moments. Kaya started to quiver as her heart began to race. She could feel every beat against her chest and was finding it difficult to breathe. *What was he waiting for? They were looking for the device, weren't they? Why wasn't he taking it?*

Increasing her confusion, the man looked away and shifted his gaze to the mass of villagers behind her. An odd look passed over his face and he grinned. To her disbelief, the man stretched out both of his arms and slowly began to lift off of the ground, emitting more and more green light as he did so. Gasps echoed through the crowd as the enormous, muscle-bound man floated several feet above the ground.

In a voice that seemed to shake the heavens he called out, "I am Velion, High Ruler and God of the Twelve Kingdoms of Tython! All who bow before me shall be spared! Behold my power and tremble!" Once he had spoken, the green glow of his armor grew brighter and brighter until after a few seconds the green light was as blinding as the sun and the earth below Kaya started to quake. Cries of fear came from the crowd as the villagers fell to the ground in terror.

Kaya held her ground, refusing to stumble like the others. Noting that the strange woman from the woods was watching her intently, she maintained a calm expression, unwilling to show any fear. She didn't know what to make of these strange beings or their peculiar powers, but she knew they weren't spirits and she would not bow to them. After a few moments the ground ceased moving, and the man above her floated gently back to the ground. He seemed quite satisfied as he looked out at the villagers, who were all cowering in fear and terror. Kaya looked over her shoulder at the people behind her. Yamara was signaling to her to bow, but Kaya refused and looked back at the man before her.

He was staring at her again, but his previous look of satisfaction was now gone. In a quiet voice he said, "You would be wise to bow, little one. You do understand the words I'm saying, don't you?"

Kaya nodded and replied, "I can understand you just fine, but I will not bow. You've come for this haven't you? Well go on, take it and leave." She extended the device out again, hoping he would do as she asked. He did not. Instead he tossed his head back and he boomed with laughter.

Collecting himself he grinned and said, "I see now why my daughter was so interested in finding you. Tell me child, what is your name?"

Kaya was dumbfounded. Of all the responses he could have had, she did not expect him to be amused. Sheepishly she replied, "My name is Kaya."

Velion smiled, his face filling with unexpected

warmth. "Well Kaya, I understand that you have the ability to use this device, is that true?" he asked, pointing to the metal cylinder. She nodded and held it out, pressing the first symbol. As before the device burst to life, creating a large holographic map in the air. A hush went over the crowd behind her as the villagers watched in awe. Kaya noticed that the shorter man with silver hair seemed to be the only one who was surprised by her actions.

Still smiling, Velion asked, "And is there anyone else here who can make it work?"

"My sister, Kira, can. But she's the only other person that's tried," Kaya answered.

"I see," Velion said. Looking back over the crowd he pointed and said, "You, come here." Kaya looked over her shoulder and saw Felmar stand. Her heart sank a little as he came walking up; she didn't despise the man the way her sister did, but she didn't like the idea of him having possession of the device. Once Felmar was next to Kaya, he fell to his knees again and made a show of worshiping Velion.

Frowning with impatience, Velion ordered Felmar to his feet and instructed Kaya to give him the device. She wanted to protest, but thought better of it. She pressed the symbol, turning the device off before she held it out to Felmar. He had a wicked look in his eyes as he snatched the device from her hands.

"Press one of the symbols," Velion instructed.

"Yes, my lord," Felmar said, clearly trying to flatter the strangers. With his wicked grin growing larger, Felmar happily obliged the order. He pressed the first symbol just as Kaya had done, but nothing happened. Still grinning, Felmar pressed it a second time and again nothing happened. His grin faded into a look of panic as he frantically pressed all of the symbols on the side of the cylinder. Still nothing happened. Kaya noticed that again, the silver-haired man seemed to be the only one surprised by the events.

"As I suspected," Velion announced. "You can leave now," he snapped. Felmar begrudgingly returned the cylinder to Kaya and glared at her before he made his way back to the others. Velion fixed his gaze on Kaya again and considered her for a moment. "Where is this sister of yours? Is she in the crowd?"

"No. She is back in the village," Kaya answered, unwilling to reveal too much to the strange man.

"Why isn't she here with you?" Velion asked, searching Kaya's face for any deception.

Kaya didn't like the way he was looking at her, but felt compelled to answer. "She's injured. Something *she* should already know," Kaya retorted, pointing at the blonde woman. Velion did not turn to look; instead he kept his gaze fixed on her.

To Kaya's surprise, Velion gave a thoroughly worried look and asked, "Would you take me to her, child?"

"I thought you came for this. What do you want with my sister?" she demanded, waving the cylinder in front of her.

Velion sighed, and with a growing look of irritation he curtly replied, "The holodisk is of no concern to me, little one, although I can understand your confusion. Let me make this clear; what I really came for was you and your sister. Now, please take me to her, before I lose my patience." He extended his hand, indicating that he wanted her to lead the way.

Kaya didn't like the idea of leading these people straight to her sister, not in her current condition, but what choice did she have? They clearly had strength and power that she didn't, so how could she refuse? Begrudgingly, she turned and started to make her way through the crowd, back towards the village. Yamara gave her a grave look as she passed by, but Kaya reassured her, whispering, "It's okay."

The villagers parted before them as she led Velion and the other strangers towards the village gate. She could tell by the looks on the villagers' faces that they were deeply concerned by the interest these strange beings were showing in her and Kira. She knew that they thought she'd angered the spirits and they'd come to punish her. She wanted to tell them off and call them fools, but she couldn't be sure that they weren't right. Maybe she and Kira *had* done something wrong by going into the Black Wood. They'd certainly found some strange things; maybe they *did* anger these three strangers in some way.

With her concern growing, Kaya decided to be bold again. She stopped short in the middle of the crowd and turned to face Velion. Holding her head high she demanded, "You aren't going to hurt her, are you? Because if you are, you might as well kill me now, because I'll never let that happen!"

The silver-haired man snorted and said, "My, my, she is a feisty one, isn't she?"

"If you think this one is feisty, you should see the sister, Thanatos. They truly are a pair," the blonde woman interjected.

Frowning, Velion replied, "Child, I have no intention to harm you or your sister. I promise that I will not lay a finger on her." Velion held up his hand, as if swearing an oath. Forcing a smile, he gestured for her to lead on.

Kaya glared at the three of them. *What was their game? Who were they and why did they care about her or Kira?* Frustrated, she spun on the spot and stamped off towards the village again, this time with a hastened pace. She wanted answers and clearly she wouldn't get any until they saw Kira.

Almost running, Kaya made her way through the village gate and up the hill. Cresting the top of the hill she stopped in front of her hut and turned back towards the three following her. She could see that several yards behind the three strangers, the entire village was following them. This was truly becoming a spectacle. Frowning, Kaya pointed at her home and said, "She's in there, but I don't know what good coming here will be. She's probably still asleep."

Velion nodded. "That's fine child, I only wish to see her for myself." Indicating to the others that he wanted them to stay outside, he went to enter the hut, but before he could, Druin emerged from inside, holding a spear in his hand. Standing tall, he held it to Velion's throat and said, "I won't let you harm them. You might frighten my niece, but I am not scared of you!" Kaya understood now what her uncle had done; he had gone to grab his weapon in order to protect them. If only he knew what these strange beings were capable of.

Kaya tried to warn him but she didn't get the chance. Before she could utter a word, the blonde woman bolted towards Druin like a blur of green and silver lightning. In the span of half a heartbeat she had moved nearly twenty feet and slammed her shoulder into Druin's side, sending him flying through the air. He landed in the dirt several yards away, lying in a crumpled heap of pain. Kaya called out, but the damage had already been done.

Druin groaned in pain as he rolled over in the dirt. Kaya looked wildly at the blonde woman. "How could you?!" she demanded.

The blonde woman laughed and said, "Oh, don't worry. He'll survive; I went easy on him." Sneering at Kaya, she turned to look at the crowd in the distance and yelled, "Let that be a lesson to anyone else who would try to stop us!" The villagers all dropped to their knees again, worshiping and praying in the distance.

Seeming amused, Velion ignored the scene and entered the hut, his huge body barely fitting through the door. Kaya looked back at her uncle, who was starting to stir. Deciding that he would be fine, she followed after Velion, entering the warm and stuffy hut.

Lying on her bed, sound asleep, was Kira. Kaya was amazed that her sister was still asleep, despite all the commotion. They'd barely left her alone before Velion showed up in his flying monstrosity. She must have been truly exhausted to have slept through that.

Velion eyed Kaya's father for a moment, but proceeded towards Kira's bed. He crouched at her bedside and began to examine her injuries, touching his hand to her bandages.

"What are you doing? You said you wouldn't lay a finger on her!" Kaya demanded.

Velion turned to look at Kaya, the irritation evident on his face. Quietly, he said, "How many times must I tell you, I mean you no harm? How am I supposed heal her wounds if I don't know what they are?" Kaya didn't know what to say, as it hadn't entered her mind that he might want to heal Kira. She was convinced that they had come to take the *holodisk,* or whatever they kept calling it. *Why would he want to help them?*

Velion turned back to Kira and pulled at her bandages, revealing the deep gashes from the sabercat's claws. The wounds were swollen and filled with puss. He shook his head. "Her wound is infected. She is going to die," he paused, "unless..."

"Unless what?!" Kaya demanded, tears forming in her eyes. Kira couldn't die, not after everything they'd been through. Kira was supposed to be the strong one! She was supposed to take care of Kaya, not the other way around! Kaya couldn't allow both her father and her sister to die; if there was a way to save either of them, she demanded to know what it was.

Velion turned back towards Kaya and said, "Unless you agree, of your own free will, to come with me and the others."

"Come with you? Where?"

"Back to my home, child," Velion replied, eyeing her closely.

"Where is your home? Would I be going alone?" Kaya didn't like the sound of this at all.

"It's a place very far from here, across a vast ocean of stars and no, you would not be alone. Part of the deal is that your sister has to come with us as well. Choose quickly, do you want me to heal her or not?" Velion stared at her, without expression.

It was such a strange request, that Kaya didn't know what to do. She looked at Kira's arm again and cringed at the gruesome sight. She'd seen infection before and knew that Velion was telling the truth. She looked back at her father, who was sleeping soundly and looking healthier than he had in days. She frowned, unable to decide. If only someone older was there to tell her what to do.

"Well?" Velion urged.

She wanted more time to think but could tell that Velion was losing his patience. She did, however, have an idea. "I agree, but on one condition," Kaya replied. "You must also heal my father and promise to leave my village in peace. No one is to be harmed!"

Velion eyed the girl, smirking as he did so. "You're very shrewd for someone so young. So be it. Do we have a deal?"

She hesitated, looking at Kira's infected wounds again. "Yes," she replied, hoping that she hadn't just made a huge mistake. Velion turned back towards Kira and pulled out a device that looked very similar to the cylinder she still had in her hand. Holding it over her arm, Velion pressed one of the symbols and immediately the object started to glow bright green, filling the hut with its light.

To her amazement the gashes on Kira's arm started to change. The blood and puss evaporated and the skin started to pull itself back together. After a few seconds the gashes were completely gone and the skin looked as if there had never been a wound at all. Velion smiled over his work and moved the device down towards Kira's ankle. Holding it a few inches above her swollen foot, the device went to work again. The swelling diminished and the bruising disappeared completely, leaving the ankle looking as normal as ever.

Kira began to stir, but did not wake up; instead she rolled on her side and let out a long groan. Velion smiled again and looked towards Kaya. "She will be as good as new when she wakes up. Now tell me, what ails your father?"

Kaya still couldn't believe what she'd witnessed. *Who was this man? How could he heal wounds like this?* She looked back and forth between Kira's healed arm and Velion's smiling face. "How?"

"All in good time, little one; but for now I need to know what is wrong with your father if I'm to uphold my end of the deal," Velion insisted.

"I don't know what's wrong with him, he's been sick with a fever for many days. That's why we were in the woods; we were looking for medicine for him." Kaya answered, walking over to her father's bed. He was sleeping quietly.

"I see. Well, I'll do what I can," Velion replied. His massive body moving in the small hut was almost comical, but Kaya was so awestruck by what had just happened, that she failed to notice. He crouched next to her father and activated the device again; this time it glowed with a yellow light instead of a green one. Velion paused and asked, "Tell me child, where is your mother?"

"She died many years ago," Kaya replied, taken aback by the question.

"I see. I'm sorry for your loss." He went back to work. Holding the device a few inches above her father's body, Velion moved it from his head all the way to his feet and back again. The changes were less dramatic, but Kaya could see the color in her father's face return to a normal pigment.

He started to shift in his bed and to Kaya's amazement he opened his eyes for a few seconds and smiled at her. Just as quickly as he had come to, he rolled over and fell back to sleep. Velion deactivated the device and stood, trying not to hit his head on the ceiling. "I've done what I could for your father but the rest is up to him. He was much closer to death than you might have guessed, little one. I'll give you a moment to say goodbye. When you are ready, come outside and we will be on our way." He walked over to Kira's bed and, putting his massive arms under her body, lifted her up. Still fast asleep in his arms, Kira looked peaceful as the two of them left the hut.

A moment later, as Kaya sat next to her father wiping the tears from her eyes, Druin burst into the hut. "What... what is the meaning of this? Where is he taking Kira?" he asked, looking disconcerted as he glanced around the hut.

"Shh... Father is resting." Kaya placed her hand on her father's shoulder and smiled to herself. "It's hard to explain, but I'll do my best." She told him as much of the story as she could manage in the short time she had.

Reaching the end of the story, she finished, "I made an agreement with him, that if he healed my father and Kira, and left the village in peace, that we would go with him."

"Go with him? I'm not letting you go anywhere with that man!" he shouted, more at the people standing outside than at Kaya.

Frowning, Druin sat on the floor next to Kaya, and looked at her father. "I'm glad the stranger was able to help my brother, but you cannot leave. You risked everything to save your father, and now you are just going to abandon him?"

Kaya shook her head; she didn't know what to do. All of this was so much for her to take in and she wished Kira was there to help; she would know what to do. "These people are different, Uncle. The villagers believe they are the spirits themselves."

"The villagers are fools! They're no spirits!" Druin yelled, again more to the door than to Kaya.

She felt trapped. She'd made a deal with Velion, and there was no turning back. "I don't think they're the spirits either, but as you saw, their strength is beyond ours; that blonde woman single-handedly killed five wolves, without even so much as a scratch. He kept his end of the deal and I gave my word; I must go."

"You don't know what you are doing; you are just a child. Let me go talk to them," Druin insisted.

"No." Kaya's eyes filled with tears. "He gave me a minute to say goodbye, but you *must* let me go with them. I don't want you to stand up to them again and get killed. Someone has to stay and watch over my dad." Her uncle did not respond right away. He sat there, deep in thought, for a long moment before eventually giving in.

Pulling Kaya into a hug, he whispered, "I love you Kaya. If your mom was here, she would be as proud of you and your sister as I am. Tell Kira that I said so, won't you?" Kaya nodded furiously, beginning to sob. "I don't know why these people want to take you, but I guess we don't have a choice," he said, squeezing her tightly. "You take care of your sister! Never leave her side if you can manage it, and please, for my sake, stay out of trouble!"

Kaya nodded furiously again, the tears rolling down her cheeks as she did. Why was this happening? She didn't want to leave! There was finally hope that their father would get better and now she had to leave him? It wasn't fair! She wouldn't go! "No, I'm going to stay!" Kaya cried out.

"I want that more than anything, but if you refuse to go, they will hurt us. Me, and Yamara, and your father too. You wouldn't want that would you?" Druin shook his head knowingly, "No, you have to go. Be strong, like your mother and sister."

"Time's up!" The blonde woman's voice called from outside the hut. Druin helped Kaya out the door.

CHAPTER 7

Kira opened her eyes and found herself in an unfamiliar place. She looked around the dimly lit room she was in and decided she must be dreaming. The room was so peculiar, but something about it seemed real. She pinched herself but nothing changed. Where was she?

She was laying on what she assumed was a bed, although it looked nothing like the one she was used to. In fact it felt much more comfortable than what she was used to. It was made of a white fabric and was soft and fluffy to the touch. She bounced her weight up and down on it and felt it spring back under her. She laughed a little. If this was a dream then she was okay with staying here for a while.

She examined her surroundings again. The bed sat in the center of a large room made out of gleaming white stone. Swinging her feet over the side, Kira hopped on to the cold floor before remembering her injured ankle. To her amazement the ankle felt as good as new, and was no longer swollen or purple. She bounced on the pads of her feet, testing its strength and was pleasantly surprised at the results. Remembering her journey, she quickly looked at her arm. The gashes from her fight with the sabercat were also gone. She rubbed her fingers across her forearm and the hair stood on end as if nothing had happened. Something didn't make sense. How could she be healed if this wasn't a dream? Everything seemed so real.

Even the white stone beneath her bare feet felt real as she wiggled her toes on the smooth, cold surface. She bent down to run her fingers across the floor. It was unlike anything she'd felt before, hard and strong, yet smooth and beautiful. Standing back up, she noticed a strange object protruding from one of the walls.

Walking over to the protrusion, she noticed that she felt lighter than normal, like she was made out of feathers. She smiled at the sensation. Whatever this place was, it was certainly different than home.

As she approached the object hanging from the wall, a most peculiar thing happened. Water began to flow out of a tube sticking out of the wall, falling into a stone basin below. Seeing the water made her realize that she was incredibly thirsty, so she cupped her hands to catch some and slurped it down. It tasted divine. It was cold and clean; cleaner than any water she'd tasted before.

After several handfuls, Kira wiped the water from her face and turned to look around again. The room was lit, but there didn't seem to be a source to the light. She searched for an opening where the sun might be shining in, but found none. There was no fire or any torches either. Something didn't seem right to her. There were no doors or windows that she could see, so how had she gotten there?

Starting to feel panicked, Kira ran her fingers along the walls as she walked around the room. Making a full circle, she was troubled to find no doors and no windows at all. The smooth rock hadn't even had so much as a crack in it except for where the stone walls sat flush against each other. She was trapped in the strange room, with nothing but a bed and a bizarre fixture that water came out of.

"Hello?!" she called out, wondering if anyone would hear her. She doubted anyone could. She was entombed in stone, with no apparent way out. "Can anyone hear me?! Hello!!!" she yelled, but there was no reply; only the echo of her own voice bouncing off of the gleaming stone walls.

Frowning, she went back to the bed and sat on it. She tried to remember how she'd gotten there, but couldn't recall anything. The last thing she remembered was telling the village elders about the cylinder they found and the strange woman in the woods, but that didn't explain anything. It didn't make sense at all, really; she should have been feverish from her wounds and laid up in bed, but here she was.

A dark thought passed through her mind, making her feel uneasy. Was she dead? Had the wounds killed her after all? Yamara had been convinced her arm was infected, so it was possible. Was this where a person went after they died? She shook her head in confusion. That didn't make sense either. She felt alive enough, and she had been thirsty, hadn't she? How could a dead person be thirsty? There had to be an explanation; she just needed to think.

Her thoughts were interrupted when, without warning, the wall to her right started to move. The large stone wall began to slide sideways, revealing a dark opening where the corner had been. She got up to make her way out of the room but was halted by a figure emerging from the darkness.

Kira couldn't believe her eyes as she stumbled back, landing softly on the bed again. It was the blonde woman from the forest, but she wasn't alone. Another, smaller figure was following her and Kira's heart skipped a beat when she saw who it was.

Kaya entered the room and with a wide grin spreading across her face, she bolted over to Kira and tackled her in a hug. "You're awake!!" she exclaimed, hugging Kira hard enough to squeeze the breath from her.

"How…" was the only word Kira could manage.

Realizing she must be crushing her sister, Kaya let go and stood back, beaming at Kira like she'd been brought back from the dead.

"What's going on? How are you here? And what are you doing with her?" Kira blurted, feeling more confused by the minute.

"I'll let her explain," the blonde woman nodded towards Kaya. "I'll have someone bring you some food, I'm sure you're both hungry," she said as she turned and left the room, the wall sliding shut behind her.

"How did we get here?" Kira asked, still disoriented. The question seemed to dampen Kaya's spirits, as she stopped smiling and hung her head, lowering her eyes to the floor.

"I'm sorry. I didn't know what to do and you were asleep, so I couldn't ask you," Kaya said, her voice wavering a little. She looked back up at Kira, and with a troubled look, she whispered, "Please don't be mad at me."

"Mad at you? Why would I be mad at you? Just tell me what's happened! Where are we, Kaya?" Kira insisted.

"I don't know how to explain it," Kaya whispered.

Feeling exasperated, Kira pulled Kaya over to the

bed and forced her to sit. Trying to remain calm, she said, "Just start from the beginning. The last thing I remember was lying in my bed and telling the elders about what happened in the Black Wood. What happened after that?"

Kaya frowned, and with an uncomfortable look she said, "They came back for the thing we found in the woods, or at least that's what I thought at first."

"Who is 'they'? That blonde woman?" Kira asked, confused again.

"Yes, but she wasn't alone. She had two others with her," Kaya replied as she started to relay the story to Kira. She explained how Velion had asked to see Kira and how he made a deal to heal her and their father, if they came with him.

"Wait, he healed Dad? Did he get better?" Kira interrupted.

Shrugging, Kaya replied, "I don't know. Velion said that he did as much as he could, but I didn't get to stay long enough to see if Dad was really better."

Kira frowned and thought to herself for a moment. "You said the deal meant we had to go with them. Where are they taking us?"

"Well, after Aeria carried you back to their ship..."

"Aeria? Who is that?" Kira interrupted again.

"Oh, the blonde woman's name is Aeria." Kaya replied. Kira nodded in understanding and gestured for her to go on. "After she carried you to the ship, we got inside and flew to some other place far away, where there were a lot of other people like them. They wouldn't let me out to see anything, but when I asked what the place was, they said it was their first settlement on the planet."

"*Their first settlement*? So they weren't from there?" Kira asked, starting to feel apprehensive about what was to come.

"No. Velion said that their home was *'across a vast ocean of stars'* when we made the agreement."

"What does that mean?" Kira asked.

Kaya shrugged again, "I don't know, but we didn't stay at that place for very long; probably only a few hours."

"Where did we go after that?" Kira asked, the feeling in her stomach getting worse.

"I'm not sure how to explain this… the ship we were in started to fly again, but not like before. This time we flew upwards, into the sky, until… there was no more sky," Kaya said with a perturbed look on her face.

"What do you mean *until there was no more sky*? How is that possible?" Things were starting to feel like a dream again.

"I don't know! We were going up until there was no more sky and everything started to look like it was night time; until all I could see were the stars. Then everything got weird and cold," Kaya shuddered.

"What do you mean *weird and cold?*"

"Well… it felt like I was lighter than normal and all the warmth seemed to disappear."

"I think I know what you mean; at least about feeling lighter. I feel that way right now, actually," Kira replied, standing up again. "What happened after that?"

"That's when they put me in a room like this one and gave me something to make me fall asleep. When I woke up, Aeria was standing over me and asked if I wanted to come see you, so I followed her here," Kaya finished, grinning again.

Kira wasn't sure what to make of the story. It seemed too farfetched to be real, yet here she was, locked in this strange room with her sister. "Did they tell you why they wanted to bring us with them?" Kira pressed.

Kaya frowned, "No, but they've been really nice so far. It's almost like they've been treating me like an honored guest or something."

Kira gave Kaya a concerned look. She wanted to ask more questions but before she could, the wall started to move again and Aeria walked in. She was followed by someone holding a tray that was covered with bowls, each filled with the strangest food Kira had ever seen.

Aeria and her armored companion came to a stop and to the sisters' astonishment, the floor started to move. It started to grow and morph its shape as if it were suddenly alive. After a few seconds it began to blossom like a mushroom might and the top started to flatten out into a rectangular shape. What once was just a part of the floor had now become a gleaming white table. On either end of the new table, the floor started to shift and morph also, until there were two rounded seats with high arching backs.

Without even flinching, Aeria commanded the armored stranger to set the tray on the table and announced, "I wasn't sure what kind of food you would like, so I brought a variety. You'll have to get used to it if you are going to be living on Tython."

Who was this woman? Kira wondered to herself, still staring at the new table and seats. *How was she able to mold hard stone without even touching it?* She looked up at Aeria in amazement. She seemed so normal to Kira; nothing about her appeared very remarkable aside from her strange armor.

Realizing that gaping at the woman might be considered rude, Kira shook off the confusion and asked, "What's Tython?"

Aeria smiled knowingly and replied, "You will see

soon enough. For now, eat. Someone will be back in a while to fetch you. My father wishes to speak to the two of you." Bowing ever so slightly she turned on her heel and left the room again, followed by her silent companion.

Kira looked to Kaya for some explanation, but all she got was a shrug followed by a grumble in her own stomach. She hadn't realized it until then, but she was terribly hungry. She walked over to one of the seats and sat in it. To her amazement, it began to morph to her body and became very comfortable; much more comfortable than she would have expected from hard stone. She watched as Kaya went to sit in the other chair, and giggled when her sister jumped in surprise.

The two girls surveyed the food before them and, shrugging at each other, started to dig in. To Kira's surprise, most of the strange food tasted quite good; in fact much of it was better than what she normally ate. There were several types of meat, some deliciously sweet fruit, a couple varieties of bread and some steaming vegetables that she didn't recognize. Everything, even a strange yellow paste, was seasoned and cooked to perfection.

Along with the assortment of meats, fruits and vegetables there were six cups filled with three different kinds of drinks. The first one Kira tried was an orange colored liquid that had a sweet but also bitter taste. She guessed that it was juice from some sort of fruit, although she didn't know what kind of fruit would produce orange liquid.

The second drink was a bitter and strong purple-colored liquid. As she drank it down, there was a warm feeling that started to fill her throat and cheeks. After a few minutes the room started to feel more relaxed and she started to giggle as she shoved food in her mouth. She smiled as her sister tried the same drink.

Making a face, Kaya shook her head and refused to finish it. Gladly, Kira took the rest of the drink and gulped it down as well.

She wasn't sure why, but she felt happy and relaxed. Everything about this new place, wherever it was, was nice. She'd never known anything outside of her village but everything about the room seemed like an improvement over her home. There was no dirt, except for what was on her clothing, and the air was fresh and cool. Everything seemed so clean and beautiful compared to the mud-brick hut she had grown up in. "You know... I think I could get used to this, *hic,*" she announced with a hiccup.

"Muh huh... meh tow," Kaya replied with a mouthful of food.

Hiccupping again, Kira clumsily grabbed for the third type of liquid and started to gulp it down. It was a dark brown, fizzing liquid that tickled her nose as she drank it. It was sweet and the bubbles in it felt incredible on her tongue. She had no idea how a person could make such a drink, but she liked it.

Leaning back in her seat, Kira let out a long and loud belch that made Kaya giggle from across the table. Biting off one last piece of meat, Kira decided that she'd had her fill. Gently rubbing her tummy, she cheerfully asked, "What do you, *hic!* Think Velion wantsh, *hic!* from ush?" Kaya, whose mouth was so full of food that her cheeks were puffed out like a squirrel's, shrugged and muttered something unintelligible.

What *would* he want? Kira wondered to herself. *What was the point of all of this?* They come across some inhuman woman in the woods, only to have her and her father collect them and take them to their home? To what end? It really didn't make sense at all. She still wasn't convinced that she hadn't died and this wasn't some strange afterlife experience.

The wall began to move again and Kira's thoughts drifted away. Expecting to see Aeria again, both girls were surprised to see a man with long, silver hair enter instead.

"Who are *you?!*" Kira blurted, feeling unnaturally bold.

Taken aback by the demanding question, the silver-haired man actually chuckled. "My, my, Aeria was right after all. You really are a bold one, aren't you? I suppose that's to be expected considering your heritage."

"My *heritage*? What would you know about my heritage?!" Kira barked with the warm feeling returning to her face. This time, however, even Kaya was surprised by her sister's tone.

The man, to Kira's surprise, was quite jovial about the conversation, and laughing again, replied, "More than you might expect, Mistress Kira. If you are done eating, will the two of you please join me? I'm to escort you to your meeting with King Velion." Bowing lower than Aeria had, the man extended his arm, indicating that he wanted them to leave the room.

Happy to explore more of her strange surroundings, Kira hopped to her feet and exited the chamber. She was followed closely by Kaya, who grabbed another piece of bread from the table before running to catch up. "You know my name, but I don't know yours," Kira said matter-of-factly, as she walked past the silver-haired man.

"With pleasure, Mistress Kira. My name is Thanatos and I am one of King Velion's generals," he replied in a diplomatic tone.

"What's a general?" Kira inquired as she walked through the passage into a long, dimly lit corridor.

"A good question. I am the commander of

Velion's first military battalion. I lead his army into battle, when required," Thanatos replied, indicating to the girls which direction to walk.

"So... like a warrior? You are a fighter?" Kaya interjected as they made their way down the long corridor.

"Simply put, but accurate none the less. I am a *warrior*," Thanatos compromised.

"Kira's a fighter too! She took on a sabercat one on one and almost won," Kaya bragged, making Kira's rosy cheeks blush even more.

"Then perhaps one day I will be fortunate enough to see her fight," Thanatos smiled. "This way," he said, turning down an adjacent hallway. "You said she *almost* won... what does that mean?"

"It means that I almost died. I was saved by Aeria, or whatever her name is, before the sabercat could finish the job," Kira said with a frown.

Thanatos stopped short and turned to look at Kira. Coolly he said, "Her name *is* Aeria, but while I have you here, alone, there is something I must tell you." He looked around, checking for onlookers. Finding none he continued, "Be very careful around Mistress Aeria, she can be quite cruel to those she sees as being below her. Right now, I think she is amused by you and won't harm you, but if you offend her, it may very well be the last thing you do."

Kira and Kaya exchanged worried glances. Wary of pressing the issue Kira asked, "Who are you people and why are we here?"

Thanatos grinned, "I cannot speak for my people or family, but I am a friend. Why you are here, I cannot say because I am as confused about it as you are. I suggest you ask Velion the same question when you meet him. Come, we are almost there." Turning away, he began to walk again. The girls followed.

As they made their way down the dimly lit corridor, Kira noticed something at the end of the hall. There were two massive, white doors with a strange green orb in the center. The doors were exceedingly bright compared to the dim corridor and as they approached them, Kira had to squint her eyes in the bright light.

Something about the doors seemed to radiate a power that could be felt in the air. She didn't know what to make of the feeling, but as the giant doors slid silently apart, she couldn't help but feel *empowered*. Something about this place was intoxicating but also... *natural*, like her entire body was absorbing power and becoming stronger. She looked over at Kaya, who had a puzzled look on her face. *Was she feeling the same thing*? Kira wondered. She wanted to ask, but as they passed beyond the doors the room they entered stole her breath away.

There were no words to describe her wonder as she looked around the cavernous room. Giant pillars, wider than she was, extended high above her. They supported a magnificently crafted dome ceiling with elliptical rafters that curved upwards. At the center of the dome was an oculus, peering out into a dark landscape filled with small white lights. Kira understood then, what Kaya meant about it looking like night outside.

Below the oculus, floating high in the air, was a strange rotating monstrosity. It was composed of spinning metal hoops rotating inside of larger spinning metal hoops. The image was mind bending and Kira began to feel queasy as she watched them spin. Looking away, she noticed that at the center of the room, there was a platform with two levels. On the higher of the two levels she saw an enormous, white haired man, sitting on a large chair that was magnificent to behold.

The chair was massive, and was made of some strange, blue, glassy material. Kira had seen stones like this in Felmar's hut back in the village, but nothing this magnificent. It looked like the chair had been carved directly from a colossal growth of sparkling stone. The long, flat facets of countless curving stones formed the back of the chair and the edges around the top looked sharp enough to slice through flesh. To either side of the man sitting in the chair was an armrest, also composed of the shimmering stone.

The spectacle was awesome to behold and Kira had to pinch herself again to be sure she wasn't dreaming. What had they gotten themselves into? She looked over at her sister and realized just how alone they were; isolated in a strange place, surrounded by strange and magnificent beings whose motives were still a mystery. The warning that Thanatos had given them in the corridor didn't bode well and she knew they needed to be careful.

As they made their way up the steps to the first platform, the enormous man on the seat opened his eyes and looked down at them. With a smile he boomed, "At last! I finally get to meet the infamous Kira in person! I trust you're both feeling better now that you've had some time to rest?"

The two girls, still in awe from the astonishing spectacle, could only manage to nod.

"Good! And I trust that you've had time to eat? What did you think of the food?" he inquired.

"It was really good!" Kaya cheerfully replied, breaking the spell the room had put on them.

"Excellent! I wouldn't want you to go hungry. You're far too important for that," he boomed again with a chuckle, his long curly beard bouncing as he laughed.

Still feeling bold from dinner, Kira interrupted his laughter and demanded, "Who are you and what do you want with me and my sister?!"

His grin faded and with a serious look he replied, "A most prudent question indeed. I apologize for the confusion, but it wasn't until I had some time to reflect on the subject, that I could be sure of the answer."

The two girls exchanged confused looks.

"You see, Kira and Kaya, the two of you are very unique among your people. There is something that sets you apart from the rest and is of great interest to me and my family..."

"What does that mean? How are we unique?" Kira interrupted again.

Frowning at her rudeness, he said, "Patience, child. I promise to answer all of your questions, but first I must ask one of my own. What have you been taught about the origin of your people? Where do they think they came from?"

Kira's anger flared. She had no idea what this had to do with anything. She was about to argue with Velion before the scolding look from her sister made her reconsider. Sighing with irritation Kira explained, "We were taught that our people were created by *the spirits*, who came from high above and molded humans in their image. They taught us how to irrigate, and work the earth to grow food. They showed us how to speak and how to use medicine, but I honestly don't see what this has to do with us."

"On the contrary, it has everything to do with you. You see, your *'spirits'* were really my people. To be exact, it was my father, Kronus, who created humans," Velion said, watching their reactions closely.

Kira's mind reeled. Could this be true? She doubted it, but why would he lie?

"I can see that you doubt my words," Velion

continued, seeming to read her thoughts. "I promise you, I am telling the truth. Many centuries ago, my father found your planet while searching for a precious resource. When he searched it, he discovered a primitive race of semi-intelligent beings that had mastered the use of fire and, for reasons unknown to me, he decided to manipulate their genetics," he explained.

"Planet? Genetics? I don't understand," Kira replied, feeling more confused.

"I see... this might be more difficult to explain than I had anticipated. We will discuss astronomy later but for now, just think of genetics as the thing that makes you different from other animals. Your people believe the spirits created humans in their own image, which is actually fairly accurate. My father changed your ancestors by molding them to be more like my people. He made them smarter and taught them how to farm and build," Velion clarified.

Kira didn't know what to think and definitely didn't know what to believe. She'd never really believed in the spirits, but this explanation seemed even more farfetched. She looked over at her sister and shrugged.

Kaya seemed to be in deep thought and had a concerned look on her face. Quietly, she asked, "Does this mean we're related to you?"

Surprised, Velion replied, "Very perceptive, little one. Humans *are* distantly related to my people, but the two of you are more precious than that. Do you know why?"

"No, not really," Kira replied truthfully.

"If I'm correct, when my father was on Earth creating humans, he must have had children with one, because the two of you share my blood. Do you understand now? The three of us are related. We are family," Velion concluded.

"Is it true, my lord? They are *direct* descendants from Kronus?" Thanatos interjected, looking at the two girls in disbelief. Velion nodded but did not speak.

Kira wasn't convinced and curtly she asked, "If he was around so long ago, how can you know?"

"The holodisk that you found confirmed it," Velion replied shortly. Seeing that neither girl seemed to understand, he continued, "You weren't aware of it, but the device you discovered in the woods can only be used by someone who shares my blood. And since both of you are the only humans who seem to be able to use the device, then you must be related to me."

Thanatos seemed to be taking the news much more seriously than either of the two girls, because he was visibly agitated. With a tone of alarm he said, "There hasn't been a new heir in the royal family for centuries! If these two truly are descendants of Kronus, then wouldn't they be entitled to a place among the royal family?"

Velion grinned and replied, "That is for the council to decide. Regardless, the implications *are* profound, which is why you were the only other person entrusted with this knowledge. I hope you will keep it to yourself until we have made it back to Tython?"

Thanatos stuttered, "Of... of course, my lord, but why the secrecy? Isn't this glorious news?"

"Because there are spies everywhere, even among my own army. We cannot risk any of them catching wind that there are two new heirs. They must be protected; do you think you can handle that?" Velion asked, eyeing Thanatos closely.

Thanatos bowed and in his typically diplomatic voice replied, "With great pleasure, my lord."

"Good. By the looks on their faces, I think we'll

conclude our discussion for today. Please take them to one of the empty officer's chambers, won't you? I suspect they'll wish to stay together for the duration of the trip, yes?" Velion asked. Kaya nodded, but Kira did not respond. Her mind was too deep in thought to notice what was going on around her.

"Then it is done. We will meet again in a few days when we return to Tython. Thanatos..." Velion concluded, gesturing for Thanatos to depart.

* * *

The three of them left the throne room and made it all the way to their new accommodations before Kira said, "Why would there be spies around, Thanatos? And why would they care about the two of us?"

Thanatos stopped just outside of their new door and turned to look at Kira; his face was filled with a grave concern and quietly he said, "I'm afraid I am sworn to secrecy on the subject. But with the utmost regard for your safety, I will tell you this... be careful who you trust. If I were the two of you, I would only trust each other and no one else."

"But if we can't trust anyone... then why should we take your advice?" Kaya asked, puzzled at the contradiction.

"You are learning quickly; there might be hope for you after all," Thanatos replied with a smirk as he led the girls into their room. "Now, this is your new home until we reach Tython. I'm afraid you'll have to remain here until then, so this door will be sealed. I will come twice a day to bring you food and drink and anything else you might feel you need. Should you find yourself in an emergency and need my attention right away, this green panel next to the door will summon me. Just press this symbol," he finished, pointing at a large symbol near the bottom.

"The door will be sealed? Does this mean we are prisoners?" Kira asked, eyeing Thanatos incredulously.

"It is for your safety, I promise," Thanatos replied, bowing diplomatically.

"Promise? I thought I wasn't supposed to trust you?" Kira asked brusquely, but Thanatos didn't respond. He merely smiled and left the room; the door behind him sealing shut with a hiss.

Once he was gone, Kaya turned to Kira and asked, "So do you think it's true? Those things that Velion said about them being the spirits?"

Kira walked over to the door and pressed up against it, trying to push it open. It wouldn't budge. Giving up, she turned to look at Kaya. "Honestly, I don't know. It all seems so incredible that it's hard to believe, but then again look where we are," she said, gesturing at their surroundings. "I don't know what to believe, but I think Thanatos is right. We should only trust one another. I don't know who these people are, or what they want from us, but something doesn't seem right."

"What do you mean?" Kaya asked.

"I... don't know. I mean, what are the chances that we would find that holodisk, or whatever they call it? And, of all the days to do so, they just happen to be there, looking for it? That seems strange, doesn't it?"

"Like we were meant to find it?" Kaya asked, troubled.

Kira shrugged, "I don't know, something about all of this just feels... off. I keep feeling like I'm in a dream and that any minute, I'm going to wake up in my bed, sick with a fever."

Kaya looked to the ground and whispered, "I wish it was a dream... I miss Dad."

Kira walked over to her sister and hugged her tightly. "Me too, kiddo... me too." Letting go and turning to look at the room, she said, "Why don't we check out our new home."

Kira and Kaya spent the next few hours exploring their new surroundings. The officer's quarters were much larger than their other rooms had been, and had significantly better furnishings. There were several comfortable-looking seats, all surrounding a large and elaborately crafted wooden table. Instead of bare stone, the floor was covered in a silky red material that felt soft under their feet. On either side of the main room were two auxiliary chambers, each with its own bed covered in finely woven coverlets.

Each auxiliary room also had a smaller, tiled room attached that Kira found to be the most peculiar. It had two bowls protruding from the wall, one like the one she had seen before, and a different one that was lower to the ground and filled with water. In the corner of the tiled room sat an even smaller room, surrounded in glass. Kaya, who was much more adventurous than Kira, decided to step inside the glass room and was immediately drenched by water falling from the ceiling.

Blinking and sputtering, Kaya blindly dashed out of the glass room, spraying water everywhere. Not used to the tile floor, she slipped and collided with Kira, knocking both of them to the ground. For several minutes afterwards, the girls just sat there, soaking wet and laughing at each other.

It wasn't until Thanatos returned with their dinner that he explained that the tiled room was a wash room and that the lower bowl, was used for relieving oneself. He showed them how to control the shower and told them about something he called "soap." After smelling both of them, he insisted that they utilize it as soon as possible in order to, in his words, "quell the stench."

Along with the tray of food, he brought both girls new clothing to wear, saying that their leather and fur tunics were, "unfit for women of their ancestry." He tried to show both of them how the clothing worked, which was quite the spectacle as he didn't seem quite sure himself. After a few failed attempts Kira assured him that they would be able to figure it out and managed to shoo him away.

Once she was finished gorging herself for a second time, Kira went to her room to try out the shower and soap. The experience was remarkable. The water was warm and exhilarating, and the soap cleaned her hair and skin in a way she had never known.

After drying off and dressing in her new garments, she stood for a long time, examining herself in the mirror. She had seen her reflection in a lake a few times, but nothing as vivid as this. *So this was what she looked like*? She wondered to herself. It felt strange to see herself as others did, and it felt even more surreal to see herself in the new clothing Thanatos had brought.

The garments were a white with blue trim and were made of a delicate, billowing type of cloth. They were soft and smooth to the touch and the outfit hugged the curves of her body in a relaxed way. As she stared at herself in the mirror, she couldn't help but feel a little surprised at how striking she looked.

She wondered what her father would think if he could see her new outfit. He'd probably laugh and say that it didn't quite fit her personality, which was true as she'd never been the type to long for fine garments. The thought made her smile, even though it made her miss him.

There was a knock at the door and Kaya's voice called, "Are you alive in there? Did you slip and fall again?"

Scoffing, Kira replied, "You're the clumsy one; I only fell because *you* slipped!"

"Well, I only slipped because you were in the way!" Kaya responded playfully.

Turning and opening the door, Kira announced, "Well, if you would have listened to me and not gotten into the shower, I wouldn't have been in the way!"

"Wow!" Kaya interrupted, gaping at Kira.

Confused by Kaya's tone and the surprised look on her face, Kira asked "What? Why are you looking at me like that?"

Grinning, Kaya jeered, "You look pretty good when you aren't covered in dirt!"

Frowning, Kira reached out and pinched Kaya in the arm.

"Hey! Can't take a compliment?" Kaya replied, rubbing her arm and grinning wickedly.

"You weren't complimenting me, you were making fun!" Kira scolded.

"Maybe a little... but you really *do* look pretty. I bet all the boys on Tython will want to meet you!" Kaya jeered again.

"Oh stop it! Like I'd want them to! You're the one who's always wishing there were more boys around, not me!" Kira retorted, poking Kaya in the shoulder. "You are just jealous of my stunning good looks," Kira said in a haughty tone.

Kaya rolled her eyes, and responded, "Keep dreaming! At least you don't smell as bad as you did before."

Scoffing again, Kira countered, "Look who's talking! I could smell you from the other room! Maybe if you go wash up, you could look half as good as I do!"

"Oh, whatever! I'll be back and we will see who's jealous of who!" Kaya snapped, stamping out of the room.

Kira laughed and returned to the wash room. Next to the sink sat a comb, something she was actually quite familiar with, although the teeth of her comb were never as straight or nice as this one. Grabbing it, she started to run it through her hair until, after a few minutes, there were no more knots. It had been a very long time since her hair shimmered, and the look felt as alien to her as the clothes she was wearing.

Staring in the mirror again, she wondered, *what if it is true? What if we really are related to these strangers... would that be such a bad thing?* Everything around her indicated that the way these people lived was better than what she was used to. There was no shortage of fresh water or good food, and everything was clean and comfortable compared to the dingy hut she'd grown up in. Even the clothes she was wearing felt more natural to her than her leather tunic did.

The reflection of her sister in the mirror interrupted her thoughts. Setting the comb back on the sink she turned to look at her.

"Well, what do you think?" Kaya asked sheepishly, but Kira couldn't respond. Kaya had always resembled their mother, but tonight, it was as if her ghost was standing before Kira.

"Is it bad?" Kaya asked, clearly worried at Kira's silence.

"No. You look... lovely," Kira replied quietly, examining the beautiful green and white gown Kaya was wearing.

"Then why do you look sad?" Kaya wondered.

Kira smiled, and said "It's just that I wish Mom was here to see you all grown up. I think she'd be proud."

Kaya blushed and asked, "You really think so?"

"Yeah, I do," Kira nodded.

"So does this mean I won?" Kaya asked, grinning broadly.

"Maybe... but don't let it go to your head!" Kira responded with a smile.

Kaya beamed and walked over to the bed. Sitting on the edge of it, she looked back at Kira. In a cheery tone she asked, "What do you think Tython will be like?"

Kira grabbed the comb again and walked over to her sister. Sitting behind her on the bed, she started to run the comb through Kaya's tangled blonde hair. "It's hard to say, but I'm guessing it might look a lot like this place does."

"You think so?" Kaya asked, cringing as Kira combed out a massive tangle.

"Maybe," Kira replied.

"I hope so, I like it here!" Kaya exclaimed.

"Let's hope it stays that way," Kira responded pensively.

"Why wouldn't it?" Kaya asked in a puzzled tone.

Kira frowned as she pulled at another tangle. "I just don't think we should get too comfortable. We need to be on our guard around these strangers, at least until we know what they want."

"Do you think they want to hurt us?" Kaya questioned.

Kira didn't respond right away. She worked at Kaya's tangles for some time before she finally replied, "I don't think they would go to so much trouble, just to hurt us, but that doesn't mean that they have our best interests at heart either. I think we are important to them for now, but I don't know how long that will last."

"What do you mean?" Kaya asked as she started to chew on one of her fingernails.

"I don't know how to explain it, but it feels like there is more to this story than we are being told," Kira replied as she finished combing Kaya's hair.

"Like they are lying to us?" Kaya turned to look at Kira again.

Kira frowned and shook her head, "It's just a feeling, don't worry about it. It's time for bed anyhow."

Kaya looked to the ground and in a quiet voice asked, "Do you think it would be okay for me to sleep in here with you? I don't want to be alone in this strange place."

Kira smiled, "Well the bed is big enough, that's for sure. That's fine, as long as you promise not to kick me in your sleep!"

"I promise!" Kaya exclaimed, standing to her feet and jumping head first on to the bed.

"Now if only I knew how to turn the lights off..." Kira mused, searching for some sort of device on one of the walls. There was no need, however, because as she said the words, the lights in the room automatically started to dim. Smiling, she crawled further onto the bed and sprawled out.

After a few minutes of thinking to herself, Kira could hear her sister's gentle snoring. She smiled again, grateful that she was not alone in the strange room. Turning on her side, she closed her eyes and drifted into a dreamless sleep.

CHAPTER 8

Two days passed as the girls spent their time confined in their quarters. The monotony of the long hours was only broken up by a game Thanatos brought them. The game was a contest between two opponents, who each raced fifteen rounded stones around a track of twenty-four triangles. Kira wasn't sure how she felt about the game, but Kaya seemed to love it; no doubt because she kept winning. Out of twenty games, Kira had only managed to win six; a fact Kaya was more than pleased to rub in.

Kira was about to lose her fifth straight game when Thanatos interrupted to tell them they would be arriving at Tython in less than an hour. Thanking the heavens, Kira quickly cleared the board, ignoring her sister's complaints.

Standing up, she turned to straighten the sofa she'd been sitting on, but Thanatos stopped her. "Don't worry about it. The servants will clean it once we've left the ship."

"Why wait?" Kira wondered.

Sighing, Thanatos replied, "You're new to this, but being the descendant of Kronus is no small thing,

Mistress Kira. On Tython you will be seen as royalty, and as royalty you will be expected to adhere to certain rules of etiquette."

"Etiquette?" Kaya asked, handing the collapsed board game back to Thanatos.

"I suppose you don't really know what that is, do you? If you're going to survive the council, you must show that you can act as one of them, and I promise you, none of them would be caught dead cleaning. That is the work of the lesser ones."

"Who are the lesser ones?" Kira asked.

Sighing again, Thanatos walked over to one of the chairs and sat in it. "There is so much you need to learn. The lesser ones are one of the races that Velion and the council rule over. They actually look quite similar to humans but they do not come from Earth. They make up the lowest caste system of the twelve kingdoms, and are regarded as little more than slaves."

"You sound like you feel bad for them," Kira suggested.

Thanatos's look of exasperation shifted to one of alarm, and with a fierce look he said, "I will forgive the error this one time, because we are alone and you didn't know better, but do not insinuate such a notion again. There are a great many things happening on Tython that concern the lesser ones and their treatment and anyone who sympathizes with them is seen as a traitor."

"I'm sorry... I didn't know." Kira said sheepishly.

Seeming to calm down, Thanatos continued, "It's fine; just don't do it again, especially around the others. As I was saying, the lesser ones make up the lowest caste system and are the servants of the royal family. But between you and me, I *do* feel a little bad for them, although not for the reason you think."

Puzzled, Kira asked, "What do you mean?"

"I don't feel bad for them because they are treated like slaves. I feel bad because so many of them are *grateful* to be treated as such. You'll soon come to find that most of the lesser ones enjoy their captivity." Thanatos clarified.

"Why would they like being treated like slaves?" Kaya asked, shocked.

"Honestly, I don't know. It's just how they are. It's probably the reason they were enslaved to begin with."

"You said they were the *lowest caste*, what does that mean?" Kaya asked.

"The twelve kingdoms include several species of intelligent life, and each of them makes up a caste level. At the very top, is the royal family, which I guess now includes the two of you." The sisters exchanged a brief look of surprise as Thanatos continued, "Each member of the royal family rules over one of the twelve kingdoms. Right below the royal family is their distant relatives, which includes me. We are charged with the lesser ruling positions. Below us is the rest of my race, or the people who come from Tython. After that are several other species, until you get to the very bottom, where the lesser ones are."

"Why isn't everyone equal?" Kira interjected.

Thanatos fixed her with a strange look before saying, "Because they aren't. On Tython, the strong rule over the weak. That's how it's always been, and it would serve you not to question it."

Kira understood the warning and changed the subject. "When we were talking with Velion, you said something about there not being an heir for centuries, what did you mean?"

Thanatos smiled, "I wondered when you'd ask me that. It's a long story but simply put, the royal family hasn't had a new addition for a very long time. The last child born to the royal bloodline was nearly eight centuries ago, and the poor thing died before his first birthday."

"If there are no heirs, then won't the royal family eventually die off? Who would rule then?" Kira asked.

Thanatos nodded, "A question that's been asked and fretted over more than you can imagine. The council has extended great effort to continue their bloodline, but until the discovery of the two of you, their efforts were in vain. "

"How so?" Kira felt uneasy at the mention of her and her sister.

"There isn't time enough to explain, so suffice it to say that the royal bloodline was found to be incompatible with any known species. That is, until we found you," Thanatos finished quietly. Kira didn't know what to make of the information. She still wasn't completely convinced that she was related to these strangers at all, let alone the answer to their procreation problems.

Interrupting, Kaya asked, "What does it mean to be part of the royal family?"

Thanatos seemed relieved at the change in subject. "It means that the people you rule over will not love you, but they *will* fear you. The members of the royal family are seen as gods by their subjects, and they will expect you to act as they do. If either of you wish to make it through this, it's important that you embrace the fear of those subjects and never exhibit weakness or sympathy. From what I have seen, both of you have unflinching nerve, so use it. You will get much more respect for being brash than for being timid. Do you understand?"

Kira and Kaya exchanged glances and nodded.

"Good. Now, before I escort you to the transport,

there is one last thing you should know. As we speak, there are groups throughout the twelve kingdoms that are fighting to free the lesser ones. Right now it's only a minor issue, especially in light of our rediscovery of Earth, but there is no telling what might come of it. This is not widely known, so I expect you to keep it to yourselves."

"What does finding Earth have to do with it?" Kira asked.

"There is no time to tell you now, but I promise to explain later. Are you ready to leave?" Thanatos asked, peering at each of the girls.

"Yes. We didn't really bring anything with us," Kira reminded him.

"Right, I guess not. Well then, let's go," he said, turning to the door. With a hiss it opened and the three of them set off down the long corridor.

After several minutes of walking they came to a large marble door that resembled the one at Velion's chamber. Thanatos walked to a panel next to it and started using the controls until the door quaked to life. Sliding open, it revealed an enormous hangar that held a solitary ship. It was the enormous vessel that Velion had flown to their village.

Kira gaped at the monstrosity and asked, "What is that thing?"

Kaya laughed and said, "I forgot, you never did see the ship they came in did you? Well that's what they flew to our village while you were asleep."

"But I thought we were in that ship already... does that mean we are in a larger ship?!" Kira wondered aloud as she looked around the enormous hangar in disbelief.

Thanatos grinned, "Both of you were asleep when it happened, but after we left Earth we docked inside this hangar, which is a part of the Trident."

"The Trident?" both girls asked in unison.

"The Trident is the royal flagship. It is the most powerful battleship we have in the fleet and you've been living on it for three days," he finished as he led them down a carpeted walkway heading to the ship.

As they approached the side of the ship, the platform came to life and started to lower. Stepping up onto it, the three of them were lifted into the belly of the vessel. Kira was amazed at the craftsmanship of the smaller ship.

"How can such a large thing fly? How can you even lift it off of the ground?" Kira wondered.

"All in good time, Mistress Kira. Velion and Aeria should be waiting for us on the bridge, so let's hurry," Thanatos instructed, hastening his pace.

Somewhat to Kira's surprise, Velion was there to greet them with a large smile. In a booming voice that seemed too big for the confined space he said, "Good! You are clean and properly dressed. Are you ready? Today is a historic day indeed!"

Kira replied, "Do we really have a choice?"

His smile fading to a frown, Velion responded, "You *did* have a choice, and your sister made it for you before we left. Now, I trust Thanatos has briefed you on what's going to happen?"

"A little, but I still don't know what to expect."

"Well, I'll tell you then. We are going to be flying down to the surface of the planet. When we arrive there, you will be escorted to the palace. Once there, I will convene the Council of Twelve and you will be presented to the others."

"What happens then?" Kaya asked.

Velion grinned again and replied, "You'll just have to wait and see. Now, both of you go sit up front. I'm sure you'll want to get a good look at your new home."

Both girls obeyed and moved to sit in the front as

the vessel's engines ignited. Feeling a sensation she'd never imagined, Kira stared out the large panoramic windows. The vessel lifted off of the ground and hovered towards two massive hangar doors at the end of the platform.

Flashing yellow lights on the hangar floor burst to life as the doors started to part, revealing an ocean of stars sitting just beyond a green force field. Kira gazed at the stars in awe; she had never seen so many. Once the doors were completely open, the ship accelerated with breakneck speed, slamming Kira back against her seat.

Passing through the green force field, the vessel shot out into space with immense speed. Kira couldn't believe her eyes as it turned to face the planet Tython. It was an enormous blue-green ball floating gracefully against a backdrop of colors that she could scarcely believe. Massive stellar dust clouds of purples, yellows and greens stretched out across the heavens in an awe inspiring backdrop of grandeur.

It seemed so strange to Kira, yet something about it felt... natural. She understood then what a *planet* was. She never guessed that her home was just a ball, floating in an ocean of emptiness and stars like this one, but now there was no denying it. Her mind reeled as she processed all the images before her. How could this be? Nothing could prepare her for this. The vastness of the scene made her feel uncomfortably small and insignificant. *What would the villagers say if they could see this? Would they change, knowing that the planet they lived on was just one of many and that places like this existed? How would she ever explain it to them if she returned to Earth? Would they even believe her?*

Thanatos walked up behind the girls and whispered "That's the Talos Nebula. It's all that's left of a giant star that collapsed billions of years ago."

"It's beautiful," Kira whispered in awe. Kaya was speechless.

Kira pried her eyes from the breathtaking nebula and focused on Tython. It was mostly covered in land, but had several vast oceans. Around the exterior of the planet floated three massive rings. "What are those?" Kira asked, pointing at them.

"Those are the planet's rings. They are the debris left over from when two of Tython's smaller moons collided with each other about one million years ago."

"Two moons?" Kira asked, gaping as the rings.

Thanatos chuckled, "Tython has fourteen moons, two of which have people living on them."

Both girls were at a loss of words. Neither one could adequately process the sights before them as the vessel headed towards the planet. Kira watched in wonder as the planet grew larger as they approached it. Soon it filled the entire window and she was no longer able to see the nebula. As they flew closer, a feeling of panic started to fill Kira's stomach. *How would they ever stop*? They were falling towards the planet with such great speed; there was no way they'd be able to stop.

Gripping the arms of her chair in panic, Kira watched in horror as the outside of the ship seemed to burst into flames, filling her view with fire and smoke. Looking around in terror, she noticed that she was the only one who seemed bothered by the new development. "Is that normal?" she asked, trying to hide her alarm.

Thanatos clapped her on the shoulder and said, "Happens every time. Don't worry, the ship has shields that prevent the atmosphere from reaching the hull. We are completely safe, Mistress Kira."

"What's wrong? Don't like flying?" Aeria taunted

from behind them, but Kira ignored her.

After a few seconds the flames disappeared and Kira was able to clearly see the clouds and ground below her. As they careened towards the surface, she could see large settlements stretching out for miles. From this altitude, she could see several individual settlements connected to each other with strange strips of flattened land. The whole scene looked like some strange spider web.

Pointing at the largest settlement, Thanatos said, "That's where we are heading: the royal city of Ishkur."

"Is that our new home?" Kaya asked anxiously.

"Perhaps, Mistress Kaya. It depends on what the council decides," Thanatos responded.

The two girls sat and watched as the city of Ishkur grew larger and larger until they were flying down wide avenues like canyons, walled in by enormous buildings. They were magnificent; taller and brighter than anything either girl had imagined, and there were so many of them, each more fantastic than the last. *How can so many people live in such a small area?* Kira wondered to herself. Every inch of the ground was covered by pavement and the city stretched as far as the eye could see. Looking towards the ground, Kira could see countless people moving about the city, apparently unaware of her flying above them.

Taking her eyes off the ground, Kira watched in awe as they headed towards a massive rounded structure. It had seven enormous tiers, each successive level encompassing a slightly smaller diameter. The bottom three levels were complete circles that supported the top of the structure. The top four levels formed crescents that wrapped around a tower standing at the center of the structure. This inner tower rose upwards and inwards, forming a point that stood high above the rest of the structure.

At the base of the colossal building sat an enormous courtyard of grass, and as they approached, Kira could see that there were thousands of people standing in it. Looking to Thanatos she asked, "What are those people doing down there?"

Smirking, he said, "They are waiting for us." Both girls exchanged looks of alarm at the news. Thanatos, noticing their distress, said, "Don't worry. I'll be with you the whole way. Just try to ignore them, if you can. Remember what I said about appearing strong."

"You didn't say anything about huge crowds of people!" Kira reprimanded.

"You'll do just fine," Thanatos tried to comfort, but his words did little to soothe their nerves. Both Kira and Kaya fidgeted anxiously in their chairs and kept exchanging worried looks.

As the ship began its descent into the courtyard, a sinking feeling filled Kira's stomach and her mind raced with anxiety. She'd never seen so many people in her life and they wanted her to just act *normal*? How was she supposed to do that with so many strangers watching her?

She wanted to protest but there was no point, as Thanatos had already walked away and was talking with Aeria. Kira squirmed in her seat as the ship landed gracefully on the ground. Through the window she could just start to make out individual faces, all of whom were either cheering or yelling. *Were these the lesser ones?* She wondered. She understood then why Thanatos had said they weren't much different than humans. They didn't look all that different from Kira, except their skin was much paler.

"It's time to go. Are you ready?" Thanatos asked as he walked back over to the girls. Kira and Kaya both nodded. Smiling, he assured them, "It will be over before you know it."

With that, the three of them made their way out of the control room and started down the ship's corridor. Each step seemed to amplify the apprehension Kira felt in her stomach and as they made their way onto the platform she had the distinct sensation that she might be ill. *Why couldn't this just be a dream? I'd give anything to wake up, sick and dying, if it meant I didn't have to walk out in front of that crowd!* Her thoughts, however, were interrupted by the feeling of her sister's clammy fingers threading themselves between her own.

Kira's anxiety melted away as she looked over at Kaya and saw the terrified look her face. She had always been able to shelter her baby sister, but she had a feeling she was out of her depth here. Instead, she smiled and squeezed Kaya's hand tightly as she leaned over and whispered, "Remember what Thanatos told us. We have to be strong, okay?"

Kaya nodded furiously and, with a look of utter terror, she stood to attention. Catching a reproachful look from Thanatos, Kira also stood up straight, holding her chin high. The platform moved, and with a hiss it started to descend. Immediately the crowd outside roared to life with cheers and whistles.

As the platform lowered to the ground, the noise from the crowd seemed to grow louder and louder until it took everything Kira had to not cover her ears. All around them, on either side of a long paved pathway, stood tens of thousands of human-like figures. Now that she could see them up close, Kira realized that they looked less like humans than she'd originally thought. They were shorter than most humans and what appeared to be pale skin, was actually a glossy, blue translucent pigment.

Additionally their mouths, noses and hair were almost normal, but their eyes were slightly bigger and set further apart, and their ears were longer, coming to a sharp point at the tip.

Thanatos indicated to the girls that they should wait a moment while Velion stepped off of the platform ahead of them. After he walked a few paces Aeria followed after him and, with a nudge from Thanatos, so did Kira and Kaya.

As they started to walk down the procession, the crowd thundered with even greater intensity. The roar was deafening and the crowd appeared to be in a frenzy, whooping and cheering as if some great spectacle was before them. Kira didn't understand. *Did they always act like this when Velion and the others returned, or was it because of her and Kaya?*

All of it was overwhelming and the walkway ahead of them seemed to stretch on forever. It didn't help that Velion was walking at a painfully slow pace and kept pausing to greet people in the front row. Aeria, on the other hand, was not nearly as cheerful as her father seemed to be. She walked resolutely behind him without so much as a glance towards the crowd.

Kira tried to mirror Aeria's disposition, standing tall and walking firmly ahead without looking at the crowd around her. More than a few times she noticed them pointing at her and Kaya as they made their way down the procession, but she did everything she could to ignore them. *Almost there... almost there,* she kept thinking to herself as they approached the end of the path.

About twenty yards away from a set of huge marble doors Velion did something unexpected. He stopped and turned on the spot to face the masses behind them, holding both of his arms in the air towards them. Unsure of what to do, Kira and Kaya kept walking, hoping to pass beyond Velion and escape the fanfare, but were forced to stop when he turned his gaze to them. With a giant smile he pulled both of them to his side and whispered, "You are doing great, now smile for the crowd!"

With that, he stepped back a pace and cleared his throat. The crowd hushed all around them, and in a voice that was somehow amplified, he called out, "Citizens of Tython! I have returned bearing wonderful news! We have made an important discovery that will change the twelve kingdoms forever!" The crowd roared back to life as thousands of lesser ones cheered with renewed vigor. After several seconds, Velion waved his hands to calm the crowd. "After searching for countless years, we have finally discovered a planet filled with resources without end. Many of our troubles are finally at an end and our future is secured!" The crowd burst to life again, but this time the cheers were mixed with the sound of murmuring and talking.

As the mood in the fanfare turned from elation to restlessness, Kira wished she was anywhere else. They were all staring and pointing at her like she was some strange creature they'd never seen before; it made her skin crawl. Shifting uncomfortably, she looked over at Kaya and noticed that her sister appeared to be handling the situation quite well. She was obviously nervous, but the smile she had on her face seemed genuine. Kira briefly wondered if her sister was actually enjoying this, but her thoughts were interrupted as Velion pulled both girls close and whispered, "I think that will do for now. Go ahead and follow Thanatos, I will see you in the council chambers shortly. Try not to wander off." Setting them free, Velion turned back to face the crowd and Thanatos beckoned for the girls to follow him.

As they made their way through the giant marble doors, Kira turned back to look at the crowd. Now that she was no longer at the center of their attention, she could lower her guard and truly take in the spectacle. Something about the way the crowd moved in unison was hypnotic. She'd never seen so many people in such a small area before, and it was as if they all melted together, moving as a single massive being. She decided that if she ever made it home, this would be one of the stories she told her people.

The doors behind them shut with a soft thud, and Kira returned her gaze ahead of her. Without so much as a word, Aeria split away from Thanatos and the girls, ducking through a dark passage to Kira's right. Thanatos didn't seem to notice as he continued to lead the girls down the cavernous hallway.

All along either side of the corridor stood massive round pillars like the ones in Velion's meditation chamber, except each of these had a statue of an armored guard standing at the base. Looking up, Kira noticed that between each set of pillars, the high vaulted ceilings had intricate floral patterns carved into them. *How is it possible to carve such beautiful designs into stone?* she wondered. Nothing in her village was made of stone, except the tools they used for farming and the spear points, but even those were rough and jagged; not smooth and graceful like the patters above her head.

Kira looked over at her sister, who seemed to be preoccupied with the stone guards they were passing. Each time they made their way past one, she would drag her fingers across the stone and look up at the carved face. Quietly she asked, "Thanatos, what are these?"

Without turning to look he merely said, "That is a story for another time."

Frowning, Kaya decided not to press the issue. Kira turned to look at the stone guard nearest to her and couldn't help but get the feeling that it was watching her as she walked by. Perhaps, she speculated, that was the reason for their presence in the first place; to give the impression that someone was always watching. She shuddered at the thought, and decided to ignore the stone guards.

The three of them walked for a long time, passing arched doorway after arched doorway until the hall ended at a wide spiraling staircase. Without a word, Thanatos began to climb up the shallow steps. Both girls followed after him, although the stairs were wide enough that all three of them could have walked side by side.

They climbed and climbed until Kira's calves started to ache and both she and Kaya were out of breath. Finally, the landing at the top of the stairs came into view, revealing a hallway that was shorter than the one below. Kira could see a set of huge doors at the end and as they made their way towards them, they took her breath away again.

They were enormous! Standing high above her, each door was half of an ornately carved mural of a huge dragon with twelve heads. The three centermost heads stood taller than the other nine, and were crowned with unique headpieces; one with a crown of lighting, the next with a crown of fire and the third with a crown of ice. The other nine heads were all feasting on different types of animals, most of which were unfamiliar to Kira, except one that looked quite like a sabercat.

As they approached, the massive doors seemed to sense their presence because they began to swing open, revealing a large semi-circular room. The room reminded Kira of Velion's meditation chamber on the

Trident, except instead of just one throne there were twelve.

The twelve seats sat around the perimeter of the semi-circular room and varied in size. The two centermost chairs were the largest, dwarfing the other ten, which were identical to each other. All twelve of the seats faced a grand auditorium of benches that sat behind a half wall and climbed row by row up towards a secondary platform. This appeared to be the place where onlookers could watch the council meetings, and by Thanatos's indication this was where Kira and Kaya were to sit.

The three of them were alone in the cavernous room and every movement seemed to echo across it. Sitting down in the first row, Kira and Kaya looked at each other in amazement. Every new experience seemed to outshine the previous one and everything seemed to be getting more and more grandiose. There was no simplicity to be had, as everything was so overwhelmingly monumental compared to what they were used to.

"Just wait here until I get back. It will be a few minutes before the council convenes, and I have a few matters to attend to." Both girls nodded and Thanatos made his way out through an auxiliary passage behind the twelve chairs.

"Do you think anyone would believe us if we told them about this place? It seems so... surreal," Kaya pondered aloud, looking around at her surroundings.

"I'm not sure I believe it myself," Kira replied honestly.

"What do you think is going to happen? What will the other people on the council be like?"

"I don't know. But whoever they are, we shouldn't be too quick to trust them. Remember we don't know what they want from us," Kira warned.

"Excellent advice. You should listen to your sister," chimed an unfamiliar voice. Turning in surprise, the girls found a peculiar figure walking down the steps behind them. The voice belonged to a short man with blond hair who was dressed in extravagant purple and black robes. Dangling from his neck was a long silver necklace, consisting of large silver medallions linked together to form a sort of chain that clinked as he walked.

"Oh, do forgive me; I've spoken without introducing myself. My name is Dolius, herald of the twelve kingdoms," he said, stopping a few steps up and bowing gracefully. Kira and Kaya exchanged confused glances. Standing back up, the man continued his way down the stairs and headed for the throne furthest to the right. Sitting in it, he grinned and said, "Perhaps it isn't customary where you are from, but when a person introduces themselves on Tython, it is considered rude not to do so in return."

"Oh... right, umm... My name is Kira and this is my sister Kaya," Kira announced uncomfortably.

The small man let out a chuckle and responded, "I of course already knew your names, but I thought it fun to tease you none the less."

"How... how do you know our names?" Kaya asked.

"Oh I'm sure you'll discover soon enough that news travels quickly here on Tython." He paused to flap his hands like a bird, and, with a wicked grin, continued, "There are always little birds flying around, spreading news and revealing secrets. Besides, what good would a Herald of the Twelve be, if he wasn't the first to know about something as important as the two of you?" he asked, laughing quietly to himself.

Kira exchanged a worried look with Kaya and asked, "What is so important about us?"

"Tsk, tsk. Now I wouldn't want to go and ruin all the fun, would I? I'm afraid you'll just have to wait for the others to arrive to find out," he replied darkly. "Although, even then, I doubt you'll truly understand your role in all of this."

Kira did not like this man already. He reminded her too much of Felmar, with his cryptic wording and reluctance to divulge any useful information. Trying to hide her irritation, she asked coolly, "Our role in all of what, exactly?" but he would not respond. As she asked the question, another person entered the room. This time it was a woman entering from the auxiliary passage Thanatos had disappeared into.

The woman had long brown shimmering hair and was dressed in a revealing green silk gown. She was tall and slender, and was, by far, the most beautiful woman Kira had ever seen; she even seemed to glow as she entered the room. On her head she wore a silver and emerald tiara that glittered in the light as she gracefully made her way towards one of the largest chairs. Sitting in it without so much as a glance at Kira or Kaya, she turned to look at Dolius. In a refined and well-mannered tone she asked, "Why have we been summoned here, Dolius? My husband was none too specific about why this was *so* urgent."

"Forgive me, Mistress Hera, but I've been asked not to reveal Lord Velion's news. I believe he will address us directly when all twelve members are present," Dolius replied gracefully.

Hera let out a sigh and gave the two girls a bored look. Frowning she asked, "And who are these two? I'm not familiar with them; some distant cousins, no doubt?"

Dolius smirked and replied, "Truer than you might suspect, Mistress Hera. This is Kira and her younger sister Kaya. They, as you no doubt can tell, will be joining us for the meeting."

Giving him an incredulous look Hera retorted, "I thought this was to be a closed session; why are they permitted to be here?"

"By order of Lord Velion himself. They are his personal guests," Dolius informed her.

Hera looked back at the girls and glared at them, "Just so long as they aren't more of his bastard children! I'm tired of discovering the fruits of his torrid love affairs."

"I assure you, Mistress, they are not. Their origin is much more of a mystery than that," Dolius replied, shifting uncomfortably in his chair. Hera didn't respond, seeming to lose interest in the subject. Kira and Kaya looked at each other, but didn't say anything.

The four of them sat in awkward silence for a few minutes as the other members of the council trickled in one by one. Kira could tell from some of the looks that were exchanged as the new members arrived that this council was anything but a happy group. Many of them seemed to despise the others, which gave the room a sort of tension as Velion, Aeria and Thanatos entered together. Aeria took a seat among the other ten, but Velion did not sit. Thanatos made his way back over to the girls and sat next to Kira, whispering, "They are about to begin. I suspect that before the end, they will wish to hear from you, so be ready to be called to the floor."

With a tone of alarm Kira whispered, "What?! I have to get up and talk to them? What am I supposed to say?"

"They will likely have questions for you. I advise you keep your answers short and concise, and try to speak up; not everyone can hear so well," he advised, nodding towards a sickly looking woman sitting on the left side of the room. She looked old beyond her years, as if plagued by some disease that had aged her prematurely.

Kira felt a lump grow in her throat and a fluttering feeling filled her stomach. She wasn't much for public speaking as it was, but the thought of having to stand before these strangers did not sit well. She looked over at her sister, who merely shrugged and gave her a consolatory look.

Velion walked to the center of the room, stopping a few feet in front of Kira and facing the council members. Clearing his throat he addressed the room in an official tone, "My beloved family, I thank you all for coming today, I know some of you have made long journeys without knowing why I've summoned you, but I assure you it will be worth your time."

An older man sitting next to Hera, who looked a great deal like Velion, interrupted in a gruff tone, "It appears that only some of us have decided to show, Brother." He pointed to the vacant seat next to Velion's empty throne.

Velion paused out of respect, but it was clear that the interruption had irritated him. He replied, "Don't worry about Hadius; we can deal with that later."

But the man didn't back down, standing and raising his voice even louder, "No, I think we should discuss this now! Why is it, when we are all summoned with the utmost urgency, that Hadius doesn't show?! This has become an unacceptable trend, and I believe it begs the question of his loyalty!"

The room erupted in argument as the council members started talking over one another. Kira wasn't sure what to make of the spectacle, but felt reassured by the amused look on Thanatos's face.

Magnifying his voice like he had done outside, Velion boomed, "SILENCE!!!!" His command seemed to make the whole room shake and, in response, the council members all went silent. Glaring at the lot of them, Velion proceeded with an indignant tone, "We will discuss Hadius's absence in a moment, but that is not why I have summoned you here!" He paused, making sure he wouldn't be interrupted again. Satisfied that they would remain silent, he continued, "As I was saying, I have summoned you here because I have important news to share with you. On our scouting expedition, my daughter Aeria made an important discovery."-Aeria beamed at the mention of her name-"After thousands of years of searching, we have finally found Earth!!"

The room did not react at first, but after a moment the man at Hera's side spoke up, looking at Aeria in shock and demanding, "Is this true? You really found it?" Aeria nodded with a smug look on her face, but did not speak.

At this, the room erupted in conversation again as all the strangers expressed their disbelief; all of them except for Dolius, who didn't seem surprised by the news. Kira watched him closely, noting that he appeared to be amused at the other's disbelief. There was something that wasn't right about him, but she couldn't put her finger on it.

A hardened looking man sitting to Kira's left spoke next, "Did you examine the planet? Was it everything Kronus claimed it to be?"

Grinning widely, Velion replied, "Yes, we did examine the planet, and yes there appears to be enough ore to sustain our technology for countless generations to come."

The hardened man looked stunned, but also deeply satisfied. Like a child asking to play with a new toy, he blurted out, "Please, Lord Velion, would you permit me to assemble a colonization expedition to the planet? I could have a mining operation up and running within the month!"

Velion's grin widened further as he replied, "My dear Aithos, there will be no need for a colonization expedition."

Looking alarmed, the hardened man asked, "What do you mean? Are we not going to mine the ore?"

Velion burst into laughter, which only confused the room even more. He explained, "Of course we are going to mine the ore, but what you don't understand is how easy it will be." No one spoke, as all of them were looking to each other in confusion.

"You see, it appears Kronus kept more details about his discovery of Earth secret than previously thought." Again the room remained silent as all eyes were fixated on Velion as he continued, "It seems that the thirty years that he claimed he was stuck in sub-space, he was actually building a mining expedition of his own, outfitted with functional transport buildings. And more than that, he was breeding a native workforce."

This news sent the room into another uproar as the council members started talking over one another, asking questions and expressing disbelief. This time Velion let them go on, seeming to enjoy the reaction. After several minutes of heated conversation, the council members finally calmed down and returned their attention to Velion, who was patiently waiting to continue.

This time Hera was the first to speak up, asking, "Would the two girls behind you have anything to do with this *native workforce* he was breeding?" At this the entire room turned their attention to Kira and

Kaya. Kira cringed as Velion turned to look at her. With a satisfied look, he gestured for her to come to the floor.

Kira stood and looked down at Kaya, who gave her an encouraging smile. Deciding it might be best for her to go alone, she stepped around Thanatos and made her way towards Velion. Stopping at his side, he put his massive arm around her shoulder and with a formal tone, he announced, "I present Kira, a daughter of Earth."

"Can she speak?" asked Aithos with a raised eyebrow.

Kira blinked in confusion and blurted, "Yes I can speak! Why wouldn't I be able to?" Everyone except Dolius and Aeria shifted in surprise, indicating that most of them had not expected her to address them directly.

"You can speak our language?" Aithos asked, dumbfounded.

"Well, I never knew it was *your* language until I met her in the woods, but yes, I can speak it," Kira retorted sarcastically, pointing at Aeria.

Aithos looked over at Aeria in confusion, and asked, "You found this one in the woods? How many more are there?"

Velion replied for Aeria, saying, "There appeared to be around a million of them, give or take."

Aithos blinked, "A *million*? How did Kronus manage to breed so many? Are they civilized?"

"It's not clear how many he originally bred, but it appears that he used genetic manipulation on a population of primitive bipeds to create them. They aren't civilized, but they have retained much of the education Kronus provided. As you just witnessed, they still have the ability to speak our language, even after thousands of years," Velion explained.

"Genetic manipulation? What kind of manipulation? She almost looks like... us," Aithos wondered, more to himself than to Velion.

Velion gestured at Aeria, who nodded and pulled out the metallic cylinder from the woods. Tossing it across the room, Velion snatched it out of the air and handed it gently to Kira. "Go ahead, show them," he whispered.

Kira looked around the room, and with a shrug, pressed down on the first symbol. Immediately the device burst to life, displaying a holoprojection of a new and unfamiliar map in the air. Everyone, even Dolius, gasped in surprise.

Kira didn't much care for the attention. She wasn't enjoying having a room full of strangers gape at her, like she was some sort of freak of nature. Shifting her weight uncomfortably, she pressed the button again and handed the device back to Velion.

"How... is this possible?" the man sitting next to Hera demanded with a truly alarmed look on his face.

Velion stood up tall, and in an official tone said, "It's possible because Kira is a descendant of Kronus."

This news *really* caused an uproar in the room as everyone stood to their feet and started arguing with one another. Even Thanatos made his way to the floor to join in the commotion. Kira didn't know what to do, so she just stood there watching as the room fell into chaos. She turned to check on her sister, but didn't have to look far. Kaya had also gotten up and was standing right behind her, wearing a look of amusement and concern.

"Do you think they are mad?" Kaya called out over the commotion of the room. Kira shrugged and pulled Kaya close to her, putting her arm around her shoulders. She didn't think they were angry, but it certainly didn't feel like they were very happy about the news.

Velion looked over at the girls, and with an unexpectedly soft expression on his face he smiled at them. Turning back to the council, he raised his voice and boomed, "ENOUGH!!" Everyone in the room seemed to freeze in place, falling silent as they looked to Velion in surprise, as he called out, "Return to your seats; there is still more business to attend to."

Looking sheepish, the group went back to their seats and sat quietly, staring at the two girls. After a few seconds of silence Velion continued, "What I tell you is the truth. Kira and her sister are descendants of my father Kronus. I know this for certain, having scanned them for the appropriate genetic markers. And as you just witnessed, they have the ability to use the royal technology."

The man next to Hera interrupted, "What about the others you found? Are they also his descendants, Brother?"

"No, Pisus. These were the only two with his genetic markers. The rest appear to be a different hybrid of our species and the native bipeds he found," Velion answered.

"What of their parents?" Pisus asked.

"I examined their father before leaving the planet and he did not have the marker. Their mother must have been the carrier, but she is deceased." Kira winced at the emotionless remark about her mother's death.

Aithos spoke up, "With respect, Father, how could the marker survive so many generations? We've been searching for Earth for thousands of years, and the chances that the markers would pass through so many variations without degradation is... unheard of.

Even our most promising attempts to pass it on had *significant* degradation after just one generation."

"It *is* remarkable, I agree, but you've seen firsthand that the child is able to use our technology. There is no mistaking that she is one of us, as is her sister..." -Velion paused to take a breath- "which leads me to the next order of business. As Pisus has so conveniently pointed out, Hadius is not here today, and we all know this isn't something new. His continued absence is starting to affect the rest of us, which is why I spoke with him a few hours ago."

"About time!" Pisus retorted with irritation.

Velion grinned, although it was obvious his patience with Pisus was wearing thin. He went on, "Together we decided it would be best to remove him from the Council of Twelve, and open his seat for appointment."

This news seemed to go over better than the previous announcements had, as Kira noticed that everyone in the room was nodding in agreement. She didn't know what to make of the situation, knowing so little about these people or their council, but what came next, she could have never anticipated.

"From now on, Aeria will take over his position and responsibilities as High Lord of the Lower Kingdoms!" All the other council members applauded as Aeria stood and bowed gracefully. "And in her place, I have decided..."-he paused, looking over at Kira with a grin- "to appoint Kira the twelfth member of the council!"

Everyone stopped clapping and gaped at Velion in horror. No one spoke, or even so much as moved a muscle for several seconds.

Kira blinked and looked up at Velion. Had she heard that right? Did he just say that he wanted her to be on the council? Surely there had been some sort of mistake. Maybe he appointed someone else named Kira to the council... that made more sense, didn't it?

"You can't be serious!" Aeria blurted out, gaping at her father.

"I am," Velion replied, standing tall.

"But she's... not even from Tython! How can she be expected to sit on the council?!" Aeria demanded.

"I have to agree with our daughter, Velion. Who is this girl from Earth that we should appoint her to the ruling council?" Hera interjected.

"She is a descendant of my father, just as all of us are, which gives her a birthright to sit on this council. We've been trying for millennia to pass on the royal marker, and none of our work has been nearly as promising as this girl is," Velion defended.

No one seemed to know how to react, least of all Kira. She blurted out, "What do you mean I'm going to be on the council?"

"Do not fear, child; it is your destiny," Velion assured her with a wide smile, as if he had bestowed a great gift upon her.

"My *destiny*? I don't even know you people, and now you're deciding my destiny?" Kira protested. "I never even agreed to come here!" she shouted, trying to ignore the pained expression that passed over Kaya's face. She wasn't angry at her sister for agreeing to come here, but this was just outrageous. How was she supposed to become a ruler among a people she hardly knew, in a place she'd never even seen before? It wasn't fair to burden her with so much responsibility without even asking.

"Hush now, don't do something you will regret later," Velion cautioned, but Kira wasn't going to listen.

"The only thing I regret is meeting you. Why couldn't you just leave us alone?" Kira yelled.

"Enough!" Velion roared. "I'll hear no more of this! The decision has been made. One day you *will* thank me! Now, return to your seats, both of you."

Kira glared at Velion, but noticing an admonishing look from her sister, she backed down and stomped back to her seat. Kaya followed after her, looking uncomfortable and avoiding eye contact with everyone in the room.

Velion shook his head and mumbled something under his breath. Collecting himself, he turned back to the council members and continued, "Now, obviously the girls are unfamiliar with Tython and its people, so this appointment will not take effect until both have had some education. Judging from where I found them, I doubt either one can read or write." This did anything but reassure the council members, who kept looking to one another for some sort of explanation. Finding none, they merely sat in quiet acquiescence.

Thanatos was the first to break the silence, with a thoughtful look on his face he said, "Lord Velion, I think there is something we are forgetting about."

"Oh?" Velion asked, looking confused.

"The inhabitants of Earth, my lord. What are we going to do with them? They aren't lesser ones, after all," Thanatos continued. Kira and Kaya exchanged anxious looks.

"I'm not sure I follow," Velion folded his arms and gave Thanatos a reproachful look.

"Well, with all due respect my lord, don't we need to decide how to treat these earthlings? They are their own species after all, and from the looks of it, they are more closely related to us than most of the lower castes are," Thanatos proceeded with a cautious tone.

Pisus interjected before Velion could respond, "He has a point, Brother. These earthlings could prove to be useful, if they can carry our genetic markers. We should be careful how we treat them; they do have rights after all."

"Rights?!" Hera spat. "What rights? They are weak and uncivilized, why should we grant them rights?"

"It's not for us to *grant* them rights, Hera; that is something they have on their own. *We* are the outsiders here, not them; or have you learned nothing from the sins of our father?"

"Oh don't start in on this again Pisus! We've heard it all before!" Hera admonished.

"Now wait just a second, I think Pisus brings up a valid point. Do we really want to continue the traditions of our father?" The sickly woman at the side of the room chimed in. Up to this point she had remained silent, even when the room had burst into chaos.

"Oh, shut it! Shouldn't you be resting? Leave the important things to those of us healthy enough to understand what's happening," Hera snapped.

"Just because I'm ill, doesn't mean I'll be as insufferable as you, dear sister! At least I have enough sense to listen before I open my mouth and say something foolish," the sickly woman retorted, snickering until she burst into a fit of coughing. Hera looked livid, but noticing a severe look from Velion, she did not respond.

Velion held up his hand, indicating that he wanted silence. "Perhaps the time for this decision is not now. We will need more information about the earthlings before we choose. For now, Aithos will begin the mining operation, using only the labor of lesser ones. Once the operation is running, he will study the humans from a distance and will report his findings back to us," Velion concluded. Aithos nodded in agreement.

CHAPTER 9

As Kira sat down in the chair she couldn't help but feel a little overwhelmed. Nothing about this experience seemed to make any sense. Just four days ago she was deathly afraid of losing her father to illness and questioning the validity of the spirits. Now she was an unimaginable distance away from home, with an alien race of *Gods* on a different planet and had been appointed one of their rulers! Was this all just a dream? Surely it had to be, there was no other explanation for it.

"Are you okay?" Kaya asked, giving her sister a worried look.

"I... I don't know," Kira responded truthfully.

"Did you know they were going to do that?" Kaya sat in the chair opposite of Kira.

"No; did you?" Kira wondered, hoping there was some clue that Kaya had forgotten to mention.

"No. I mean who would? They don't even know us and now you're going to be on their council? I guess they think you're special or something..." Kaya's voice trailed off and she shook her head.

"Not just me. Velion mentioned you too," Kira reminded her.

Kaya frowned and said, "Maybe there is something we are missing. I mean, I understand we're supposed to have some sort of 'marker,' but there must be something else to it. Who would appoint practical strangers to such a high status if there wasn't more to the story?" Kira shrugged, but Kaya wasn't paying attention as she continued, "Who is this Hadius person anyway?"

"I think Velion said it was his brother," Kira remembered.

"Well whoever he is, they must not be happy with him," Kaya guessed.

"I did get that feeling from the way Pisus, or whatever his name was, questioned his loyalty. Do you think it has anything to do with what Thanatos told us on the Trident?"

"You mean about the lesser ones trying to get freedom?"

"Yeah; do you think that's what Pisus meant?" Kira wondered, but Kaya just shook her head and shrugged her shoulders. Both of them sat there a while, quietly thinking to themselves before Kaya started to giggle.

"What?" Kira asked suspiciously.

"Just this place! Isn't it spectacular?" Kaya asked, gesturing at their surroundings. Kira looked around at their new home.

The room truly was spectacular. It was beautiful beyond anything Kira could have imagined; so clean and precisely crafted. Everything in it was made of the same white stone as the rest of the palace and it was almost as grandiose as the council chamber had been.

There were three chairs and a long couch sitting at the center of a large and cavernous antechamber, and the bedrooms just beyond were equally grandiose. Unlike the quarters on the Trident, these apartments were semicircular and had a breathtaking, hanging veranda that looked over the capital city. If Kira was to be held against her will, this was as nice a prison as she could have asked for.

"It really is something, isn't it?" Kira asked, smiling for the first time that day.

"I can't wait to tell the others about this place! They'll never believe us!" Kaya exclaimed. Kira nodded and smiled. She didn't have the heart to tell Kaya of her growing worry that they'd never see their home again.

Trying to change the subject, Kira asked, "How do you think they built this place? It's so large and beautiful."

"I don't know," Kaya shrugged. "Maybe they will show us? Velion did say something about us getting an *education,* whatever that means."

"Maybe," Kira shrugged as she stared out over the veranda at the city. "So much of what they do seems like... magic or something. It all defies what I thought was even possible," Kira said thoughtfully, watching ships fly across the horizon. "I bet even slimy old Felmar would be at a loss for words if he could see this."

"Oh, you should have seen him when they landed at the village! He was down on his hands and knees worshiping them out of fear before they even said a word!" Kaya laughed.

"Really? Doesn't surprise me; he always was a wimp." Kira jeered.

And that was how it was for the first few days as Kira and Kaya learned how to live in their new home.

Thanatos would come to visit each day to check on the girls and bring them new clothing and games, but for the most part they spent their time in solitude. Becoming familiar with their new surroundings, they learned how to use the controls in their home, they discovered there was a holoprojection system in both of their rooms as well as the antechamber that had channels broadcasting various programs throughout the day.

There was one program that caught Kira's attention more than the others. It featured various finely dressed Tythonians debating the various happenings throughout the twelve kingdoms and relaying information about the weather predictions on various planets. She initially took an interest in the channel when she stumbled across it broadcasting a story about her and Kaya. They had somehow captured the images of their arrival and were playing them over and over again, speculating on who they were and where they came from. They were calling them the 'mystery girls' and their guesses about their origins ranged from distant cousins of the royal family, to illegitimate offspring of another of Velion's love affairs. Apparently that was something that happened fairly often.

When Thanatos came the next day, Kira inquired about the broadcast, wondering what it was and how it could replay images of their arrival. He explained that the channel was called "the news," and that the images were made possible by a technology that could record events as they happened and display those images afterwards. He explained that almost every corner of the central planets was recorded in order to, "keep a watchful eye over their subjects."

"You mean there is always someone watching?" Kira asked with alarm, but Thanatos merely laughed and assured her there was nothing to worry about; they had complete privacy in their home as cameras were forbidden within the palace walls.

* * *

After about a week in their new home, things started to feel normal again. The strangeness of the situation never fully faded from their minds, but their new surroundings and acquaintances started to feel natural. Between the comforts, conveniences, and abundant food, it was hard to complain about anything. Even though Kira disliked the idea of sitting on the council, the plethora of servants that were now constantly attending to her and Kaya's every whim and need did make her feel less anxious about the idea of ruling.

Living as one of these *Gods* was rather blissful, at least until the girls met Master Yu-On. He was an elderly, grey-haired lesser one who was to become their private tutor and chaperone around the palace.

"I am not your friend," Yu-On announced when he first met them. "I am not your mother or your father, your brother or your sister. I am not family and I will not be easy on you. I have been teaching children my entire life and have already seen all the tricks and pranks you could ever think of! I highly advise you spare us all a lot of time and frustration, and just do as I tell you."

Kira and Kaya were bemused by this strange new man, and found many of his quirks quite humorous; a fact that they soon learned was best kept to themselves, as Yu-On carried a wooden cane he was prone to using as a disciplinary rod whenever he felt slighted.

Despite his prickly exterior, Master Yu-On was actually a very interesting and engaging teacher. He rarely seemed irritated by questions or interruptions so long as they led to opportunities for learning, and after a few weeks of working with the girls he even seemed to become proud of them. Kira even overheard him telling Thanatos how amazed he was at how rapidly they were learning.

As much as she doubted she would enjoy learning, Kira found she had an insatiable hunger for the knowledge and lessons Yu-On offered. Learning to read and write came naturally, both to her and Kaya, and after only a month they were nearly fluent in the strange written language of Tython.

Once they had nearly mastered reading and writing, Master Yu-On began to teach them more advanced subjects. Each day they studied astronomy, physics and mathematics, and history and culture. Both girls were fascinated by all of it, but Kira was particularly entranced by the study of astronomy. She learned about the stars in the heavens and how they were created. She even started to understand things she could have never guessed at before, like how the rising and falling of the sun was really an illusion due to planetary rotation and how it was this rotation that created the gravity that kept them on the ground.

Yu-On also taught them about the twelve kingdoms and the planets that supported them. He explained that the kingdoms encompassed only a small portion of the galaxy, and that aside from the very recent discovery of Earth, no new life or civilizations had been discovered for thousands of years.

"Master Yu-on, how did the twelve kingdoms begin? Were there always twelve?" Kaya asked one day during their history lesson.

"An intriguing question, and perhaps my favorite to answer," he replied, beaming with pride. "Do you want the short explanation or the long one?"

"Maybe just the short version, for today," Kira teased, knowing full well that when Yu-On gave the long version of anything, he could go on for hours.

Yu-On shrugged, "So be it. Long ago, before there were twelve kingdoms, the galaxy was chaotic and uncivilized. The various planets that now comprise the heavenly kingdoms were mostly overrun with vegetation and wild beasts, except for one. Tython was ruled over by the Gods, even then, and was the only *truly* civilized planet in the galaxy. One day, Velion's father Kronus decided to explore the galaxy and colonize the wild planets. On the first planet he searched, he discovered the lesser ones, who at the time were an uncivilized and weak species. In his greatness and charity, Kronus decided to take the lesser ones under his wing and teach them to be civilized. He taught them how to read and write, and eventually molded them into the hard-working, industrious people we now know."

"Sort of how he did on Earth?" Kira wondered

"Yes, apparently so; although he spent more time with the lesser ones than he did with your people."

"What happened next?!" Kaya interrupted, apparently worried that Kira's comment had derailed the story.

"Glad you are so eager to learn, little one. Well, after Kronus taught the lesser ones how to be civilized, he took them from their planet and spread them across the galaxy."

"Why did he do that?" Kaya asked.

"Well you see, Kronus, in his infinite wisdom, saw the usefulness of the lesser ones, and spread them across the inhabitable planets in the galaxy in order to expand his kingdom."

"You mean he enslaved them to do the work for him," Kira snapped sarcastically.

Master Yu-On did not reply right away, but instead leveled Kira with an ambiguous stare. Seeming to decide something he said, "Yes. He did enslave them, Mistress Kira."

"What gave him that right?" Kira asked, ignoring the dismayed look on Kaya's face.

Yu-On paused again, squinting at Kira with curiosity. "Well, that is the right of a God over his subjects, is it not?"

Kira sighed and crossed her arms. "Maybe, but how do we know that he was a God?"

This time Yu-On forced a smile. "An honest question, which I am obligated not to answer. Only a God, such as yourself, is permitted to question such things," he finished, lowering his eyes to the ground diplomatically.

Kira was confused. Exchanging a concerned look with Kaya, she asked, "Wait... you *really* think we are Gods?"

"Why of course, Mistress Kira. You have been appointed a seat on the Council of Twelve, which only a God is permitted to be on." Yu-On maintained his lowered gaze, appearing to be frightened. It was the first time in months of knowing him that he showed any sort of weakness. From the minute they met, he commanded such respect and fierceness that this was not like him at all.

"Yu-On... are you frightened?" Kira asked, confused.

Yu-On did not reply at first, but after a moment he spoke with a trembling voice, saying, "I do not wish to displease you, Mistress Kira."

"Displease me? I thought you were my teacher, how would you displease me?" Kira asked, bewildered.

"It is true that I am your teacher, but you are my ruler and superior, Mistress Kira. I am afraid that you are trying to get me to blaspheme the Gods, which I will not do." He looked back up at her with a fierce gaze.

Taken aback by the sudden change in her teacher, Kira was unsure of how to respond. Uncrossing her arms she said, "Master Yu-On, I am not trying to get you to blaspheme anything. I was just asking a question. You have to forgive me; I do not come from Tython and am not always aware of how to act. On Earth, there are no lesser ones and certainly no slaves."

Yu-On looked thoroughly confused. "You mean, when you were a God on Earth, you let your people live in freedom?"

Both Kira and Kaya burst into laughter, which only served to further confuse Yu-On. "No, no. You misunderstand. On Earth I wasn't a God. I was just a girl who liked to hunt."

Yu-On looked mortified at first, but after a moment he grinned broadly and said, "You are playing a joke on me, aren't you, Mistress Kira? Not a God!" he exclaimed, laughing nervously.

Kira looked at Kaya, who just shrugged. Feeling a pang of sadness, Kira realized that Yu-On would never really understand. He had been a slave his whole life, and was taught that it was right for the *Gods* to rule over him. Shaking her head, Kira replied softly, "Just... never mind. You were telling us about Kronus and the lesser ones, weren't you?"

Yu-On still looked confused, but seemed relieved at the changing of the subject. "Yes! Where was I... oh yes! Kronus commanded the lesser ones to spread his kingdom across the galaxy and so they did, but not without strife. Even though most of the inhabitable planets were uncivilized, there were several that did have primitive civilizations on them."

"What happened to those?" Kaya asked anxiously.

"Well, in short they were either destroyed, or taken over. All of them resisted the rightful rule of Kronus at first, but only a few were wise enough to surrender in time. In fact there are many battles recorded in the history texts that talk about the great powers of Kronus and how, with his powerful scythe, he was able to defeat whole armies singlehandedly."

"Wow, and he did this all by himself?" Kaya gasped.

"Well, yes and no. History does have a tendency to exaggerate the facts. Kronus did have some impressive victories of his own, but most of the time he was supported by his three sons, Hadius, Velion, and Pisus; all of whom are quite powerful in their own regard."

"So if Kronus was such a legend, then why isn't he ruling the twelve kingdoms now?" Kira asked. The question had been bothering her for some time now, having heard so much about the *great Kronus*.

"A most interesting tale, and perhaps my favorite. After conquering and civilizing many of the planets that now comprise the twelve kingdoms, the Gods stumbled across an ancient civilization, called the Centuri."

"Who were they?" Kaya asked, completely enthralled.

"They were a highly advanced species, with great technology and power, but when they met Kronus they deceived him."

"What do you mean?"

"It is hard to explain, but I'll do my best. You see, at that time, Kronus had grown weary from fighting war after war. He desired an era of peace, but as powerful as the Gods were, they didn't have the means to keep order on all of the conquered planets. So he made a deal with the Centuri, agreeing to make them a noble caste only answerable to him, if they would use their strength to police the planets. But what Kronus didn't know, was that the Centuri plotted to overthrow his kingdom and rule the planets in his stead. So through craft and deceit the leader of the Centuri, Ophiron, formulated a plan to lure Kronus away and kill him, but somehow Kronus learned of the treachery. Instead of going alone, he brought his three sons with him."

"What happened? Did Ophiron kill Kronus?" Kaya interrupted anxiously.

Yu-On smiled, "No. Because Kronus had brought his sons with him, they were able to overpower Ophiron and kill him. But the three brothers knew that if the Centuri found out about Ophiron's death, they would rebel and wreak havoc across the galaxy, plunging it into a never ending war."

"So what did they do?" Kira asked, finding herself also engrossed in the story.

Yu-On seemed pleased and pressed on, "In order to avoid such a long conflict, Hadius, Velion and Pisus formulated a plan. They went to Ophiron's second in command and told him what had occurred."

"But you said if the Centuri found out they would declare war. How did the brothers avoid that?" Kira objected, confused.

"They made an agreement with Ophiron's second in command, that if the three brothers overthrew their father and cast him into prison for his crime, the

Centuri would leave the galaxy peacefully, never to return."

"Did it work?" Kaya blurted.

"Surprisingly, it did. I can't explain it, honestly. The three brothers captured Kronus and as promised, they stripped him of his armor and scythe, and cast him into an unbreakable prison on the planet Nyxia."

"And the Centuri just left? Never to come back?" Kira asked in disbelief.

"Yes, which is the part that I cannot explain. They had complete control over the kingdom and could have possibly overthrown the Gods, but they chose not to. There are rumors that the three brothers gave something to the Centuri to convince them to leave, but there is no proof to back such a claim. Whatever the reason, the Centuri left and haven't been seen in thousands of years."

Kira was burning with questions, but before she could ask any, there was a chime at the door and Velion himself strode into the room. Beaming from ear to ear he walked up to the girls and asked, "How are we today? I trust Master Yu-On isn't boring you too much?"

Kira was still wary of Velion, having spent very little time with him, so she didn't respond. Kaya apparently didn't share that reservation, as she exclaimed, "Not at all! He was just telling us about how you and your brothers threw your father Kronus in prison!!"

Kira glared at Kaya and gulped hard, unsure of how Velion would react to such a glib description of the incident. To her surprise he seemed to take it in stride. "Oh, that story? I think it must be his favorite, as he does love to tell it whenever he can."

Deciding to be bold, Kira asked, "Was it a difficult decision to overthrow Kronus?"

Velion paused, leveling an approving look at her. "You know what I like about you, Kira? You aren't afraid to speak your mind, even if you sometimes shouldn't. The short answer is no, it was not a difficult decision. My father didn't really give us any choice, honestly. If we hadn't made our bargain with the Centuri, we would probably still be fighting a war as we speak."

"Does Kronus see it that way?" Kira pressed, ignoring an alarmed look on Yu-On's face.

Velion's smile faded, and with a more serious tone he replied, "My father was always more hungry for power than he should have been, and in the end it was his undoing. What Yu-On hasn't told you and doesn't know, is how my father became the supreme ruler to begin with." Yu-On looked thoroughly surprised and with wide, eager eyes, sat down to listen to Velion.

Unflinching at Velion's change in demeanor Kira asked, "How did he?"

"My grandfather, Varuna, was once the supreme ruler of the galaxy, and saw fit to leave it as it was, primordial and natural, but my father Kronus disagreed with him. You see, my father felt that we were wasting the resources available to us and were failing to achieve our potential as supreme rulers over all life. So one day, after failing to convince Varuna that the people of Tython should colonize the other planets, my father conceived a plan to betray him. Pretending to apologize for his lack of respect, my father lured Varuna to a ship that was in orbit above Tython, asking him to come alone. Once Varuna boarded the ship, my father captured him and imprisoned him."

"Is Varuna still alive?" Kira inquired.

Velion considered her for a moment, finally saying, "It's hard to say. Although he would never tell me what happened, I believe that my father flew his ship as close as he could to the center of the galaxy, and set my grandfather adrift towards the black hole that resides there." He finished, looking melancholic.

Kira shuddered at the thought, having learned just a few days earlier what a black hole was. "How do you know, if he never told you?" Kira wondered.

Velion's look of melancholy was replaced with a softer expression of pride. "Very clever, Kira. I know because when he returned to Tython without my grandfather, I checked the ship's navigation log."

"Why didn't you go after Varuna if you knew where he was?" Kaya interjected.

Velion gave a halfhearted smile and said, "I tried. But when my father figured out what I was doing, he stopped me and told me that if I continued, he would kill Aeria. She was just an infant at the time."

Everyone remained silent after he finished, not knowing what to say to break the silence. Finally, after a few awkward moments, Velion spoke up. "I almost forgot why I came. It's time that the two of you had these. I'm sorry it took so long to get them too you, but Aithos is the one who makes them, and he has been busy." Velion pulled out two small, gleaming cylinders, similar to the one they found in the Black Wood, and handed one to each girl. "It is customary for members of the royal family to have one of these. Keep them with you at all times, understand?" He asked, giving them a reproachful look until both girls nodded.

"What exactly are they? I mean I know I found one, but I don't really know what they do."

"They are personal holodisks and they serve a great number of functions. As you are already aware, they have a mapping system that will work anywhere you go in the galaxy, but they also serve as communication devices. If you get separated or lost, you can use it to contact any of the council members, and to set it as an emergency beacon that will summon a life pod." He indicated each button as he described their function.

"A *life pod*?" Kaya repeated, curiously.

"It's an emergency ship that follows your holodisk around. Right now, there is one in orbit above Tython for each of you. If you press the last button that says emergency... not now!" Velion scolded, stopping Kaya from pressing the button. She gave him a sheepish look and set the holodisk down. "As I was saying, if you press that button, your life pod will respond and will come rescue you wherever you are, even if you are underground or in a building. Once it finds you, it will serve both as a shuttle to take you to the nearest civilized planet, and as a medical bay that heals most injuries and ailments."

Kira was impressed at the idea, but hoped that she would never need use that function. "Does it do anything else?" she wondered, noticing that there were several more buttons that he hadn't addressed.

"Yes. As your sister witnessed, it can heal most ailments and cure most diseases. Also it can turn any organic material into an edible substance if needed, although I wouldn't advise relying on that unless you must. It might be edible, but it is usually far from appetizing," he warned. "It can also purify any water source of bacteria or parasites, and has a powerful cutting laser, in case you find yourself trapped somewhere or need to cut through something. Lastly, it can serve as a camera and audio recorder."

"Wow... this thing can really do anything, can't it? Why are we the only ones who get these?" Kira wondered.

Velion seemed amused at the question. "Well first, because we are the only ones who can use them. If you gave yours to Yu-On, he wouldn't be able to make it work. Second, because they are extremely difficult to make and require rare materials... well I guess the materials aren't as rare as they used to be, now that we've found Earth."

The room went awkwardly silent after he finished his sentence. The cavalier mention of Earth was unexpected, but Kira jumped on the opportunity, asking, "How is the mining operation going? Has Aithos been able to study my people?"

Velion looked at her uncomfortably. "So far he has submitted two reports, both of which were promising. I'd like to say that all has gone as planned, but there was a skirmish between the soldiers we left and a local population," he said quietly. "Not your village of course!" he added quickly before she could respond.

"What kind of skirmish?" Kira inquired.

"Well, apparently a roaming party of bandits stumbled across my soldiers, and for some reason decided to attack them. Only one of my men was injured, but most of the bandits were killed before being driven off," he finished awkwardly.

Kira didn't know how to take the news. She didn't love the idea that humans were dying at the hands of Velion's men, but she had seen firsthand how vicious bandits could be. "Well if they attacked first, then I guess it serves them right," she concluded.

"Will we ever get to go back to Earth?" Kaya interrupted without really thinking.

Velion seemed taken aback by the question and stuttered, "Uh... yes... eventually. But for now just try to enjoy your time on Tython, and try to learn as much as you can from Yu-On. He is our best instructor." Velion smiled awkwardly and turned to leave the room.

Before he made it to the door Kira spoke up, "Velion..." He stopped short and turned to look at her with an inquisitive expression. "Thank you... for the holodisks." Kira said, holding the metallic cylinder in the air. He smiled and turned to leave again. "And everything else too," Kira finished, but this time Velion didn't turn. He just hesitated a moment before leaving the room.

Master Yu-On stood again as the girls examined their holodisks. "Now where were we? Perhaps we've had enough history for today. Let's learn about algebra!"

Kaya groaned, but Kira smiled. Maybe being stuck on Tython wouldn't be so bad after all.

CHAPTER 10

Days turned into weeks and weeks into months, until the two girls had spent nearly half a year on Tython. Each day spending the majority of their time with Master Yu-On, learning more and more until both girls were brimming with new knowledge and understanding.

"Can you believe we've been here so long?" Kaya asked Kira as they sat on their veranda, looking over the city as the first of Tython's two suns hung low on the horizon.

"It really doesn't feel like it's been that long, honestly," Kira replied thoughtfully. "Must be because of all the time we've spent studying."

"Do you think Dad misses us?" Kaya asked.

Kira was taken aback by the sudden question and didn't know how to answer. The obvious answer was "yes" but there was no guarantee that he had made it through his illness. For all either of them knew, he could have died shortly after their departure, and vile old Felmar was running the village. There hadn't been any news about their village from Aithos, so there was no telling. Not wanting to dampen her sister's spirits Kira replied, "Of course Dad misses us. I'm sure they all do. I'd even bet Felmar misses us from time to time."

Kaya shrugged and looked back over the cityscape, ignoring Kira's joke. If Kira wasn't mistaken, her sister was succumbing to homesickness, as the frequency of her asking about Earth was increasing dramatically.

Kira understood, even if she didn't share the emotion. Sure, she missed her father and uncle, but there never really was anything for her on Earth, except perhaps hunting. If there was one thing she missed more than anything, it was the hunting trips she used to go on. She longed to wander around untamed lands, tracking her prey, but as she stared out at the tall buildings and bustling traffic of the capital, she realized those days might very well be behind her.

The familiar chime of the door rang out from behind them, and a few seconds later Thanatos came striding out onto the veranda. He had a quickened pace and a concerned look on his face as he approached. Raising an eyebrow, Kira inquired, "What is it?"

"There's been another uprising on one of the outer planets," he announced, looking grim. This was becoming a common occurrence as their time on Tython passed by. Shortly after arriving, Kira learned from news broadcasts and information from Thanatos that organized militants on the outer planets were growing in number, and were orchestrating riots and attacks on supply lines. At first these groups and their attacks were sporadic and unpredictable, but as time went by, they were becoming more frequent and more effective. Twice, the ruling Council of Twelve was called together to discuss the attacks, and twice they had dismissed them as inconsequential. Kira wasn't sure she agreed with their assessment, but as she wasn't permitted to take her place on the council yet, she couldn't express that opinion.

"Is it bad?" Kira asked, noting the worried look on Thanatos's face.

"Bad enough that the council is being convened again. I'm here to bring both of you to the council chamber immediately," he finished, gesturing for them to follow him.

"Sure. Just let me change," Kira said, ignoring the exasperated look on his face.

A few minutes later, Kira was attired in yet another spectacular ensemble (a gift she had reluctantly accepted from one of her chamber servants) and the three of them were making their way towards the other side of the palace to the council chamber. They were the last to arrive, which drew a number of reproachful looks from the council members as they took their familiar seats.

"Now that we are all here, I have some regretful news to give you," Velion began, standing in the center of the room like he normally did. "It seems that our assessment of the stability of the outer planets was incorrect." Kira tried not to snort, but couldn't catch it in time. Velion glared at her, but didn't say anything. Kira blushed and sheepishly looked to the ground.

"What's happened this time?" Pisus asked, ignoring Kira and looking grave.

"There's been another attack, this time on a supply depot on Gaius 5. The local governor has lost all control over the situation, and his district is being held captive by the militants," Velion informed them.

"I warned you that this would happen, Brother," Pisus scolded. "I told you that if we kept treating them this way, they would eventually rebel against us."

"Oh, I hardly think we have anything to fear, Pisus. Most of the lesser ones seem to enjoy their bondage, honestly," Hera jeered.

"We have more to fear than you might imagine, actually. They do outnumber us, several billion to twelve," Pisus reminded her.

"Except only a few colonies seem to have the nerve, or rather, the *stupidity* to rebel against us. I think we'll be able to handle such a small number," Hera finished confidently.

"As usual, your short sightedness stuns me. It may be a small number now, but if we don't handle this situation carefully, that number might increase dramatically," Pisus cautioned. Returning his gaze to Velion he asked, "Do we know what their demands are?"

"Their *demands?* Since when do *we* take demands?" A fierce looking man to Kira's right asked. He was wearing armor similar to Aeria's, except his had a bright red cloak hanging from the shoulders. Although Kira hadn't met the man directly, she knew he was Aeria's brother and was charged with any affairs dealing with war. His name was Deimos and he was anything but friendly.

"I'm sorry Pisus, but I have to agree with my son on this one. We cannot allow this sort of rebellious behavior to continue." Velion shook his head and continued, "I wish that it didn't have to come to this, but I believe it's time for us to remind the lesser ones why we are their gods." Several of the council members nodded in agreement, but Pisus wouldn't relent.

"Am I the only one here who remembers that it was the cruelty of our father that turned us into their *gods?* Have all of you forgotten that these *slaves*, used to be free? Do we not have a responsibility to take care of them?"

"Oh, shut it, Pisus. No one cares about your empathy and love for the lesser ones," Hera snapped. The room was becoming hostile as the council members started to glare at one another, but Velion remained calm.

"I understand your concern, Pisus, but I do not agree that being soft is the answer, at least not this time. We have been too soft for too long, and now look where we are. Open rebellion on an outer planet? That is unacceptable."

"But if we show compassion instead of strength, the lesser ones would be placated and would likely return to work. If we respond with force, we would just be fueling the fire of their reasons for rebelling to begin with!" Pisus protested, but his words fell on deaf ears. Kira could tell by the faces of the council members that most of them disagreed with him.

"You've spoken your piece and we have all heard it. We will put it to a vote. All of those in favor of responding to the rebellion with military force, raise your hand." Velion looked around as six of the ten seated council members raised their hands; all but Pisus, Aithos, Rhea, and Vesta.

"Then we have our decision. Aeria and Deimos will go to the planet and sort this mess out. Because this planet is rich in thorium ore I want minimal casualties; only the leaders. We can't afford to destroy the whole operation, do you understand?" Velion asked, giving Deimos a stern look. Both Aeria and Deimos nodded in agreement. Pisus just shook his head in disappointment and stood to leave.

"Not yet, Brother," Velion halted Pisus. "There are other matters I wish to attend to while I have you here." Everyone seemed intrigued at the news as Pisus returned to his seat. "First, I have been in close contact with Master Yu-On, and based on his recommendation, I believe it is time we begin the appointment process for Kira." This time there was some murmuring and uncomfortable shifting. "I know many of you still harbor reservations about her appointment, but if this council is to be complete again, we must proceed. So beginning tomorrow, Kira will be given her royal vestments and will begin her training under Thanatos. Are there any protests?" Velion looked hard at the other council members, almost daring them to speak up, but none of them did. "Good, then it will be done."

Kira blinked in confusion, looking to Thanatos for answers. With a grin, he nodded and whispered, "I'll explain later." She wanted to press the issue and ask for details but didn't get the chance before Velion continued.

"Lastly, I think it's time to make a decision about our involvement on Earth. Aithos, you've been observing the humans for six months now, what is your analysis?" Velion asked, yielding the floor to Aithos and sitting in his throne.

Aithos made his way to the center of the room and cleared his throat, "At first we had very little contact with the humans, but after a few weeks we started interacting with them. The first few encounters were brief, mostly just wandering or curious individuals that had found their way into our encampments, but that didn't last long. Those individuals must have told others, because after another week or so, we were practically overrun with them."

"Did they attack you?" Pisus interrupted with an alarmed look.

"No, actually, quite the opposite. I'm a little embarrassed to say it, but the humans have assumed that we are gods and have begun ritual worshipping around our camps."

"Just like the lesser ones did, so long ago. I knew there was too much fuss over these uncivilized barbarians. I guess the debate is over then?" Hera interjected condescendingly. Kira glared at her with as much vigor as she could muster. Since the day she had met Hera, she hadn't liked the woman.

"Not quite, Mother. They may be worshipping us, but they are very different than the lesser ones. When grandfather enslaved the lesser ones, they almost begged for it. They had somewhat of a *hive* mentality before we found them, as if working as a drone was an instinct. The humans do not wish to work, they..." Aithos paused, looking unsure of how to continue.

"Well spit it out!" Deimos demanded impatiently.

"They want to understand the purpose of their existence," Aithos continued uncomfortably.

"What nonsense is this?" Hera snapped.

"No, let him continue. What do you mean Aithos? How do you know this?" Pisus inquired, sitting forward and looking transfixed by this new information.

"Well... they keep coming and asking why we created them; asking what purpose we wanted them to fulfill. And..."-Aithos paused again, grimacing-"they want to know how we are doing the things we are doing; they've become so curious I've practically had to fight some of them off. I don't know what it is, but there is something very strange about them."

"Something stranger than how they've managed to survive on their own for so long?" Hera mocked.

Kira fumed, having to fight an overwhelming urge to walk across the room and slap Hera. Kaya must have been able to tell that she was angry, because she put her hand on Kira's leg and shook her head.

"Well that's the thing. They managed to almost completely retain the knowledge Grandfather left them thousands of years ago, and they seem anxious to learn more. I have doubts that the lesser ones could have managed such a feat. And what of them?" Aithos directed his attention to Kira and Kaya. "I've also spoken with Yu-On and he is amazed at how quickly they've learned. He's even asserted that they are learning faster than any student he's ever taught."

"What are you suggesting?" Pisus inquired with a strange look on his face.

"Well... I don't think Grandfather was trying to engineer a local workforce when he created the humans. I think he might have had a different purpose for them. I'm beginning to suspect that he created them to be a compatible species for us to merge with," Aithos continued warily. The news quieted the chamber, as each of the council members digested the idea. "I would of course need to conduct some genetic research and perform some lab tests to be certain."

Thanatos shifted uncomfortably next to Kira but didn't speak. Velion turned to look at Kira and Kaya with a strange expression, almost as if he were seeing them for the first time again.

Velion turned back to look at the council members and with a cautionary tone said, "I think that might be something worth investigating and, based on your other observations, I've decided how to proceed. I want you to expand the mining operation into a colonization effort. If these humans are so curious and capable of higher intelligence then it would suit us to civilize them, especially if we're able to mix with them."

"Is that a good idea?" Aeria spoke this time, looking astounded. "I'm not convinced that these *humans* are any more impressive than the lesser ones. Do we really want to bring them to our level? Couldn't that be dangerous?"

"What's dangerous is the fact that we haven't been able to procreate in centuries. Our technology allows us to live long lives, but without future generations to benefit from our work, then all of this is for nothing," Velion reminded her.

"But we might still find a way without... *soiling* our bloodline." Aeria looked horrified at the idea.

Velion frowned at her the way only a father could and said, "Perhaps you are right, but this is the best lead we've had in hundreds of years, too good to not pursue... unless the rest of you also disagree?" Velion scanned the council chamber for any dissent, but all of the other members were nodding in somber agreement, even Hera. "Then it is settled. I suggest we begin building settlements as soon as possible. We will need to bring some of the lesser ones with us, in order to teach the humans. I think that Kira and Kaya have displayed how quickly humans can learn our culture and history, so I doubt it will take long to teach the others."

"I will begin right away, Father," Aithos said as he stood and bowed before Velion.

"Very good, unless there is anything else to discuss, you're all dismissed," Velion announced. Everyone stood to leave but as they started to make their way out of the chamber Velion continued, "Except you, Aeria. I need to have a word with you before you leave." The other members exchanged knowing looks, but continued to leave.

As Kira and Kaya made their way out of the room Aithos approached them with a grin. Although the girls had never spoken with him directly, he spoke with a friendly and familiar tone, saying, "I will have your vestments ready for you in the morning. I trust that Velion has already given you the holodisks?" Both girls nodded. "Good, I hope they are working to your satisfaction?" Again they both nodded. "Excellent! If you ever have problems with them, just come see me and I'll fix them for you." With that, he bowed graciously and left with a smile.

The two girls made their way back to their room, each one silently going over events of the meeting in their heads.

* * *

As the council chamber doors closed, Velion turned to look at Aeria. He had a disapproving expression on his face as he commanded her to sit down. Standing before her he shook his head and began, "I have tolerated your distaste for the lesser ones for too long. Perhaps it was out of love that I allowed it, or maybe foolishness, but either way, it's time to put it to rest, Aeria."

"I don't understand," she replied, frowning up at him.

"Yes, you do. You've always looked down on them, and believed yourself to be better than they were, and although I can't deny that we rule over them, it is *unacceptable* to treat them as you do. I watched my father give in to his power over them, as his compassion was replaced with tyranny, but I will not watch you take his path!" Velion glared at his daughter.

"Did you ever stop to think that maybe he was right?!" Aeria protested, which only seemed to infuriate Velion more.

"*Maybe he was right?* Do you have any idea the atrocities your grandfather committed? You were just a child, but I had to watch him murder countless innocents, just to satisfy his hunger for power! And what did it profit him? He nearly destroyed the kingdom he built, all because he wanted complete control over his subjects. Subjects that he looked down on, in exactly the same way you do," Velion scolded.

Aeria looked away, and in a curt tone asked, "Can I leave now?"

Velion fumed, the anger in his voice evident as he said, "You were given Hadius's seat on the council because you showed you could handle yourself when the situation required it, but if you wish to continue to rule in his stead then I suggest you learn to treat those below you with some dignity! A cruel ruler may motivate with fear, but they always breed resentment and rebellion at the same time. You cannot control your subjects with force alone; you must also inspire them to follow your command!"

"Wise words coming from the man who just instructed me to crush a rebellion!" Aeria spat back.

Wide eyed and furious, Velion reach out his hand to strike Aeria, but stopped himself. Lowering his hand with a deep breath he said, "Sometimes there is no other option, but it should always be a last resort. I expect this mission to be clean and precise. We can't afford any mistakes. Now go, before you anger me further." Velion pointed at the door.

Aeria stood to leave and made her way out of the chamber without another word, although there was plenty more that she wanted to say. *How could be such a hypocrite?* She wondered to herself as she made her way towards the hangar. *He is the one who acts all high and mighty, the way he puts on such a show in front of them! And I'm the one without dignity?!* She scoffed and shook her head.

When she arrived at the hangar, her brother Deimos was waiting next to her ship. The last thing Aeria wanted to do right now was spend a few hours in a confined space with her irritating brother but there was no choice. In a gruff tone she commanded, "Get in the ship. Let's get this over with!"

Deimos grinned broadly and in a smug voice asked, "So did big sister get chewed out then?"

"Shut it!" Aeria snapped.

Deimos laughed and with a giant smile replied, "Ooooh... looks like Daddy's favorite got in trouble! Are you going to be this crabby the entire trip?" but Aeria didn't respond. She ignored him as they climbed into her ship and continued to avoid his attempts to pry until they were past Tython's atmosphere.

"Fine, I'll stop teasing, but seriously, what did he want?" Deimos tried to conceal his elation that she'd been reprimanded, but was doing a poor job of it.

Sighing, Aeria gave in and let go of her frustration. "He thinks that I need to change the way I treat the lesser ones."

Deimos laughed again, but cut it short once he noticed the glare Aeria gave him. "Well, he always was a softie when it came to them. I think he feels bad for them, even if he doesn't say it."

Aeria rolled her eyes as she punched in the navigation coordinates. It would take a few hours to get to the outer systems, so manual navigation was out of the question. "Not as much as Pisus does," she scoffed.

Deimos nodded in agreement, "You won't hear me argue with that. Honestly I think his sympathy towards them makes him weak. He never fights anymore, not since the last war. I wonder if he even remembers how to?"

Aeria shrugged, "It's hard to say, but if you listen to the historians, they say he was just as strong, if not stronger, than father was."

Deimos laughed, "I doubt it! We've both seen father fight. I doubt anyone could take him on alone."

Aeria snorted and smugly said, "I could."

Deimos looked shocked. "Oh come off it! There is no way you could take Dad on! Even together, I think we might have a hard time."

Aeria shrugged but secretly disagreed. She'd spent the last six months training harder than ever and knew her skills would outmatch Velion's, but there was no use arguing with Deimos.

"So what do you think about the humans?" Deimos asked, searching her expression.

"Which ones? The ones on Earth or the two pretending to be gods like the rest of us?" Aeria replied derisively.

"I take it you don't like the two girls then?"

"Honestly, I don't know how I feel about them." Aeria shrugged again.

"Well you've known them the longest, haven't you? Speaking of, you never did tell me how you found them," Deimos pressed.

Sighing, Aeria sat back in her chair as the ship's autopilot made the jump into subspace. "I found them by tracking down the holodisk they had on them. Supposedly they'd just found it when we arrived."

"You don't believe them then?"

"I don't know, it seems... odd that the only two humans that could use the device, would just happen across it a few hours before we arrived. I mean what are the chances?"

"Unheard of, I'm sure, but if they had the device for longer, then the log would have indicated that," Deimos surmised.

"That's the logical conclusion, but it just doesn't feel right." Aeria shrugged, getting bored with the conversation.

"So what were they doing when you found them?"

"Oddly enough, the older one was fighting a beast similar to a pervian angmar."

"Seriously? Hand to hand?" Deimos asked in disbelief.

Aeria nodded, "I think she had some sort of spear at first, but by the time I arrived she had dropped it."

"Was she able to kill it?"

"No, it was about to overtake her when I intervened," Aeria replied bashfully, not wanting Deimos to tease her again.

"Intervened?" Deimos seemed confused.

"I didn't want her to die before I figured out why she had a holodisk. She was pinned against a tree and only had a small knife," Aeria said, defensively. "I'm fairly certain she'd come to terms with her death and was trying to take the cat with her. I couldn't let that happen."

"Well why was she fighting the beast to begin with?" he inquired.

Aeria shrugged. "I don't know. I think she was trying to protect her sister."

Deimos seemed impressed as he said, "There is great honor in such a death. Perhaps father is right to have put her on the council after all."

Aeria scoffed, "Honor? More like stupidity! Why would you sacrifice yourself? It seems foolish to me."

Deimos frowned, "What would you have done then? Just let the sister die?"

Aeria shook her head, "No... but self-sacrifice wouldn't have been my first choice."

"Perhaps there wasn't another choice. I still call it honor, even if you don't agree," Deimos concluded. Aeria didn't respond. The two of them sat in silence for a long time before Deimos fell asleep.

He'd always been like that, Aeria recalled fondly. As much as she couldn't stand her baby brother sometimes, he was a good man. He was as tough as nails and was a great warrior, if not a little too single-minded. After centuries of fighting side by side she discovered that it was his only downfall in battle; his inability to see beyond the fight at hand. He was unmatched in brutality but he was a terrible tactician, always opting to go with the head on approach instead of thinking things through. He lacked the subtlety and foresight that winning a war required, but she didn't hold it against him. It was in his nature and, if anything, it had opened the door for her to show her strengths in warfare.

* * *

It wasn't until they had made their way to the Gaius system that Aeria shook Deimos awake. "We're here," she announced as he wiped the sleep from his eyes.

After a moment he asked, "So what's the plan, sis? I vote we just kick the door down and show them who's boss!"

Aeria smiled but shook her head. "No, we need to be a little more subtle than that. Father wants this to be a clean operation, so try to keep the bloodlust in check, okay?" She gave him a stern look.

"Yeah, yeah, I'll be *real* nice. That's why you brought me right?" he mocked, but she didn't play along.

Working at the console in front of her, Aeria pulled up a holoprojection of the supply depot. "According to the latest intelligence report, the militants are holed up in this building, with the leaders here," she pointed at the command center buried deep in the complex.

"Yep, that's where I would be if I were running the show. Only one way in; easy to bottleneck any attackers," he nodded appreciatively, as if it were a game.

Aeria grinned wickedly and said, "And that's why you'd be in as much trouble as they are. Sure there is only one way in, but there is also no escape. So long as we can outlast their bottleneck, they have nowhere to run."

Deimos frowned. "I guess I hadn't thought about escape, but then again I don't normally have to run away. Would rather stand and fight," he finished gruffly.

"Now, we have the element of surprise," Aeria continued despite the doubtful look on Deimos's face. "They are anticipating a full-on military invasion. The poor fools never considered that we might come in person to deal with them, so we can use that to our advantage."

"How so?"

"If we come in from the west, we should be able to land without anyone noticing. From there we can make our way quietly through the hills here..."-she pointed at an area of the map outside the complex- "We'll be able to take out any guards they have on the walls pretty quietly, and can make our way inside the complex here..." she pointed to an entrance on the second level. "We will have to fight our way down, but I don't think that should be a problem. From our reports the militants aren't well armed and have minimal training, so it should be a breeze."

Deimos frowned, "I guess we could do it that way, although I still like the idea of the full on attack. You sure you're not down for some shock and awe?" he asked like an excited kid. To his disappointment, Aeria shook her head.

"No, but maybe if things get too boring, I'll let you have some fun," she grinned mischievously.

"Deal!" Deimos replied excitedly.

Shutting down the holoprojection, Aeria started working at the controls of the ship again, plotting their course towards Gaius 5. Although the ship had built in radar deflection making it almost invisible to planetary sensors, she was grateful the supply depot was on the dark side of the planet. The night sky would make their descent less noticeable, and if she could manage to keep the ship low to the ground, they would never see them coming.

She knew Deimos was never much for sneak attacks, but it was honestly the best approach to minimize any damage to the supply depot. Even though Velion scolded her about the way she treated the lesser ones, she still had a hard time worrying about wellbeing of the militants. If they had the nerve to rebel, then they deserved to be crushed and humiliated, and this plan would accomplish both.

As the ship made its way through the thin atmosphere of Gaius 5, Aeria started to feel something... unfamiliar. She wasn't sure, but something felt off about all of it, like she was missing something. She pulled up the holoprojection again to double check the plan but couldn't see any error in it.

Deimos seemed to notice her anxiety as he asked, "Is there something wrong?"

Aeria shook her head, "No, it's nothing. Just wanted to make sure I had the layout of the compound memorized," she lied. She tried to suppress the feeling but it wouldn't go away. Deciding to ignore it, she increased the speed of the ship, wishing to get the mission over with as quickly as possible.

It wasn't long before the ship made its way to the chosen landing spot, and although she knew it would be unattended, she breathed a sigh of relief when the scanners indicated they were alone. Landing the ship was a bit tricky as there wasn't much room to maneuver, but Aeria was able to set the ship down in such a way that it was almost completely invisible from a distance.

Stepping out into the warm and muggy air of the mining planet, Aeria surveyed their surroundings. The supply depot was on the outskirts of the mining town and most of the area around it was undeveloped forest. As she expected there was a pathway into the woods that surrounded the depot. She would bet anything it led directly to the compound.

"This way." Aeria pointed towards the pathway. Still feeling apprehensive, she looked around and noticed that Deimos was still only wearing half of his armor. He loved to show off his body for the women, so he rarely wore the top half of his armor. Frowning, Aeria whispered, "There aren't any pretty girls around to impress, so put on all of your armor."

Deimos grinned and replied, "If I didn't know better, I'd say you were worried about me."

"Well I wouldn't want you getting a scar would I? I'd never hear the end of it," she jeered.

Deimos laughed quietly and said, "Fine, I'll put the rest on, but I'm telling everyone how worried you were about me!" Aeria made a show of rolling her eyes, but secretly she was relieved. As they walked, the armor on Deimos's legs started to shift and move, until the metal expanded and grew up and over his shoulders, molding perfectly to his upper body in a matter of seconds.

As they moved quietly through the woods towards the supply depot the feeling of worry seemed to grow in intensity. Aeria tried to shake the feeling but it wouldn't abate. *Why do I feel like this? There is nothing to worry about; they are just lesser ones!* she tried to remind herself, but it didn't help. In fact, as they moved closer to the supply depot, she started to get the feeling that they were walking into a trap.

After a few minutes, they reached the edge of the woods and could see the supply depot. It was a solid and rectangular complex, built like a military compound with high walls surrounding an interior courtyard. The majority of the complex was underground in order to protect the inhabitants from aerial bombardment. There was only one entrance on the ground level; a large, reinforced gate that would normally be guarded all day and all night, although such work ethic couldn't be relied on this far away from the central systems. Not when most of the exterior systems were run by corrupt governors that liked to cut spending in order to line their own pockets with royal credits.

Lack of security was undoubtedly the reason such a formidable complex was so easily overrun, but the militant miners didn't seem to be following suit. From where they were crouching, Aeria and Deimos could make out no fewer than eight guards on the exterior wall, and they could only see half of the building. There was no telling how many there were around the whole complex, but apparently their entrance wouldn't be as easy as previously thought. *It's no matter*, Aeria assured herself. *These lesser ones will make for child's play.*

Looking to Deimos, Aeria nodded that she was ready. He nodded back and with a grin he leapt high into the air, Aeria following after him. Together, with blinding speed and strength, they dispatched the first two guards, one at a time; Deimos hitting them high and Aeria sweeping them low. Both fell off the high wall and hit the courtyard ground with a thud. The other guards, hearing the scuffle, started to panic, and called for backup. The next two guards went down almost as easily as the first two, still not having time to react to the lightning fast speed of their attackers. Aeria elbowed her second guard off the wall with great satisfaction and sized up the third.

This time she pulled out her twin blades and leapt towards the third guard, driving the swords through his armor and into chest. As he choked in pain, she put her foot on his torso and shoved him off the blades, sending him into the courtyard with the others. By this time the remaining guards around the four walls were aware of what was happening, and, to Aeria's surprise, had readied weapons. From all across the courtyard a flurry of chaotic plasma blasts went flying in all directions. One narrowly missed Aeria while another hit the wall next to her, causing an explosion and sending debris flying into the woods.

Aeria realized there was no time to hesitate, as she hadn't expected them to be armed with such sophisticated weapons. With as much speed as she could muster, she dashed from one guard to the next, driving her blades through their pale blue skin. Out of nowhere a plasma ball hit the wall in front of her and knocked her back, sending her flying several feet through the air. Landing hard against the wall's walkway, she felt rage surge through her veins. *How dare they! I'll kill them all!*

Fuming, she climbed to her feet, and decided the fun and games were over. Up to now she was just toying with them, taking them on one at a time, but obviously that wasn't going to work anymore. Surveying the walls she counted five guards. Putting both of her blades together, she started to gather energy, causing the blades to glow. Once enough had been gathered she shot the energy in waves towards the remaining guards. None of them expected this and in a matter of moments all five had either been blown off of the wall or were unconscious.

Slightly out of breath, Aeria looked around again, making sure that none of them had been missed. Deimos leapt from where he was over to his sister. "What's the deal? I thought you said they wouldn't be armed?" he demanded, also winded.

Aeria shook her head, "I don't know. The intelligence report said that they weren't armed. There was nothing about plasma weapons!"

"Do you think we've been set up?" he wondered.

"Maybe, but by whom? It's no matter, we'll just have to be a bit more careful. I don't want to have to send you home in your life pod," Aeria jeered.

"Me? More likely to be you, but I agree. We should be more cautious."

The two of them made their way towards the entrance on their right. Now that the circumstances had changed, Aeria suspected that taking the shorter route might actually *be* what the militants would expect. *Was this why she'd felt so uneasy? Had she somehow know that things would go this way?* She shook the thought off, deciding that there was no time to figure it out. They needed to focus on accomplishing the mission, especially if it was going to be this difficult.

When they reached the door, both of them hesitated. Silently counting to three, Aeria ripped the door off the hinges and Deimos dashed in. There was no one waiting for them. Breathing a sigh of relief, Aeria indicated the direction they needed to go. There was a service stairwell a few yards away that would take them to the lower levels.

Cautiously they made their way down the stairs, but no one was in sight. Coming to the first floor landing, Aeria held up her hand to indicate that they should stop. Pulling out her holodisk she held it up to a glowing panel next to the landing. She pressed one of the buttons and a map of the compound burst forth. Pressing and holding a secondary button, the map flickered while it synced with the building's network. A moment later three red dots appeared on the map. They were moving, and all three were heading directly for Aeria and Deimos. The two of them grinned and waited; crouched and ready to attack once the landing door opened. Moments later all three of the lesser ones poured into the stairwell and the two deities dispatched them with ease; the hammer of Deimos knocking one out and the blades of Aeria dismembering the other two.

This is too easy, Aeria thought darkly, pulling out the holodisk again. Scanning again revealed that there were no more life forms in the building, except for three more red dots huddled in the command room. Deimos frowned and said, "That's it? This won't even be fun!"

Aeria didn't like it. Something wasn't making sense. The Intel reports indicated that dozens of militants were holed up in the compound, why were there only fourteen now? "Something's not right

Deimos. There should be way more militants than this," she warned.

"Do you think it's a trap?" Deimos asked, looking unsure.

"It's hard to say, but we should be cautious. Let's go. Just keep an eye out for anything strange."

"Right." Deimos agreed, following after his sister. They made their way across the first level towards a secondary stairwell that led to the lower levels. They moved quickly, keeping an eye out for anything out of the ordinary, but nothing was amiss; if anything, the supplies of the depot were too organized. As they passed by dozens of pallets loaded with neatly stacked and labeled supplies Aeria decided to stop and look around.

"Is it just me, or is everything *too* neat?" she asked, examining the supply stores.

"Huh?" Deimos was at a loss.

"Think about it, if there had been a rebellion and the supply depot was ransacked, wouldn't all of this stuff be in a giant mess? I've never known a riot to leave things in an organized and clean fashion before, have you?" she finished, gesturing at the room.

Deimos looked around puzzled. "You're right, but what does it mean?"

Aeria frowned in irritation. "It means we've been set up. There's been no rebellion here, but I'd bet all my credits that the three in the command bunker know what's going on. This time let's just disarm them. We need answers." Deimos nodded in agreement.

The two made their way down another set of stairs that ended in a long narrow corridor. This was the chokepoint they'd seen on the map, so both of them moved slowly and quietly down the hallway. At the end was a reinforced door that led to the command bunker; it was closed and most likely sealed shut. For anyone else it would be an almost impenetrable barrier, but for the two of them it would make for short work.

As they approached the door, both were on their toes, waiting for something unexpected to happen, but nothing did. Counting silently to three again, Deimos kicked the door with all of his strength, bending the metal and sending it flying into the command room. Dashing in, Aeria quickly disarmed and knocked down the three lesser ones inside, but they were not alone.

Looking around the large room she was stunned to find large piles of lifeless bodies. There had to be thirty or forty of them in total, and the stench was something awful. Clearly whoever was planning this intended for it to look like Aeria and Deimos had killed all the militants.

Anger surged through Aeria's veins once more as she tried to comprehend what was happening. Reaching down to one of the stunned lesser ones, she yanked him to his feet and shook him. "I want answers! NOW!" she roared.

The pale blue-skinned lesser one started to laugh. "You walked... right into it, just like he said you would," he sneered at Aeria.

Fury burned through her mind as she demanded, "Who? Who set this up?! Tell me now!" but he just shook his head in refusal. Fuming, Aeria looked around at the other two lesser ones who were being held against the ground by Deimos. "Fine! You won't talk, then maybe they will. You two! If you value your friend's life, then I suggest you start talking!" She held her blade to the lesser one's throat in a threatening manner, but the threat didn't work.

The one she was holding spoke up again, "It's too late. We've already set the building to blow. You walked right into the trap, just like he said you would."

Aeria looked around in alarm and noticed that one of the consoles was displaying a timer and the numbers were counting down. Three minutes and twenty-five seconds still remaining. *Plenty of time to get some answers,* she thought furiously. Driving her blade into the lesser one's leg she screamed, "Who?! Who said we'd walk right in?!"

The lesser one cried out in anguish as she twisted the blade. Coughing in pain he said, "Can't tell you… didn't see his face. But he had… a message for you…" Aeria's eyes widened in surprise. *A message?*

Pulling the blade out of his leg she held it to his throat again. "What message?"

The lesser one sneered again and said, "He said to tell you: beware the human girls, they aren't who you think they are." He finished with another sneer. Aeria wanted to press him for more information but before she could he bit down hard on something in his mouth, and before she could do anything he was dead.

Deimos looked at him in alarm and quickly tried to open the mouths of the other two he was holding, but it was too late. Both had already bitten into their poisoned capsules and were dead. Aeria's heart sank. Now they would never get the answers.

"Damnit!!" she shouted. "What did that even mean? The humans can't be trusted?"

"There is no time! We need to go before this places blows!" Deimos shouted, pulling her by the hand as he dashed out of the command room. Aeria looked back at the timer, two minutes flat. Barely enough time to get out of the complex.

Together they ran as quickly as they could, dashing down the hall and up the stairs, running past the depot's supplies and then out into the courtyard. Leaping high into the air they jumped to the walkway on the wall, but as they did so Aeria noticed something.

"Look!" she shouted, stopping and pulling hard on Deimos's hand. He turned, bewildered and frantic. The two of them looked out across the mining settlement and were shocked to see that it was completely destroyed. Large pillars of smoke billowed up from crumbled and burning buildings, and lifeless bodies were strewn through the streets. "This was more than just a setup, this was a massacre."

"We need to go, quickly!" Deimos pulled on her hand again, and Aeria felt her body start to run without her telling it to. She was stunned, not knowing what to think. *Who had done this? Even she didn't hate the lesser ones enough to massacre a whole settlement!*

They ran, dashing through the trees, trying to get as far away as they could. Just as they made their way out of the trees and could see the ship, an enormous explosion shook the ground, knocking both of them down. Turning over, Aeria looked back to see a massive fireball rising up into the air over the spot where the compound had been.

"Quick!" Deimos yelled, trying to get up and run towards the ship, but it was no use. Before they could get to their feet, both of them watched in horror as Aeria's ship exploded, sending pieces of it flying in all directions.

CHAPTER 11

"No!!!" Kira sat up, panting and sweating. She blinked, looking around her room with bleary eyes, her heart pounding in her ears. *It was just a dream*, she realized as she lay back down. It had felt so real, watching the ship explode like that. Glancing toward the window, she saw that it wasn't quite dawn, but she could tell from the orange glow that the first of Tython's suns would be rising soon.

Sitting up again, she hopped out of her bed and made her way towards the bathroom. Splashing cool water on her face seemed to drive the residual anxiety from the dream away. After drying off, she stared at herself in the mirror for a few minutes, trying to remember the details of the dream, but they slipped away. Shrugging, she made her way out of the bathroom and headed towards the kitchen to find some food. She would need to eat something if she was going to survive her training that morning.

She wondered what it would be like. No one gave her any details about these *royal vestments* or why they required training. *And why was Thanatos going to train her? Wasn't he some sort of general or something? Was this some kind of military training?* The thought was actually more pleasing than some of the others she'd come up with the night before. Learning to fight was something she could actually have fun doing.

Grabbing a plate of fruit, Kira made her way out onto the veranda to watch the suns rise. The city of Ishkur was glorious in the morning, the way the orange light gleamed on the shiny, tall buildings and the people on the streets below started to bustle and move.

Hearing soft footsteps approaching, Kira smiled and held out her plate. "Good morning, did you sleep well?" she asked as Kaya sleepily walked up to her and grabbed a piece of fruit from the plate.

"Better than you, probably. Were you dreaming again?" she asked, flopping into the chair next to Kira.

"Yeah, it was a weird dream about a building blowing up and then a spaceship exploding," Kira shuddered at the jarring memory.

"That does sound weird, but then again you always were the weird one," Kaya jeered with a sleepy smile. Kira snorted but didn't reply.

Changing the subject, Kaya asked, "What do you think this training is supposed to be?"

"I have no idea, honestly. Are you going to come with and see?" Kira asked hopefully.

"What, and miss out on Master Yu-On teaching me math? I don't know if I could pry myself away from *that*," Kaya replied sarcastically.

"That's what I figured," Kira laughed, playing along.

To their surprise, the familiar chime of the door rang out behind them. Confused, Kira wondered aloud,

"Thanatos isn't supposed to be here for another hour; I wonder who it could be?" but the question was answered before she could even stand up.

Thanatos came strutting in, but when he saw the girls on the veranda he gave them a disappointed look. Walking out onto the veranda he said, "I was hoping to come and rudely awaken you, the way they did when I was given my vestments, but I see you are already up."

Kira shook her head and teased, "Well how nice of you to stop by so early!"

"Naturally. I trust you've had enough breakfast, so let's be on our way!" He grinned and took the plate of fruit from her hands as he pulled her to her feet.

Aghast, Kira protested, "But I haven't even dressed yet!"

"No need, you'll be given clothes shortly," he responded archly. "Kaya, you can stay here and get ready if you want. We'll be down in the armory; I trust you know where that is?"

"Muh-huh," Kaya replied with her mouth full.

"Good. We will see you there shortly," he called back as he and Kira made their way out of the apartment.

Several minutes later he and Kira arrived at the armory and made their way into an open courtyard filled with dirt. "So what's this training about, anyway?" Kira asked.

"You see this armor I'm always wearing?" Thanatos pointed to his breastplate and Kira nodded. "Well, you are getting yours today!"

"Really? You mean I get my own?" Kira exclaimed, suddenly much more enthusiastic about the training.

"Yes, well sort of. You will get different armor than I have," he clarified.

"Different? How so?" Kira didn't understand.

"Well, to put it simply, your armor will be much more powerful than mine," he continued.

Giving him an inquisitive look, Kira repeated, "More powerful?"

Thanatos sighed in exasperation. "I suppose you wouldn't understand, would you? This armor is unlike any technology you had on Earth. It does more than just protect my body; it also allows me to... bend physics."

"*Bend physics?*"

"Perhaps a demonstration will help." He turned towards the courtyard and with a motion of his hands the ground began to move. Several yards away a large piece of stone rose up and formed a jagged boulder.

Kira gaped at him, "You mean... you can make the ground move?"

Thanatos grinned and said, "Oh, I can do much more than that, but you are getting the idea. This armor allows me to manipulate the magnetics of my surroundings as well as other things. I can also do this." Again with a peculiar motion, Thanatos waved his arms in a circle and then shot them forward. When he did so a visible shockwave shot out from his hands and flew towards the newly created boulder. With a loud bang the boulder disintegrated, sending rocks and dirt flying through the courtyard.

Kira's jaw dropped as she stared at the heap of dirt that had just been a boulder. "What was that?"

"What I just did was amass energy that acts like a shock wave from an explosion. It can be used to blow apart hard materials like that boulder, or can be used to knock an opponent back," he explained.

Kira couldn't believe her eyes. Was she really going to learn how to do this? She was so excited she could barely contain herself. "So when do I get the armor?"

"Well, looks like right now." He nodded in the direction behind Kira. She turned to see Aithos beaming at her and approaching with a strange type of suitcase in his hand.

"I see you two are up and at it bright and early!" Aithos exclaimed, looking satisfied. "This is good; I have things to attend to and was worried I'd be delayed."

"Is that my armor?" Kira blurted out, staring at the object in his hands.

"Yes, it is. I'm glad to see you're so excited, but before I give this to you, I must warn you about it. This is not a toy, and can be *very* dangerous if you are not careful. I don't want you wearing it around until you've completed your training with Thanatos, do you understand?" Kira nodded furiously, bouncing up and down anxiously. "You could very well blow up the entire palace if you aren't careful!"

Kira stopped short and looked at Thanatos. "I thought you said I couldn't blow things up?"

"No, I said *I couldn't*. You're armor is different and grants many abilities that mine doesn't," he replied with some impatience.

"He's right; the royal vestments have significantly stronger abilities than the military armors. One day I'll have to give you a lesson or two, myself, although I'm not nearly as good of a fighter as Aeria or Deimos are. If you really want to learn the ins and outs you should seek them out," Aithos said thoughtfully as he lowered the case to the ground. Bending to a knee he opened it and pulled out a pair of metallic boots.

"That's it? Boots?" Kira asked disappointedly.

Aithos and Thanatos both chuckled and Aithos said, "You'll see when you put them on." He handed them to her with a knowing smile. Kira shrugged and sat them on the ground, putting one foot in after the other.

At first nothing happened, but after a few seconds something about the boots seemed to change. They started to move, adhering to the contours of her feet. Kira giggled as the sensation tickled her toes. To her amazement, the boots started to morph and grow, creeping up her legs until they had gone past her knees. She was grateful she hadn't changed out of her pajamas; if she'd been wearing a dress like she usually did, this might not have gone so well.

Up and up the metallic material climbed, until it wrapped itself over her shoulders and started down her arms. After a few seconds she was entirely covered in armor,, from her feet up to her neck. "How did it do that?" she wondered, looking to Aithos for an explanation.

He smiled and said, "A master of his trade never reveals his secrets. Besides, I doubt you'd understand even if I did try to explain it."

"It's true, Kira. I asked him once, and the explanation went on for days, but I still don't understand how it works." Thanatos assured her.

"Try to walk around. Test it out a little; make sure it fits before I leave," Aithos encouraged.

Kira shrugged and started to walk around. The armor contoured to her body perfectly, but wasn't uncomfortable or restrictive. It wasn't heavy either, not like she would have thought it would be. It was like the metal was made out of some sort of light elastic material, because as she moved her legs and arms around, the material bent and stretched with ease. She took a few more steps and found that as she moved, she even felt lighter, like she was in space. The sensation was unreal.

"Try and run, see how it feels," Aithos suggested.

Kira smiled and started to jog around the courtyard. It was almost as if she wasn't wearing anything at all, even though the metal armor clinked softly as she jogged.

"*Not jog*, I said run. See how fast you can go," Aithos clarified.

Kira hastened her pace and found that as she did so, she started moving more quickly than she'd ever moved before. She kept running faster and faster until the entire courtyard was a blur and she was moving so quickly that even Thanatos and Aithos could no longer keep track of her. Laughing at the exhilarating speed, Kira decided to try something more. She stopped short and dashed across the courtyard. She moved so quickly that it almost appeared as though she teleported from one spot to the other. Tracking her movements at such a speed would be nearly impossible, were it not for the dust cloud she left in her wake.

"I think she's getting the hang of it," Thanatos said to Aithos, who nodded in agreement.

"Okay, one last thing before I go. Try to jump as high as you can," Aithos instructed.

Grinning again, Kira bent her knees and leapt into the air. She shot off of the ground like a rocket, flying nearly a hundred feet into the air. She went so high that as she started to fall back towards the ground, she worried that she would break her legs on the landing. But as she hit the ground, it felt no different than if she had hopped out of bed.

"Whoa! That was amazing! How did you do that?" a familiar voice exclaimed. The three of them turned to see Kaya running out into the courtyard with a look of astonishment on her face.

Aithos smiled and laughed, saying, "I'm glad you're impressed at my handiwork. Who knows, in a few years you might even have a set of armor yourself." Kaya gasped with excitement. Still beaming Aithos continued, "Well on that note, I think I'll take my leave. I have a lot of work to do back on Earth."

Kira stopped him. "Before you go, there is a small village near where Aeria found us. That's our home. Will you make sure that nothing bad happens to them?"

Aithos gave her an appraising look and with a smile said, "Ah, so that's where you are from, is it? I've seen that village, and was planning on starting the colonization efforts there. I believe there is a human named Felmar that lives there, correct?"

"Felmar?! You've met him?" Kira was surprised.

Aithos laughed and said, "I wouldn't say I've *met* him, as much as I've driven him off a few times. He's sort of a nosy human, I've found."

"Well whatever you do, don't give him any authority in the colony! He can't be trusted," Kira warned.

"I see... well in that case I'll make sure to keep an eye on him. Is there anyone else you'd like me to know about?"

"If it's not too much trouble, will you let Druin and Yamara know that we are here and that we are okay? They're probably pretty worried about us, and I don't know when we will get to see them again..." Kira trailed off.

"For a member of the council, I think I can do that," Aithos said with a smile and a slight bow. He turned to leave but Kaya also stopped him.

"And can you find out if our father is okay? Velion healed him before we left but we haven't heard any news since then," Kaya pleaded.

"I'll do what I can, little one. But I really must be going now." Moving to leave once again, he was thwarted one last time by Kaya attacking him with a hug. Clearly not expecting the affection, Aithos blushed as Kaya squeezed him. After a moment or two she released him and beamed up at him, as if he'd given her a great gift. He bowed graciously and finally made his way out of the courtyard.

"All right, that's enough fun for today. Let the training begin!" Thanatos announced.

Despite her excitement, Kira made every effort she could to be an example student. She hung on every word that Thanatos spoke and followed every instruction as precisely as she could. Together they spent hours training, with Kira learning everything from how to generate the shock waves to bending the matter around her. She wasn't nearly as formidable as Thanatos but she was learning quickly. By time they stopped to eat lunch she'd progressed from creating small puffs of dirt in the air, to molding a rather large mound of mud.

"Don't worry; you'll get the hang of it. You are learning much faster than I did. It took me nearly a week to get anything more than a cloud of dust, and I was the best in my class!" Thanatos encouraged her. "After we eat, we will spar and I'll teach you how to mold your armor into shapes."

"I can do that?" Kira exclaimed, examining her armor more closely.

"Yes, you can form basic shapes, so long as the continuity of the armor isn't broken."

"What do you mean?"

"You can't make anything that isn't continuous, like a detachable weapon you hold in your hand, but you *can* turn your arm into a weapon. Watch." He held out his right arm, and after a moment the armor around his hand started to morph and change until it became a long, sharp blade. "See?"

"Wow! What else can you make?" Kira probed.

"Plenty of things, but let's go eat first. I'm starving!" he pleaded, turning to leave the courtyard. The girls agreed and went to follow after him, but were stopped by the approach of Velion.

At the sight of him, Thanatos stood to attention and bowed politely, saying, "Lord Velion, it is good to see you."

"There is no time for formality, Thanatos. Something has happened." Velion looked grim, far more so than Kira had ever seen him look.

"What is it, my lord?" Thanatos asked in a worried tone.

"It's Aeria and Deimos. There's been an incident," Velion continued, his grim look turning to anger. Seeming to just notice Kira, his face softened a bit. "The armor looks good on you, Kira, almost as if you were meant to wear it. I'm sorry to interrupt, but your training lessons will have to continue later. Right now I need you and Thanatos to come with me. Kaya, please go back to your room. I'll have your sister back to you in a while."

Kira didn't know what to think, but looking over at her sister she nodded and indicated that Kaya should do as he told her. Velion turned and started to walk towards the council chamber, as Kira and Thanatos followed behind.

Once inside the council chamber Velion instructed Thanatos and Kira to sit in their usual spots, while he sat next to them. In a quiet voice he said,

"There has been an incident on Gaius 5. A few hours ago the communications from the supply depot went down and the relay beacon from Aeria's ship also disappeared. We've received confirmation that both Aeria and Deimos summoned their emergency pods and are currently making their way towards the nearest system.

"What do you want us to do, my lord?" Thanatos asked. It was exactly the question Kira was wondering herself. *Why was she here, what could she do?* She frowned, feeling like she was in way over her head.

"I need the two of you to go and find them. You can take a ship and intercept their pods much faster than it will take for them to get to safety."

"Why me?" Kira asked, unable to suppress her curiosity any longer.

Velion grinned the way he always did when she spoke her mind. "It's time for you to start learning what it means to be a council member, and handling delicate situations like this will be part of your responsibilities. Also, it's time you learn how to pilot a ship."

Kira gulped hard. *I'm going to learn how to fly?* The thought was both exciting and terrifying. Space was something that she'd always been called towards, but at the same time she was beginning to understand how dangerous it was.

"Forgive my doubt, my lord, but are you certain this is the appropriate time? Kira has barely learned how to use her armor, and if the situation on Gaius 5 is as bad as we think it is, then there might be trouble following after Aeria and Deimos," Thanatos interjected.

"I appreciate your concern, but I believe Kira can handle herself, so long as she does as you tell her." Velion gave Kira a stern look. She stared back at him, still reeling from the idea of learning to fly a ship. "There is a ship ready for your departure in the hangar. Please gather whatever you need and leave as soon as possible."

"As you command," Thanatos said as he stood and bowed again. Kira just gave Velion a halfhearted smile and followed after Thanatos as he left the council chamber.

* * *

After a rushed meal, Thanatos and Kira were on their way toward the hangars. As promised, there was a ship awaiting their arrival, and by the looks of it, it was brand new. This suspicion was confirmed once they entered the cockpit. There, on the pilot's seat, Kira discovered a note that read:

"To Kira:

No council member should be without their own shuttle. If you take care of this ship, it will take care of you.
I hope you like it.

-Velion
P.S. Try not to crash it"

Kira couldn't believe her eyes. Was this really happening? Her very own space ship? She showed the note to Thanatos. A strange look passed over his face and quietly he said, "Congratulations. Not many are lucky enough to own their own shuttles, so I guess I had better show you how to fly this thing."

After spending several minutes showing Kira how to use the controls, Thanatos explained that the majority of the ship's functions were self-controlled; even taking off from a planet or landing on one could be left to autopilot. Despite this feature, he forced Kira to manually take off, saying, "In case something ever happens to the autopilot you should have at least some practice."

The feeling of flying the ship was exhilarating, and despite the fact that her wild flying nearly gave Thanatos heart failure a couple of times, they made it out of Tython's atmosphere unscathed. He showed her how to program the navigation system and how to initiate a jump to subspace. He explained that the computer would always calculate the jump for her, that way there was no worry of accidently jumping into the middle of a star or coming out too close to a black hole, a thought that made Kira shudder.

Before she knew it, she had successfully programmed the computer and they were on their way to the Gaius system. Because the ship was new, the jump took less time than expected. "Must be the new Marc VII engine. Aren't you a lucky girl?" Thanatos said with the same strange look passing over his face. "I bet there are only a handful of ships that could go as fast as this one."

"Really? You think so?" Kira exclaimed, still reeling from the excitement of having her own ship.

"Really. It will take a couple hours to get there, so I'm going to close my eyes and rest. I'd suggest you do the same but I think it would be better for you to read this." He tossed her a large and heavy book that said "Owner's Manual" on the cover. With a sly smile he leaned his seat back and closed his eyes. It wasn't long before he was asleep, leaving Kira alone with her new study material.

The ship ride was boring and the excitement of the owner's manual wore off rather quickly, leaving

Kira with nothing to do but stare out at the passing colors of subspace. It was magnificent to behold, now that she understood what it meant to travel in subspace. Even though she didn't *completely* grasp the physics that it required, Master Yu-On had done a decent job of explaining it to her. It was amazing to her that the ship could bend space in such a way that traveling impossible distances only took a few short hours.

She imagined telling her father about it, but realized that he probably wouldn't be able to understand, not really. None of the people from home would be able to grasp the things she now understood. In some ways she missed the naivety, as everything was starting to lose its mystery, but she knew it was better to understand reality than to believe in mysticism.

In many ways, if she went back to Earth possessing her newfound understanding along with her armor, she really would be like a god to them, able to do and know things they'd never dreamed of. She wondered what it would be like to go home, after seeing and learning so much. Would it still feel like home? Would she still love the things she had once enjoyed, or would all of it seem too simple for her? Living on Tython for the better part of a year had revealed a beauty and wonder that she didn't think Earth could match. There were no expansive cities, or tall buildings. There were no flying vehicles or technologies of luxury and ease. There wasn't even reading or writing.

And what of her sister? Had she also spent enough time around the *Gods* that Earth would lose its appeal for her as well? Kira doubted it. Every chance Kaya got, she talked or asked about home. It was a little irritating, if Kira was honest with herself, but she never tried to stop her. She understood that Kaya needed to hold on to the thoughts of home in order to cope with all the changes. If Kira hadn't been so close to adulthood she might have felt the same, but there was something so liberating about all of it. No longer was she doomed to live the boring and repetitive lifestyle of her village. No longer did she have to listen to the elders drone on and on about *the spirits.* Now she *knew* the spirits. Now she *was* a spirit, soaring through the heavens in her very own ship.

She smiled to herself as she thought about the freedom that having her own ship would mean. Velion would of course place restrictions on when she could leave or where she could go, but that wouldn't last forever. Eventually she'd be a full member of the council and would be free to do as she pleased. She could travel to every corner of the twelve kingdoms if she wanted to. Maybe she would even travel to some other, unexplored places. Maybe she could discover a new planet with a new civilization on it! The possibilities seemed endless.

Her wandering thoughts were interrupted by a beeping noise coming from the console in front of her. Unsure of what it meant, she reached over and shook Thanatos by the shoulder. Yawning and looking a little lost, he asked, "Wha... What is it? Are we there?"

"I don't know, the console just started beeping. I think it means we are close."

Thanatos gave her a confused look and turned to examine the console. After a few seconds he said, "It looks like we are ten minutes away from our destination. There is no telling where Aeria and Deimos might be right now so I suggest we drop out of subspace sooner than that. Just press that symbol right there. It will ask you if you are sure; just hit yes."

Kira pressed the symbol as instructed and then hit yes when it asked if she was sure she wanted to drop from subspace. Almost immediately the ship slowed and the familiar color patters of subspace faded away to a deep, dark ocean of stars.

Thanatos showed her how to use the radar system and after a few seconds of searching they discovered two emergency beacons emitting a signal some distance behind them. "It seems we went too far. No trouble, we'll just have to double back to pick them up. Do you think you can set a heading to catch up to them?" he asked.

Feeling unsure of herself, Kira worked at the console and after nearly sending them back into subspace twice, she was able to properly set the coordinates. Once she told the computer to "execute," the space ship burst to life as the engines rotated the ship 180 degrees before propelling them towards the beacons. At first Kira felt as though she was going to be sick from the force of the accelerators but a moment later the inertial dampeners compensated for the engines, and everything went back to normal.

Fifteen minutes later they had nearly caught up with the two emergency pods. Thanatos hailed the two of them and it didn't take long for the three vessels to meet. Having read enough of the owner's manual to know that there were two docking hatches on the ship, Kira had the three vessels hooked together in no time at all.

Deimos was the first to make his way through the hatch, and with a wide grin he greeted Thanatos saying, "Nice ship! You have no idea how glad I am to see you. I'm not sure I could have survived another day in that cramp emergency pod. Maybe I'll have to talk with Aithos about making those a little more spacious." Thanatos agreed enthusiastically. Deimos seemed genuinely relieved at being out of the pod until his eyes drifted to Kira. With a severe change of expression he asked, "What is *she* doing here?"

Thanatos turned to look at Kira as if he'd forgotten who was behind him. "Oh, your father insisted I bring her along. You know, show her the ropes of flying a ship and such. Why?" Deimos didn't answer; instead he moved towards the other docking hatch and helped Aeria on to the shuttle. With a grave look he nodded towards Kira.

Aeria turned to look and with a flash of anger she pushed past Thanatos and headed straight for Kira. Grabbing her by the shoulders, Aeria pushed Kira up against the hull of the shuttle and demanded, "What do you know about what happened on Gaius 5?!"

Kira blinked and squirmed, trying to escape the death grip, but it was no use. "What's your problem? Let go of me! I don't know anything about Gaius 5!"

"Don't lie to me girl, I'll end you if I have to!" Aeria hissed with a wild look in her eyes.

"I'm not lying! Let go of me!" Kira's anger bubbled and without realizing her strength shoved Aeria as hard as she could, sending her stumbling backwards into the other side of the ship.

"Stop it! Both of you! What's this about?" Thanatos yelled, forcing his way between the two of them.

"You tell me! You're the one who's so close to this *human*," Aeria spat.

"What? Wait a second, just slow down. We don't know anything about what happened on Gaius 5, that's why we were sent to pick you up. Velion wants to know what happened down there."

"What happened was that we were set up! Someone destroyed that town before we even arrived and then tried to kill *us* by blowing up the supply depot! Not to mention destroying my ship! And your girl here knows something about it!" Aeria lunged at Kira again, but Thanatos was able to hold her back.

"Just calm down! How could she possibly know anything about this? She's been confined to the Palace until now," Thanatos protested.

Aeria seemed to relent, throwing her arms up in the air. "Then explain to me why the whelp who tried to blow me up, gave me a warning about her!"

Thanatos gaped at her, and then with a bewildered look turned to peer at Kira. Kira didn't understand what was happening but she certainly didn't like being attacked. It took a great deal of composure not to go right back after Aeria, but she knew it would only make things worse. *They had a message about me?* she wondered. *How did they even know who I was?*

"Wait... what warning? I don't understand," Thanatos shook his head.

"Aren't you listening?! Clean out your ears, fool; whoever set us up said she was part of it!" Aeria shouted, starting to lose her composer again.

"Well, not *exactly*," Deimos interjected, causing Aeria to shift her infuriated gaze to him. "The lesser one said that the person who set us up gave him a message: *'to beware, that the humans aren't who you think they are.'* Whatever that's supposed to mean," he finished, trying to ignore Aeria's wild look.

"*Aren't who we think they are?* How did this lesser one even know about them? I know they've been on the news but no one outside of the council knows that they are from Earth." Thanatos looked perplexed.

"That's what he said, and since he swallowed poison before we could interrogate him, that's all we know," Deimos shrugged, eyeing Kira warily.

"*Poison?* You mean he killed himself? Have you ever heard of a lesser one doing that before?" Thanatos asked but Deimos didn't respond. He just shook his head and moved to sit down on one of the passenger chairs.

"We need to get back to Tython as soon as possible. Velion needs to hear this. I'll take us home," Thanatos finished, moving over to the navigation computer and putting in the coordinates. A moment later the ship made the jump to subspace and was heading back towards Tython.

"You better hope you're telling the truth, *girl*. I swear, if I find out that you had something to do with this, I will destroy you," Aeria glared at Kira before moving to sit in one of the other passenger seats.

"I didn't and you couldn't even if you tried," Kira spat back at her. Aeria looked livid, but decided to let the boast go unanswered.

* * *

The flight back was filled with awkward silence as none of them dared say anything. Kira couldn't help but let her mind linger on the warning. *Aren't who you think they are? What does that even mean?* Had she done something she couldn't recall? Had she somehow told someone to destroy the town without knowing it? That was absurd. She had been confined to the palace for over six months and the only people she ever talked to were her sister, Thanatos, Master Yu-On, and occasionally Velion. Before the last meeting she wasn't even aware of Gaius 5, so how could she be behind an attack on it?

It was hard to believe how little excitement she derived from landing the ship back on Tython. A few hours earlier she was dreaming about the adventures she could have in her ship, but now it seemed more like trouble than anything, especially with the way Aeria was treating her. She felt as though she were being punished, but had no idea what she had done to deserve it.

The four of them made their way from the hangar to the council chamber, where Velion was anxiously waiting for them. Kira expected him to have a relieved look on his face when they returned but to her surprise he looked furious. With a wild gesture he indicated that he wanted them to sit.

"What the hell have the two of you done?! I told you to keep it clean!" Velion shouted, making the entire room shake. Aeria and Deimos exchanged confused looks. "It's all over the network! Every news outlet showing the devastation that the two of you wrought on that settlement! Do you have any idea how much damage you've caused?!"

"It wasn't us!" Aeria protested, but Velion didn't seem interested.

"I sent you there to quell an uprising, not to give the entire kingdom a reason to rebel! If we thought things were unstable before, what do you think this is going to do?" he shouted, holding a remote out and turning on a large holoprojection at the end of the room. The projection showed a newscast displaying images of destroyed buildings and piles of dead lesser ones with a caption that read 'Council Punishes Uprising by Destroying Entire Settlement.' Turning back to face his daughter, Velion shouted, "Do you understand now?!"

"But it wasn't us! The town was destroyed before we even got there!" Aeria yelled, standing up. "Someone set us up!"

"Don't you lie to me!" Velion bellowed.

"She's not, father. What she says is true. The town was massacred before we arrived," Deimos interjected. Velion looked confused and yet somehow more angry than before. "The intelligence reports were wrong. There was no rebellion on Gaius 5. Someone set us up so that it would look like we destroyed the town. When we got to the compound there were only a handful of lesser ones, but they were trained and very well armed."

Velion didn't seem to know how to react as he walked over to his throne and sat down, covering his face with his hands. After a few seconds of silence he looked back up at them and quietly asked, "If it was a setup, then did you at least find out who was behind it?"

Deimos shook his head, "No father. The lesser ones in the compound killed themselves and set the building to blow before we could get any real answers from them."

"Then how do you know it was a setup?" Velion demanded, the irritation returning to his voice.

"We were able to get some information from their leader before he swallowed his poison."

"*Poison?* Since when do lesser ones commit suicide? I'm not sure I've ever known one to purposely kill themselves. Are you certain that's what happened?"

"Yes, it was unmistakable. All three of the leaders killed themselves rather than submit to our interrogations," Deimos clarified.

"What information did you get then?" Velion put his face back in his hands and let out a long sigh while he waited for the response.

Aeria spoke up, glaring over at Kira as she did so. "They indicated a man had instructed them we would be coming; that we would walk right into the trap he set for us."

Still holding his face in his hands, Velion asked, "Did they tell you who it was?"

"No, the lesser one said that he hadn't seen his face so he couldn't say. Whether that was a lie or not, I do not know. But there was more," Aeria paused, glaring at Kira again. "This mystery person wanted to pass along a message, telling us 'not to trust the humans as they aren't who we think they are'."

At that Velion looked back up at them with an alarmed expression. "The humans?"

"I believe he meant Kira and Kaya," Aeria clarified.

"*Kira and Kaya?* They aren't who we think they are, that's what he told you?" Velion inquired.

"Those were his exact words," Aeria finished.

Velion looked at Kira with a piercing gaze and asked, "Do you know anything about this? Do you have any idea why this lesser one would have said this?"

Kira shook her head, "None whatsoever."

Velion stared at her, searching her expression for any hint of deception but found none. Shaking his head he said, "Of course you don't; you've been here under careful watch ever since you arrived."

"*That's it?* We get a lead that she might be a spy or worse, and all you're going to do is take her word for it?" Aeria demanded.

"Enough! There is no possibility that Kira had anything to do with this treachery. If anything, this is ploy to throw us off the scent of who's truly behind it," Velion replied harshly.

"Unbelievable," Aeria mumbled, but Velion ignored her.

"I need time to process this. If what you say is true then we have a much larger problem on our hands than some rebellious lesser ones. You said that they were well armed, Deimos?"

"Yes. They were equipped with military grade plasma rifles; weapons that wouldn't have been readily available in a mining settlement."

"My Lord, isn't there something we are forgetting about?" Thanatos asked, nodding towards the holoprojection. "What of the spread of this news? Have we done anything to suppress it?"

"Yes, I ordered that it be shut down as soon as I saw it, but there is no telling how many of the systems saw it before then. Its effect won't be apparent for a few days. I've ordered all of our intelligence officers to give hourly reports on the activities of the central systems."

"Just the central systems?" Thanatos questioned.

"For the time being, that's all our resources will allow. The outer systems aren't as important as the inner ones. If the central systems start to collapse then we will have a much larger problem on our hands. We can't afford to lose those." Velion stood and turned the recorded holoprojection off. "I need some time to think about our next move. All of you, go to your quarters and stay there. If you have to leave, please try to stay near the palace."

CHAPTER 12

The next few days passed without incident. Kira kept watching the news for any signs of rebellion but either the news wasn't reporting it, or nothing was happening. In order to keep her mind off of the warning Aeria had brought back, Kira focused as hard as she could on her training.

Thanatos wasn't able to dedicate as much time to training her as before, but each morning he would spend an hour or two showing her new techniques and sparring with her. She learned not only how to move the earth around her, but how to pull large portions of the ground up and throw them across the courtyard. After a few days she could manipulate the ground around her with such precision that she was able to build almost any structure from the dirt; all without lifting a finger.

Even her shockwaves were getting better. Now she could amass them more quickly, enabling her to shoot several of them in rapid succession. She finally understood what Aithos meant when he said she could very well destroy the whole palace. With enough time and concentration, she could amass a shockwave so large and so strong that it would crumble an entire building, not that she had tested that.

All of these abilities seemed to come naturally to her, the same way Druin's fighting lessons always had. It wasn't long before Kira was able to outperform Thanatos, which was no small feat given that he was Velion's top general and had almost 200 years of experience.

Despite the demands of her rigorous training, the warning kept creeping back into her mind. She hadn't told Kaya about it, which was unheard of. Ordinarily she never would have withheld such important information from her sister, but for some reason, she just couldn't find the words. Kaya already had so much to think about as it was, between Master Yu-On's lessons and her constant homesickness. It just didn't seem fair to give her something else to worry about.

And so Kira trained, and trained, from dawn until dark. She was obsessed with her progress, working harder than she'd ever worked at anything before. When Kaya asked her why she was training so much, Kira told her that it was so she could be the best, but that was a lie. Secretly, Kira was worried. Worried that at any moment she might be called into battle. Worried that whoever had set Aeria up, might be coming for her. If they were, she wanted to be ready.

It wasn't until two weeks had passed that Velion called the council together. Again Kira was summoned while Kaya was asked to stay in her chamber.

"Why can't I come? This isn't fair! First you get a space ship and armor, and now you keep getting called to meetings without me! I thought I was important too," Kaya protested, standing in front of their apartment with her arms crossed in defiance.

"Kaya, don't be like this. I know you want to come, and if it were up to me, I'd bring you along, but they specifically asked for you to stay here," Kira tried to console her.

"Not fair! What's so important about this meeting anyway?" Kaya demanded.

Kira sighed, "I don't know, they didn't say. I just know that I *have* to go, and if I don't leave right now I'll be late again!"

"I wish we had never come here! All I get to do is study and do homework! It's not fair at all!" Kaya shouted, stomping off toward her room in a huff. Kira wanted to go console her, but there was no time. As upset as Kaya might be, she was nothing compared to the reproachful looks the council members gave when Kira was late.

"I'll be back as soon as I can, I promise!" Kira called back as she left the apartment. A few minutes later she entered the council chamber and was grateful to not be the last to arrive. Only half of the council had shown up and Velion wasn't there yet. Going to her normal spot Kira sat quietly, watching the others as they chatted with each other.

Aithos noticed her sitting quietly and decided to walk over to her. "I hear you are getting pretty good with your armor. I even heard you beat up on poor Thanatos yesterday morning?"

Kira blushed a little, "Well, it's not really a fair fight, is it? I mean my armor allows me to do things that his doesn't, so the odds were stacked in my favor."

"I wouldn't be so sure. Yes, the armor makes a difference, but Thanatos didn't get to where he is by losing many battles, even against stronger opponents," Aithos smiled broadly and put his hand on her head, messing up her hair.

Kira made a face, but she didn't care. She didn't really worry much about her appearance and having someone to talk to made the council more bearable. It took a while for her to feel comfortable around them, but she noticed that the longer she was around, the less resentful the others seemed to be towards her.

"Oh, I've been meaning to catch up with you. Do you remember the thing you asked me to do?" Aithos asked, lowering his voice and leaning in closer. "You will be glad to know that your father is in good health, and is doing very well with the transitions we've implemented."

Kira's heart nearly stopped in place. "Really?! You've seen him?" She asked, a little more loudly than she intended.

Hushing her, he continued, "I actually had a long conversation with him and another man named... Druin?"

"Yes. That's my uncle!"

"Well, they were both quite pleased to know that you and Kaya were safe and sound. It seems they were quite worried about you after you left."

"Gee, I wonder why?" Kira replied sarcastically.

"Who knows?" Aithos played along. Looking around to make sure they weren't being listened to he lowered his voice again, "I shouldn't have done it, but I promised them that I'd let you and your sister return home for a short while to see them. If you want to go that is..."

Kira's eyes widened in disbelief. "Really? Are you serious? I don't know that Velion would like us going back."

"Well, I thought the same thing, but your father was so insistent I couldn't really say no. He said he had something very important to tell you. Any idea what it is?" Aithos inquired, looking around again to check for eavesdroppers. No one was listening, but Aeria was glaring at Kira the way she had been since the incident on Gaius 5. Kira made a face at her, which drove Aeria to break her gaze.

Kira looked back at Aithos. "He has something important to tell me? He didn't say what it was?" Kira had no idea what her father wanted to tell her that would be so important.

"No, he refused to tell me, but he said the information could mean life and death," Aithos frowned, looking somewhat concerned.

Kira sat back in her seat and folded her arms. *Life and death? What could he possibly know that would make such a difference?* she wondered to herself. "When can we go? How do we get there without anyone noticing?" Kira asked, trying to think of a way to escape.

"A truly ingenious plan, if I do say so myself. But now isn't the time. I'll let you know what you need to do, just keep an eye out," Aithos grinned mischievously and turned to walk away. Kira thought about stopping him, but noticing the glare from Aeria again, she decided not to.

Kaya is going to freak out when I tell her! Kira thought as she tried to ignore Aeria's disdainful look. The excitement of getting to see her family again made it difficult to sit still as the last few members filtered into the council chamber.

When Velion made his way to the center of the room, everyone took their seats except Thanatos, who was nowhere to be seen. That was unusual, as he had attended every meeting since Kira arrived. She looked around for him but there was no sign of him.

"My dear friends, I've called you here today because I have some disturbing news. As all of you are aware, there was an incident on Gaius 5 not long ago, but what most of you have yet to learn is that there is more to the story. The truth of the incident is that we were setup by an unknown third party who has access not only to our intelligence network, but also to some of our most deadly weapons." Velion paused as the news swept across the room. Several of the members seemed stunned by the news, while others did not react. Velion continued, "I have spent the last several days gathering as much intelligence about the incident as I can, and what I have surmised is that there is an unknown, but very well connected, branch of militants operating throughout the outer systems."

"Which outer systems?" Pisus interrupted.

"I'm sorry to say it, but it appears to be all of them," Velion replied. This news was taken much more seriously as the council members started murmuring to each other in alarmed tones. "It gets worse," Velion interrupted, causing the room to go quiet again. "It seems that this militant group is planning several more of the same type of attack."

"Why? Do we know their objective?" Pisus asked, looking deeply concerned.

"Unfortunately, no. Right now we can only guess, and our best guess is that they wish to incite a wide scale rebellion by making it look as though we are slaughtering our people when they disobey. They tried to do this by leaking images of Gaius 5 to the networks, but their plan failed when we suppressed the news."

"Is there anything we can do?" Hera asked.

"We are working on that as we speak. I have ordered several divisions of the military to patrol the outer systems while our best agents try to infiltrate the organization," Velion explained.

"Will that work?" Deimos chimed in.

"Honestly, it is hard to say. Whoever is running this organization has gone to great lengths to hide themselves and their operatives. What little we know indicates that this group is most likely run by someone in the higher castes, possibly even a Tythonian." Velion shook his head.

"If it's a Tythonian, then who could it be? Surely you aren't suggesting it's one of us!" Pisus protested.

"Right now I cannot say, but the evidence we have so far is that the man behind the Gaius 5 incident was well connected and wealthy. Based on his understanding of our intelligence network, it's highly likely that he used to work for us," Velion finished, looking tired.

"I hate to say it, but... there is someone who used to be part of this council that hasn't been heard from in a very long time," Pisus suggested warily.

"Oh, did you mean me, Brother?" An unfamiliar voice called out from behind Kira. She turned to see who it was and was surprised to find someone she had never seen before. A tall man with jet black hair came walking down the steps with a wide grin on his face. He was handsome but looked weathered, as if he'd been living in harsh conditions for many years. His eyes were dark brown and he squinted as he looked around the room. He was dressed in armor like Kira's, except it was a dark grey color instead of silver and had a long black cloak hanging from the shoulders. "I'm glad to know how quickly my own brother is to suggest me a traitor!" he announced as he reached the bottom of the stairs.

Stopping for a moment, he turned his gaze to Kira. With a soft smile he walked over to her and bent to one knee. Taking her hand in his he kissed it and said, "My dear Kira, I'm sorry I have not come to see you sooner. I've wanted to congratulate you on your appointment to the council, but I just haven't had the time. I'm sure you will make an excellent ruler."

Kira didn't know what to say to this stranger, so all she could manage was a quiet, "Thank you..."

"Hadius has been working very closely with me over the past few days, Pisus. If it weren't for him we wouldn't have nearly as much information about the militants as we do," Velion clarified. Hadius gave Kira an odd look and returned to his feet, turning to look at the council.

"And how is it he knows so much about them?" Pisus asked, looking skeptical.

"Have you already forgotten what my previous duties were? Was I not charged with running the intelligence network of the kingdom?" Hadius asked in a spiteful tone as he moved to stand next to Velion.

"And a fine job you've done! Where was your *intelligence* before Gaius 5?" Pisus jeered.

"A fair point, but as I had been relieved of my seat on the council, I was no longer charged with running the network, was I? A job that I believe fell to *you*, being second in command." Hadius smiled wickedly. Pisus was clearly angered by the blow, but after receiving a reproving glare from Velion he chose not to respond.

"As Velion was saying, our intelligence suggests that the traitor is one of our own. Most likely a disgruntled military officer, heaven knows we have quite a few of those, don't we?" Hadius laughed, but no one else seemed to find it funny. Kira couldn't help but stare at the man. There was something... *familiar* about him. Something she couldn't explain, but it was almost as if she had met him before.

"I have narrowed the list down to a possible twenty, but as most of these people haven't been seen for many years, it will take some time to track them down. I will remain in close contact while I'm assisting in this endeavor," Hadius finished.

Velion thanked him and announced, "That is all for now. There will be individual briefings later as the systems in question fall into several different jurisdictions, but the rest of you will be free to go. Please keep an eye out for anything out of the ordinary; we can't be sure the militants haven't found their way on to Tython."

As the room started to disperse, Kira couldn't help but notice the way Hadius watched her leave. Again she was struck with the feeling that she'd met him before, but how could that be? In all her time on Tython she'd never once seen him and she surely hadn't met him back on Earth. Deciding to worry about it later, Kira rushed back to her apartment to give Kaya the exciting news.

* * *

Aeria left the council chambers feeling a sense of resentment. She couldn't believe that after the warning they received about the humans, that Velion hadn't even mentioned it to the council. What was worse was that he specifically instructed her to keep it to herself. How could he be so sure about the human girls? It was odd enough that they were able to use the royal technology, but now their enemy was keeping tabs on them? Something didn't feel right. And what was this business with Hadius returning? He hadn't been seen in a long time and now, without warning, he decides to show up and lend a helping hand?

She shook her head as she made her way to her chambers. Her room in the palace lacked the luxury that her home on Olympa had, but it was comfortable enough. She didn't particularly enjoy spending so much of her time on Tython, but with the new developments in the rebellion there wasn't enough time to spare for travel. She didn't like being away for so long, in fact she had noticed that the longer she was away from Olympa, the more the problems her governors usually caused. She could only imagine the issues she would need to unravel once she returned.

Sitting down on one of the couches, she let out a long sigh. *They aren't who you think they are,* she repeated in her mind for the thousandth time. *What a strange message to pass along.* It wasn't unreasonable for her father to dismiss it as a poor attempt at causing distraction, but what kind of fool would tell such a blatant lie? Surely this mysterious puppeteer would have realized that such an obvious ploy would be figured out almost immediately.

She knew there had to be more to it, but If it wasn't a ploy, then how did the humans fit in with the massacre on Gaius 5? Or with the militants for that matter? If they had been confined to the palace since their arrival as everyone assumed, then there was no chance they could set something like this up. Besides, no one outside of the council knew anything about them or where they were staying. Of course the media had guessed at their identities and location, but unless someone on the council leaked their whereabouts there was no way for the militants to contact them.

That didn't make things better either. If there was a leak on the council then one of them was a traitor, but to what end? All twelve of them were treated in the highest regard, and were given a fair amount of autonomy in their districts, so why betray the council? It was a death sentence for sure, so what benefit could there be?

She closed her eyes and tried to push the thoughts away, feeling a headache coming on. Maybe she was making too much of the warning, just as her father suggested. He was usually right about things like this, whether she wanted to admit it or not.

A chime at the door interrupted her thoughts. "Come in," she called out, keeping her eyes closed, but no one entered. "I said come in!" she called out, a bit louder. Again no one entered the room. Opening her eyes, she looked over at the door and yelled, "Come in!" but nothing happened. Letting out a sigh of exasperation she got to her feet and walked over to the door.

As usual the door slid open, but no one was on the other side. Stepping out into the expansive hallway she looked around for any signs of a visitor, but like normal, the passage was empty. Frowning, she called out, "If this is some kind of joke, I am *not* amused!" Her words echoed down the hallway but nothing stirred. Deciding that the door must have malfunctioned she went back into her room, collapsing on the couch once again and closing her eyes.

No sooner had she gotten comfortable before the chime rang out again. Sitting up, she yelled "Come in!!" but no one did. Getting to her feet in irritation she marched over to the door. Again no one was there to greet her, nor was there any sign of a person in the corridor. Letting out a loud sigh, she turned to go call for maintenance, but was stopped when she noticed something at her feet. A small piece of folded paper was lying on the floor just outside the door. Looking around again, Aeria bent down to pick up the folded paper.

Unfolding it in her hand she found a note inside that read:

*"They are meeting with their co-conspirators tonight. If you want to find out who they really are,
follow them.*

-A friend"

Aeria reread the note several times before the words sunk in. *So I was right!* she thought to herself. The humans were more than they seemed after all!

She started walking back towards the council chamber, deciding the best course of action was to tell her father. He would want to know immediately. But as she made her way down the corridor, she slowed to a stop. *Would he even believe the note?* The way he seemed to adore the human girls had blinded his judgment once before, why would this be any different? No, she needed more than a vague note as evidence. If they were leaving that night, then she would follow them and find the truth of the matter. After all, she was *Lord* Aeria now that she had been given Hadius's seat, which meant she didn't have to answer to anyone.

A smiled passed over her face. She liked the sound of that; Lord Aeria, ruler of the lower kingdoms, accountable to none but feared by all. She would prove her worth once and for all by exposing the humans and their treachery.

* * *

As Kira expected, Kaya was still sulking in her room when she returned. After revealing the news about their father's health her spirits seemed to brighten, but it was nothing compared to her excitement at the chance to go home.

"Are you serious?! You better not be playing a trick on me!" Kaya scolded.

"Cross my heart and hope to die," Kira declared, making a cross over her chest with her fingers. The news elicited the highest-pitched shriek Kira had ever heard as Kaya jumped up and down on her bed in excitement. "Shhh! Keep it down," Kira warned. "We're not really supposed to be going, but Aithos found a way to sneak us back for the night."

Kaya stopped the shrieking but continued to jump on the bed as she asked, "When are we going?"

"I don't know," Kira shrugged apologetically. "He said he would let me know what we needed to do."

"Well how is he going to..." Kaya started before being interrupted by the chime of the door. Kira smiled and went to see who it was, but was surprised to find the stoop empty. No one was in the hall either, but looking around she discovered a folded piece of paper lying on the ground. Picking it up, she read:

> *"Meet me in the hangar right after sunset.*
> *Try not to be seen.*
>
> *-A friend"*

Kira folded the paper and put it inside of her armor next to her holodisk. Checking the hall once more and finding no one, she went back inside the apartment.

"Who was it?" Kaya asked, looking puzzled.

"No one, but I know when we are supposed to meet Aithos."

Kaya's expression lit up with excitement again, "When?"

"After sunset, we need to go to the hangar." Kira smiled.

"And then what?" Kaya asked as she started jumping on the bed again.

"I don't know, the note didn't say." Kira shrugged.

The several hours that remained before sunset seemed to drag on, until they were interrupted with a visit by Thanatos. He apologized for not making the council meeting, explaining that he'd been given a task by Velion that he couldn't elaborate on.

"As an apology, I decided to swipe a few of these." He explained, grinning mischievously as he presented the girls with four sweet rolls from palace kitchen. Kaya cheered and thanked him, snatching a roll from the plate and taking it out on the veranda. Kira also thanked him for the rolls before explaining what he missed from the council.

"Hadius was there? That's odd. He hasn't been around for a long time. I knew Velion was working with him on the situation with the militants, but I can't recall the last time he was actually on Tython."

"What do you know about him?" Kira inquired.

"Well, he's sort of an enigma, honestly. It's hard to tell when he's being genuine and when he isn't but as far as I can tell he's loyal to the kingdom," Thanatos shrugged.

"You said he hadn't been on Tython for a long time, where does he normally stay?" Kira asked, taking a bite out of one of the sweet rolls.

"He lives on a planet called Draco. It's in the lower kingdom and is the furthest planet from the center of the galaxy; a very inhospitable place." With a sigh, Thanatos walked over to the couch and sat down.

Following him, Kira sat on the couch across from him and asked, "How is it inhospitable?"

Thanatos frowned and said, "For one, it's a prison planet where all of the worst criminals are sent for hard labor. Second, it's a primordial planet littered with volcanoes and lava. As far as I know there is no natural life on Draco, except for the prisoners and Hadius's servants."

"Why would he want to live there with prisoners?" Kira asked in amazement.

"I honestly don't know, but that is where he stays. As for the prisoners I don't think it was his choice to make it a prison planet, but when Velion took over for Kronus that's where he decided to put them."

"That seems kind of mean, doesn't it? Why would Velion put them there when he knew his brother was living there?" Kira asked, sensing that there was more to the story.

"I don't know the whole reason, but when the three brothers overthrew Kronus they had a difference of opinion about what to do with him. I don't know what Hadius suggested, but whatever it was, it earned him the lower kingdoms and the third seat on the council instead of the first or second," Thanatos explained.

"What's wrong with the lower kingdoms?" Kira couldn't recall Master Yu-On ever describing the difference between the three.

"Simply put, the lower kingdom isn't as nice as the other two are. It has a lot of undeveloped planets that aren't nearly as rich in resources. In a way, it was a sort of an exile for Hadius, although he never seemed to treat it as such." Thanatos's voice drifted off and he finished speaking with a preoccupied look on his face. After a few seconds, he continued, "Well, I still have a lot of things to do for Velion, so I should be going. Try not to spoil your appetite with the sweet rolls." And with an almost melancholic smile, Thanatos stood to his feet and left the apartment.

Kira watched him as he left, noting that he seemed more down than she had ever seen him. It was almost as if the militant rebellions were getting to him, changing him into a quieter and more reclusive person. She'd hardly seen him since the incident on Gaius 5 and with each passing day he seemed to be around less and less. *Was he avoiding her and Kaya? Maybe he thought the warning about them was true?* Kira wondered as she finished her sweet roll.

Deciding not to worry about it, she spent the remaining hours before sunset helping Kaya decide what to wear for their trip. In all their time on Tython they had accumulated a decent-sized wardrobe from the many gifts of Velion and the other council members. Although Kira had many outfits of her own, she decided she was just going to stay in her armor. By now it was almost second nature to wear it, and she was looking forward to showing off some of her newfound abilities.

* * *

Some time later, when they had finally found the right outfit for Kaya, the two girls prepared to leave their apartment. Stopping right outside their door, Kira checked the hallway for any passing guards or servants. Finding none, the two girls quickly made their way towards the hangars. The trip was easier than expected, as they managed to make it all the way to the hangar entrance without seeing a single person, but as Kira peered into the hangar she knew their luck had run out.

Inside the hangar, there were nearly a dozen servants and guards loading a transport vehicle with large containers. Luckily none of them were facing the entrance, but sneaking into the hangar unnoticed would be tricky. Peering around, Kira noticed a stack of empty cargo containers to the left of the door. Looking back at Kaya she silently indicated that they would need to go to the left. Kaya nodded in comprehension and readied herself to make a run for it. Kira looked back at the guards and servants, watching for any opportunity to move without being noticed.

Just as she was beginning to think it was hopeless, one of the servants at the other end of the hangar dropped a cargo container with a loud crash, spilling the contents across the floor. The accident created the perfect distraction, so with a quick signal, the two of them dashed into the hangar while the workers weren't looking.

Kira was able to travel the distance in half a second, thanks to her armor, but Kaya was forced to run at normal speed. Thankfully the spilled container created enough of a ruckus that no one in the hangar was paying any attention, allowing the girls to move unnoticed. Sneaking along the empty containers, the girls continued to move until they found a dark and secluded area under some scaffolding. Hiding beneath the scaffolding, Kira tried to figure out what to do next. Aithos's note hadn't elaborated on where he wanted to meet them, so she decided to just wait it out.

A few minutes later, Kira noticed Aithos enter the hangar from an entrance near the recently-spilled cargo container. In a loud voice he reprimanded the clumsy servants and ordered them out of the hangar, saying that he would take care of it. Kira glanced over at Kaya and whispered, "We'll wait until they are all gone and then we'll make our way over to him, okay?" Kaya nodded in agreement.

Together they watched as the servants made their way sheepishly out of the hangar. Once all of them were gone, Aithos walked over to the entrance he had come through and shut the door, locking it behind the servants. He waited a moment before turning around and looking directly at the two girls. With a wave of his hand he gestured for them to come over to him. Exchanging puzzled looks, the sisters crawled out from under the scaffolding and made their way across the hangar.

"How did you know we were there?" Kira asked as they walked up to him.

With a wry smile he replied, "I was watching your every move once you were in the hangar. Well done on waiting for a distraction before coming in. The guards would have likely seen you if you hadn't."

"You were watching us? How? I thought there were no cameras in the palace." Kira looked around the room, trying to spot any surveillance cameras.

"There aren't, but there is more than one way to keep track of you. Remember your holodisks? They have a tracking beacon in them, which is different from the emergency beacon that helped Aeria find you on Earth, and which only I know how to monitor. I trust you weren't followed?"

Kira didn't know how she felt about being *monitored*, but decided it wasn't worth arguing about. "I don't think so; we didn't see anyone on our way in."

"Well that will just have to be good enough. Are you ready to go?" He asked, looking from one sister to the other. Both girls looked to each other and nodded in agreement. "Good! Your trip is going to be a little rough, but I trust it will be worth the discomfort. Follow me," Aithos said as he started walking towards the cargo vehicle parked a few yards away.

"What kind of *discomfort* are we talking about?" Kira inquired, suddenly feeling apprehensive as they approached the vehicle.

"It won't be *that* bad. Besides it should only take about twenty minutes or so." He paused, stopping next to a set of cargo containers on the floor. Bending down, he pulled one of the boxes open, and to Kira's surprise it was empty. "You're going to be traveling in this." Aithos grinned, pointing inside the container.

"Are you serious?" Kaya gaped at him in disbelief. Kira started to panic as she stared into the container. It was long enough that she would be able lay down in it, but it reminded her of a coffin.

"If you want to see your father, this is how it has to be done. I know it's not very luxurious, but at least there are two of them," he explained, pointing to another container a few feet away. Kira breathed a sigh of relief, feeling glad that at least she didn't have to share one with her sister. "Each of you will get inside, and I will seal them from out here. They are ventilated, so you shouldn't run out of air, but it's going to be dark and cramped in there, so try not to panic."

Great! I get to be locked in a dark and cramped box and all he can say is 'don't panic'? Kira protested to herself. With a wary smile, Kira nodded and climbed inside the cargo container, lying down on its hard interior. With an apologetic look, Aithos lowered the container's lid and locked it in place.

Cramped and dark was a serious understatement of this experience. The container was barely big enough for her to shift her weight and with each passing second, it felt as though it was collapsing in on her. Suddenly she was second guessing the plan, wondering if she hadn't placed her trust in the wrong person. What if Aithos wasn't really taking them to Earth, but to some other place? What if he was the one behind the militant attacks and this was all just a ruse to capture her and Kaya? He *had* insisted on secrecy after all.

Trying to stay calm, Kira concentrated on her breathing, taking in long slow breaths. After a moment or two her eyes adjusted to the darkness and she could see a small amount of light coming in from one of the ventilation holes. Shifting as much as she could, she positioned herself so she could see out of the hole. She could just barely see the outline of Kaya getting in the other container and Aithos sealing it shut. Without so much as a grunt of effort, Aithos picked up the massive container Kaya was in, and walked over to the transport vehicle. He gently set the container down and turned to do the same with Kira's container. The feeling of being lifted into the air was surreal, but Aithos seemed to be taking extra care not to make the move any more uncomfortable than it already was.

Once they were on the vehicle, Kira heard Aithos walk around to the front and climb into the driver's seat. A few seconds later, they were out of the hangar and were soaring over the city of Ishkur in the fading light of the second sun.

The ride was short, although it didn't really feel that way inside the oppressive container. Each passing second drove more and more doubt into Kira's mind. Was Aithos truly to be trusted? There was no telling where they were heading, as she had never been allowed to explore the city. As she felt the vehicle start to slow down she looked out the ventilation hole and was able to catch a glimpse of their destination. It was a massive, squared pyramid that stood hundreds of feet tall, with a smooth white exterior that glimmered in the orange glow of the twilight. They seemed to be landing in front of it, as Kira was able to make out a large causeway leading up to an open passage.

As the vehicle came to a stop, Kira could hear Aithos talking with another person. Peering through the hole again, she saw that there were two guards greeting Aithos in a familiar tone. The conversation was indiscernible from within the container, but the guards didn't seem to be suspicious of the transport. After a short conversation, the vehicle started to move again and within moments it was inside of the massive pyramid. There was a loud thud from behind them and the vehicle came to another stop.

This time Aithos was alone, and as he walked around the vehicle he softly called, "Just sit tight for a few minutes. I have to go initiate the transport process, but I'll be back shortly." And with that he disappeared into the depths of the pyramid. Kira tried to look around at her surroundings but the room was too dark to make anything out.

Left with just her thoughts, Kira tried to soothe her doubts. The trip seemed to be going as scheduled and there was no indication that Aithos was deceiving them, but she still couldn't figure out what her father needed to tell her. She couldn't imagine what was so important that they would need to go to such extreme measures to meet, but she decided that it didn't matter. Just the thought of being home and seeing him alive made all of the discomfort worth it. She just hoped Kaya was handling the trip as well as she was.

It felt like ages before Aithos returned to the vehicle. When he did, he called out, "This will only take a minute and then you will be back on Earth. I will warn you that this trip might be a little... nauseating. Most people feel a bit sick after their first transport, so just try to stay calm"

Kira had always been anxious to use one of these transport buildings, but now that she was about to, she wasn't feeling quite as enthusiastic. During her lessons, Master Yu-On explained that the transport buildings formed a temporary tear in space, similar to a black hole, that allowed a person to travel extreme distances almost instantly. The idea was not only mind bending, but also frightening. What if something went wrong?

Without warning, the room they were in started to vibrate and fill with light. Peering out through the ventilation hole, Kira was alarmed to see that the wall they were facing was glowing. After a moment, a small circle of white light appeared in the middle of the wall and started to grow in size. As it grew, the wall appeared to disintegrate until it had completely disappeared, revealing a swirling tunnel of light and wind behind it. There was a loud hissing noise as all of the air in the room was sucked into the swirling vortex and Kira could feel herself being pulled into it as well. Little by little she could feel her body being stretched as the vehicle moved into the light tunnel.

Everything seemed to collapse in on her as if she and the container were being forced through the tiniest of holes. Gravity lost all of its effect and for a brief moment she felt as though she was hovering in an indefinite expanse of nothingness where time stopped and all matter ceased to exist. Then, without warning, there was sickening pulling feeling as her body was torn apart, particle by particle. She didn't know how but she could feel herself being flung through space and time at blinding speed. And then suddenly everything was normal again.

Kira blinked rapidly and tried to get her bearings. She was still inside of the container and it was still sitting on the back of the transport vehicle, but the blinding light from the room was gone.

"Everyone make it through okay?" Aithos called out. Kira pounded her fist against the side of the container to show she was alright. "Good! A few more minutes and I'll be able to let you out. Just try not to get sick inside my brand new containers!"

Kira made no promises as she felt an overwhelming desire to retch when the vehicle started to move again. Luckily it was a short ride, and after only another three or four minutes they came to a stop. Aithos hopped out of the driver's seat and walked back to containers, releasing the latches as quickly as he could. The familiar night sky of Earth revealed itself to Kira as Aithos opened the container lid. Sitting up Kira tried to smile, but before she could stop herself she threw up over the side of the container, narrowly missing Aithos's feet.

"Whoa! Watch the boots, girl!" Aithos cried out, jumping out of the way and laughing. "I told you the first trip is always rough." He shook his head as he made his way over to the other container and unlatched it. Kaya sat up, looking green and mumbling something before her eyes widened and she also vomited over the side her container. This time Aithos was ready and was already out of the way.

Once she felt normal enough, Kaya looked up at Aithos and asked, "What was that? It felt so... weird."

"You, my little friend, just traveled thousands of light-years in the matter of a few seconds. Fun, right?" he jeered with a knowing grin.

"Fun is not the word I'd use, but at least we made it. Where are we?" Kira looked around at the surroundings and noticed that she recognized the area. They were at a grove of trees not far from her village. She knew this because she recognized a deformed tree that had been struck by lightning once, many years earlier.

"We aren't far from your home. Your father should be coming shortly. Maybe you should walk around a bit, try to shake of the effects of the transport. We certainly don't want you getting sick on your father when he arrives," Aithos added sarcastically.

Kira rolled her eyes, but took the advice nonetheless. She still wasn't feeling quite like herself and walking around sounded like it might actually help. Climbing out of her container she walked over to Kaya and helped her get out. Kaya was still looking pretty pale and clammy, but was able to stand on her own. Hopping off of the transport vehicle, Kira looked up at the sky.

The night sky on Earth seemed so quiet and peaceful compared to Tython's, but Kira preferred it this way. There was something about the simplicity that felt *natural* to her in a way Tython's heavens never had. Now that she knew what the stars were, she would be able to tell the elders of her village that they *were* important, that there was more to them than they thought.

She tore her eyes away from the stars and looked around at the grove of trees again, getting a fond feeling of familiarity; something she had gone without for the greater part of a year. Sure, the palace no longer felt foreign to her, but it never felt quite like this. Her thoughts faded as she noticed a shadow in the trees move. Squinting in the dim moonlight she had a hard time keeping track of it, and after a moment she lost it completely.

"Kira, look!" Kaya called out from behind her. Turning around, she noticed three figures approaching from the direction of the village. It was her father, accompanied by Yamara and her uncle Druin.

Running over to where Kaya was, Kira put her arm around her sister and whispered, "We're finally home, aren't we?" Kaya turned to look at her, and with a tear sliding down her cheek she nodded furiously. The three figures broke out into a run, closing the distance between themselves and the girls.

Their father was the first to reach them. He ran up to the girls and wrapped his arms around both of them crying out, "You're here!" The three of them embraced for a long time, all succumbing to their emotions and crying. Pushing away but keeping his hands on their shoulders, he examined each of them. "You both look so different... so grown up," he said, wiping the water from his eyes.

"We were so worried about you!" Kaya managed, trying to calm her emotions.

"*Me?* Why were you worried about me? You were the ones who were taken! Imagine how I felt!" He shook his head, choking up again.

"I'm sorry, Dad, it's all my fault! I told them we would go with them..." Kaya explained, looking guilty.

"No, no, child, you have nothing to apologize for. I know why you went, and it was the right thing to do," he consoled her, hugging her again.

Kira left their side and walked over to Druin and Yamara. Hugging each of them, she said, "I've missed both of you so much. I can't believe we are here; I thought for sure we would be stuck on Tython forever."

Druin beamed at her and said, "Those are some fancy clothes you've got on; thought you were one of them at first."

Kira looked down at her armor, forgetting that she had it on. With a grin she said, "It was a gift from Velion. I think you've met him, haven't you?"

Druin's smile faded, and with a grim look he said, "How could I forget? He only terrified the entire village into thinking he would destroy it if we didn't let him take you and your sister."

Kira didn't know how to respond. She had forgotten that all of this had begun that way. It seemed so long ago, and so much had happened since then.

"Oh child, I've spent every night since you left worrying about you! I'm so happy you are safe and sound!" Yamara interjected, hugging Kira again.

Kira blushed in the dim moonlight, not knowing where to begin. "I'm sorry we've been gone for so long. There was just no way to come home until now. A lot has happened since we left. I'm not sure where to begin," Kira frowned as Yamara let go of her.

"I do," her father called out from behind her. Kira turned to look at him as he walked over to them, holding his arm over Kaya's shoulder. "I'm afraid there are some things that I haven't been completely honest about," he continued, looking pained as he spoke. "Maybe we should start a fire and sit? There is a lot I have to tell you."

Kira wasn't sure what to make of this new pained expression on her father's face but she didn't like it. He was always collected and unemotional, but now he wasn't either of those things. The tears in his eyes had slowed, but the worried and guilty look on his face told Kira that there was something wrong. Perhaps the message he had really *was* important.

Collecting herself Kira started working on finding firewood. Using the speed and strength that her armor granted her, she dashed around the grove of trees with lightning fast speed and was able to collect enough wood for a fire in the matter of seconds. Once she had the wood she used her armor to bend the earth to form a fire pit. As she stacked the wood into the newly formed pit she noticed the alarmed expressions her family had on their faces. With a nervous laugh, she said, "I guess you didn't expect that huh? Well, I'll try to explain later."

Forgetting herself again, she reached into her armor and fished out her holodisk. Putting her finger on the symbol for laser, she aimed the device at the wood and pressed it. Immediately a green laser shot out of the cylinder and ignited the wood. Again she saw the horrified looks on their faces, but decided to just ignore them as she sat on the ground. The others hesitated and exchanged bewildered looks before following suit.

A few moments later the fire was burning strong and the surprised expressions had faded. "You said there was something you hadn't been honest about?" Kira asked, trying to break the silence.

"Oh, right," her father said, the pained expression returning to his face. "I have a confession to make. I don't know how to put this, so I'm just going to say it." He paused and swallowed hard. "I'm not your real father."

Kira blinked, thinking that she must have misheard him. "Wait, what? I don't think I heard you right."

"No, you did. I am not your real father, neither of you," he repeated, looking grave. Druin and Yamara seemed to be just as surprised by the news as Kira was.

"What do you mean you aren't our father?!" Kira raised her voice, feeling angry and confused. *Was this some sort of sick joke?* She wondered.

"I don't know how else to put it," he replied bleakly.

Kaya appeared absolutely horrified as she looked back and forth between Kira and their father. Kira leveled a fierce gaze at him and demanded, "If you aren't our father, then who is?"

He took a deep breath and closed his eyes, "it was a long time ago, right after I bonded with your mother. We were trying so hard to have children then, but nothing seemed to work until something strange happened. At the time we didn't know how to explain it, so we didn't tell anyone."

"I don't understand. What are you talking about?" Kira demanded, feeling even more lost.

"One night, your mother and I were out on a walk, when a strange man appeared out of nowhere. He did something to us... *took* us someplace we'd never been before; someplace deep in the Black Wood. I don't know how he got us there; it's sort of a blur, but there was a building there, where he cast some sort of magic that took us somewhere else, somewhere... not here."

Kira was horribly confused when Aithos, who had been sitting quietly on the transport vehicle, spoke up, "Wait, was the building he took you to tall and half-finished? Like a ruin that had been abandoned?"

Their father nodded, seeming to remember something, "Yes; it was covered in growth from the woods, but it was clearly abandoned. It was a strange building with a hidden door."

"What happened when he brought you there?" Aithos asked anxiously.

"He took us inside it, and cast some sort of magic. All I remember was light and a strange sensation of being crushed, and then we were someplace we had never seen before. Like a distant land that didn't look anything like here."

Aithos looked positively alarmed at the description. Looking at Kira he said, "I think your father is describing the transport building we just came through. They must have been abducted by one of my people. What happened then? It's very important that you give me as many details as you can."

"It's difficult to explain but it was a dark, cold place, devoid of life and covered in snow and ice. The sky looked different too; there were strange colors in the heavens, bright reds and oranges. The stranger took us to another building, where he separated us. He locked me in a dark room and took their mother somewhere else. All I remember after that is feeling very tired and falling asleep. When I woke up, I was back inside my hut, lying next to their mother. The only thing different was that I had a scar on my abdomen, but I couldn't remember where I got it."

"You don't remember coming back?" Aithos pressed.

"No, I don't recall anything, but when I asked my wife about it she said she remembered the same trip. The only difference was that after he had separated us, he... he made love to her..." their father trailed off and looked down in shame. Kira's mind raced as she tried to process what he was telling them. Kaya shook her head in disbelief and looked to Kira for answers, but there were none to be had. "Nine months later Kira was born."

"But you said you weren't Kaya's father either," Kira reminded him.

"That's because it happened again, several years later. This time he only took your mother, but when he returned her, he spoke to me."

"He spoke to you? What did this man look like? What did he say to you?" Aithos demanded.

"I don't know what he looked like. I could never get a good look at him as he was wearing a large black cloak but what he said to me, I'll never forget." He paused, giving Kira an apologetic look before continuing, "He told me that my wife would be pregnant again. He said that one day others like him would come and take both of the children, and that I would *have* to let them go. He said that it was necessary if they were to fulfill their destinies and if I didn't let them go, that he would return and destroy the Earth. Then he disappeared, right in front of me. I thought for certain it was a dream, but a few weeks later my wife was with child again."

"It makes sense now! I knew you couldn't just be the distant descendants of Kronus! There was no way the royal markers would survive so many generations. If this stranger was part of my family then that explains why you can use the royal armor and holodisks. We must tell Velion immediately!" Aithos commanded, walking over to Kira and picking her up by the arm.

"Wait, what if there is more?" Kira protested, pulling her arm from his grasp.

"There is," her father spoke up. Aithos halted and looked at him impatiently. Grasping the urgency, their father rushed on, "The hunter who came back sick so long ago, had a message for me. He said that while he was in the woods alone, a man in a black cloak appeared to him and instructed him to tell me: 'they are coming,'" he finished, looking somber.

"You mean he was here, on Earth just days before we arrived? And you are certain that he said the girls were important?" Aithos pressed.

"I'll never forget his words; I assure you they meant a great deal to him." Walking over to Kira and Kaya, their father looked dismal. "I'm so sorry, I should have told you ages ago. I just didn't want to believe it. When I recovered and they told me the spirits had taken you into the heavens I knew I had failed you. Can you ever forgive me?" He reached out to touch Kira's arm.

She recoiled and shook her head. She loved their father but this secret was too big, too great for her to just dismiss. Kaya did not move but quietly said, "You did what you had to do."

"We really must be going; I'm sorry to cut this short but there are events happening that the three of you cannot understand, and this information will be absolutely vital. I will bring them back again as soon as I can, but for now we must leave," Aithos implored, grabbing Kira by the arm again. This time she did not fight, but just stared at her father as she was dragged back to the vehicle. He started to cry, his expression imploring her to forgive him, but she couldn't; not now, maybe not ever.

Kaya frowned, and hugged their father. She waved to the other two and said, "We really have missed you, but don't worry about us. The palace is very nice and they treat us like royalty. We love you." With that she turned and walked to the transport vehicle. This time Aithos did not make them to get into the containers, but said that there was no longer any need for deception.

A few moments later the vehicle crested a hill and the girls could no longer see their father or the fire. Kira closed her eyes and let the enormity of all she had just heard wash over her.

CHAPTER 13

It was just as the note suggested. The humans *were* meeting in secret, far from prying eyes. It was difficult to hear much of the conversation but Aeria had the proof she needed. Just as she suspected, the warning *was* correct. The human girls really weren't who everyone thought they were. As Aeria watched the transport vehicle fly away, she tried to decide what to do. How many times had the humans slipped past security to engage in these secret meetings? How long had they been conspiring against the council? Her father was such a fool to trust them.

She missed most of the conversation but from what she gathered, the humans were in contact with a cloaked stranger; most likely the same person that was behind the rebellion. The real question was whether or not this information would persuade her father to take appropriate action. She had her doubts.

As the three remaining humans put out the fire, and started to leave, Aeria decided she would deal with them later. Kira and her sister were more important, so she made her move to chase after the vehicle. They would never see her, just as Aithos and the sisters hadn't seen her follow them. Sure there were a few close calls, but she was certain she still remained undetected. Dashing out of the trees she ran after the transport with lighting fast speed. She had to be careful not to be spotted but she couldn't let them get to the transport building without her either.

There was no telling what role the human girls were playing in the rebellion's plans but she couldn't risk letting them escape. How far Aithos's treachery went was unclear, but he couldn't be trusted to hand the humans over. She would have to take things into her own hands.

Aeria ran, always keeping as much distance between her and the vehicle as she could until they entered the woods. Once there she moved in closer, ensuring that she wouldn't lose sight of them. She regretted having to harm her own men, but the guards outside of the transport building would need to be taken out if she was to succeed. There was no time to explain Aithos's treachery and she couldn't risk having them come to his aid.

As the vehicle came to a stop outside of the transport building, Aeria stopped to watch the encounter. Aithos had smuggled the humans through the first time, so having extra passengers this time required some explanation, but the guards didn't give much of a fuss. After only a few seconds they waved them through, and returned to their posts.

Now was the time to strike. Dashing out of the trees with blinding speed, Aeria dispatched both guards before either had time to react. Luckily they went down quietly so she remained undetected.

Sneaking through the entrance, she made her way to the transport chamber, hiding in the shadows. As she entered the corridor, she spied Aithos leaving the chamber to initiate the transport sequence, which presented an ideal situation to dispatch him without the humans knowing. She waited a moment before following after him. Neither of the girls were paying any attention, so slipping past them was easy.

Making her way to the control room, Aeria arrived just as Aithos was activating the console. If her plan was to go off without a hitch then she needed to knock him out without being detected, so she waited for the ideal moment when his guard was down. He worked at the controls for a few moments until he paused, putting his hand up to his mouth and yawning.

There it is! Without delay she dashed into the chamber and drove her elbow into his back, just between the shoulders, sending him flying across the room into the chamber wall. With a loud crash his body collapsed against the floor and did not move. She walked over to him to check his pulse and was pleased to find that he was still quite alive. It would do no good to kill him before the council could interrogate him about the meeting and his involvement with the rebellion. He would be out for a good while, giving her time to alert Thanatos once she was back on Tython.

Smirking at her handiwork, she turned and went back to the control console. Aithos had already completed most of the system checks, so finishing the sequence took no time at all. The building roared to life as the timer for the transport sequence started counting down. Aeria quickly made her way out of the room and headed back to the transport chamber. The time had come to reveal herself.

Entering the room, the two girls turned to look at her. Clearly expecting Aithos instead of her, both of them looked quite surprised as she entered.

* * *

"Aeria? What are you doing here? Where is Aithos?" Kira asked, unable to hide her alarm.

"Aithos has some business to attend to, so he can't leave the planet yet. He asked me to escort you back to the palace," Aeria replied with a strange look on her face.

"Oh..." Kira replied, unconvinced.

"Don't worry, you're safe in my hands. Besides, it will give us a chance to get to know one another."

Kira didn't like where this was going. Something didn't seem right about it. "Sure, I guess," she replied dryly, giving Aeria a suspicious look.

The conversation ground to a halt as the transport room came to life. Aeria got into the driver's seat of the transport and waited without saying anything. Again the wall at the end lit up and started disintegrating, revealing a swirling vortex. Everything in the room started to slide into it as it had before and a few uncomfortable seconds later, they were on Tython again.

Coming to on the other side of the portal, Kira shook her head, trying to shake off the effects of the transporter. She was pleased to find that she didn't feel nearly as nauseous this time but that did little to ease the anxious feeling she had. She didn't trust Aeria one bit, and something about the way the goddess was acting made Kira trust her even less. "Let's hurry; we need to speak with Velion." Kira insisted, eyeing Aeria suspiciously.

Aeria smiled again and said, "Of course. Just try to hang on; I drive a bit faster than Aithos does." With that Aeria walked over to the driver's seat and powered the vehicle on. Driving out of the transport building at breakneck speed the three of them sped wildly out into the night air of Ishkur. It took everything both girls had to not fall off the vehicle as Aeria sped through the city.

After a few minutes Kira was relieved to see the palace ahead, meaning that Aeria had been true to her word. The sisters exchanged relieved looks and prepared to disembark as the transport approached the palace hangar. Aeria flew into the hangar and gracefully came to a stop near the previously spilled container.

The three of them disembarked and Kira and Kaya started walking towards the hangar exit. Before they could make it there, Aeria spoke up, saying "Where are you going?"

Both girls stopped and turned to look at her. With an impatient tone Kira replied, "To see Velion, of course."

"You won't find him in the palace. If you wish to speak with him we will need to take a ship up to the Trident," Aeria explained.

Kira squinted at her, trying to decide if Aeria was being truthful. "How do you know he isn't here?" she asked skeptically.

Aeria sighed in exasperation, rolling her eyes as she replied, "I do know a thing or two more than you do, young one. I didn't get to be third on the council by not knowing the plans of my father. I assure you, he is not in the palace."

Kira looked to Kaya who just shrugged with a "how would I know" look on her face. Sighing, Kira decided there was no other choice. If Velion wasn't in the palace, as Aeria insisted, then their only chance to speak to him would be to go with her again. "Fine. Take us to the Trident," Kira gave in.

Aeria grinned and said, "This way; we'll take that ship over there." She pointed to a cargo ship parked about twenty yards away. The three of them made their way to the ship and boarded it once the doors were opened. It became clear that Aeria wasn't overly familiar with this type of vessel as it took her several attempts to open the doors and a few more to get the ship up and running.

"Never flown this type before?" Kira jeered.

Aeria fixed her with a reproachful look and said, "A member of the ruling family rarely has the occasion to perform menial labor like cargo transport; so no, I *haven't* flown this type of ship before." The catty response satisfied Kira, so she didn't press the issue. Instead she sat in one of the co-pilot seats and strapped herself in, suspecting that it might be a bumpy ride. She was right.

The takeoff was one of the most terrifying experiences she'd ever had, as Aeria nearly crashed the shuttle into the hangar wall twice, something that only seemed to sour the goddess's mood further. Once Aeria finally gained an understanding of the controls things went better, but leaving the atmosphere was still more jarring than her last experience. This made Kira regret not suggesting that they take her ship, which had been parked in the next hangar bay.

Aside from the rough start, everything seemed to be going as planned until Aeria started navigating away from the Trident. Kira didn't notice at first as she was lost in her thoughts about the news her father had given her; if she could even call him her father anymore. She kept wondering who the stranger was, and why he picked their mother to have children with. Why would he leave them alone on an uncivilized planet? Why hadn't he told them that he was their father?

The questions just kept piling up and it wasn't until she decided to push the thoughts away that she noticed something was amiss. The trip to the Trident shouldn't be taking as long as it was, and by the uncomfortable look on Aeria's face, something was wrong.

"Where are you taking us? Why don't I see the Trident anymore?" Kira asked, realizing she shouldn't have let her guard down.

"I'm taking care of a problem first," Aeria replied coldly.

There was a sinking feeling in Kira's stomach. "Problem? What are you talking about? We *need* to meet with Velion, we have very important news."

"What news? *That you aren't who we thought you were*?" Aeria spat back at her, engaging the autopilot and getting to her feet. Kira blinked, not knowing how to respond. Aeria, taking her silence as confirmation of her guilt, continued, "Oh don't you think I already know? How long have you been plotting in secret with the rebellion? What are they planning?!"

Kira's heart sank as she realized her folly. Aeria had followed them and had watched the conversation with their father. She was the shadow in the trees. "Aeria, it's not what you think. We weren't meeting with the rebellion!"

"Spare me your lies! I saw your treachery first hand, just as the note said I would. What were you meeting about? What is the rebellion planning? Who is the cloaked figure you discussed?" Aeria demanded wildly.

"Note? What note?" Kira didn't understand.

"Don't play stupid with me! I know your treason! Tell me what I want to know right now!" Aeria screamed.

"Treason? Aeria it's not like that. We went to see our family, that's all. We aren't part of the rebellion," Kira pleaded with her, but her words fell on deaf ears.

Aeria shook her head and said, "So be it. You can take your secrets to your grave. I'm putting an end to this, once and for all." Aeria unlatched Kira's restraints and ripped her out of her seat. Kira tried to fight back but Aeria was too strong for her, and before she knew it, they were leaving the cabin of the ship. Using her immense speed and strength Aeria drove Kira to the back of the ship, into the cargo bay.

Kaya came running up after them and screamed, "No! Leave her alone! We didn't do anything wrong!" She started pounding on Aeria with her fists, but the blows did nothing. With a motion as if she was swatting an annoying fly, Aeria swung her left hand behind her and knocked Kaya to the ground. This drove Kira to madness, but it was too late. Before she could do anything Aeria threw her into the back wall of the cargo container. With lighting fast speed the goddess pressed a button on the bulkhead, and before Kira could recover, the interior cargo bay door closed, sealing itself shut.

Immediately bright yellow lights started flashing and an automated female voice rang out, "Emergency evacuation procedure initiated. Thirty seconds until total decompression." Kira's heart sank as she realized what was about to happen. The cargo bay doors would open in thirty seconds and she would be thrown out into space. Running over to the interior door, Kira peered through the glass at Aeria and desperately screamed, "Fine! You caught me! I'm the traitor! Not Kaya. She didn't know, she's innocent. Whatever you do, don't hurt her! If you want to kill me then that's fine, but she never did anything!"

Aeria turned to look at Kaya, who had crawled over to her knees and was sobbing and begging her to open the cargo doors. Turning back to Kira she pressed the com button and said, "So be it, I won't kill her. But before the end, she will wish that I had. We'll see how she handles the wastelands of the underworld after we torture her for information."

"Twenty seconds to total decompression. Manual override will be locked in ten seconds," the automated voice called out.

Kira looked down towards Kaya and yelled, "I'm sorry! I love you, Kaya!"

Kaya sobbed harder and screamed, "No!! Let her out! She's lying! She's not a traitor!" but Aeria wouldn't budge.

"Ten seconds to total decompression. Manual override is now locked," the voice called out as the air in the room started to move. Kira could feel the air getting thinner as the room grew horribly cold. She looked at her sister one last time, and mouthed the word "goodbye" before turning to face the door. If she was going to be thrown into the depths of space then she would meet her demise head on, greeting death with a smile instead of fear.

"Five. Four. Three. Two. One." The cargo bay door opened and everything was sucked out into the void, including Kira.

* * *

Falling... spinning... innumerable white lights rotating in all directions. Kira tried to scream but couldn't find any air. Was this the end? Flexing all of her muscles she found that she had great strength, abnormal strength; more than she could have ever imagined. Gritting her teeth she managed to slow the spin; the blurring lights twisted less quickly and she was able to get some bearings. She could see something below her now, a large blue and green sphere. It floated silently in the ocean of stars and fabulous colors of the nebula behind it. She remembered back to her dream so long ago. Now she understood where she was and why the planet looked familiar. Straining with all of her might, she was able to stop the spin, but she was still falling, and gaining speed by the second. She knew this wasn't good; she knew that she had failed.

Hopelessness filled her stomach as she watched the large blue-green ball grow larger and larger as she fell towards it. She knew she wouldn't survive the fall, so she stopped fighting and let go. There was nothing she could do but accept her demise, so she closed her eyes and prayed, *Spirits, if you do exist, please don't let her kill Kaya. She is just a child...*

Tears welled in her eyes. First she hadn't forgiven her father, and now she had failed her sister. It wasn't fair! She'd done everything she could, but somehow it wasn't enough. She looked up and saw the Trident floating just behind the cargo ship she'd fallen from. The sight of it did something to her and she knew she couldn't give up. The hopeless feeling in her stomach turned to rage and anger boiled in every fiber of her being. Somehow there was air again and she was able to find her voice to roar, "NO!! Not like this! I will not let you take her!!!!!"

Remembering her training, she knew the armor would react to her thoughts, as it must have already done. She didn't know how she had managed to create air, but there was no time to question it. She was falling faster and faster towards Tython's atmosphere and would soon be feeling the heat from her re-entry. If she didn't do something the friction from the atmosphere would burn her to a crisp. She closed her eyes and tried to think of a way to protect herself. How did ships enter the atmosphere unharmed? And then she had it. With just a few seconds to spare her armor shifted and morphed around her until it completely encapsulated her, forming a metal barrier.

Just as the armor finished molding its spear-like shape, Kira felt the friction from the atmosphere start to pull against her. After a few seconds the metal around her was so hot she was certain she would be roasted alive, but somehow the armor managed to reduce the heat. Sweating profusely, she tried to keep her senses about her, knowing that once she passed through the upper atmosphere she would still have to worry about how quickly she was falling.

Without warning the heat and friction of the atmosphere came to an end and she could feel the metal around her cooling off as she entered the colder sections of the upper stratosphere. Knowing that she needed to start slowing her descent she closed her eyes again, causing the armor around her to morph back to its original form.

She could see the surface of Tython growing larger and larger as she plummeted towards it, but she had no idea how to slow down. Tython's ships all had inertial dampeners that allowed them to slow down, but she didn't think her armor could replicate that. Trying to think, she closed her eyes again searching for something helpful, when an image came to her. It was brilliant! With a bit of a smile she willed her armor to change again.

After a few seconds she opened her eyes and to her great surprise and satisfaction the armor around her arms had become like the wings of a bird, with metal facets forming individual feathers. Looking down at her legs she saw they had also changed, locking her feet together and forming long tail feathers that she could move with her thoughts.

Stretching her arms out she felt the air catch under her metal wings, and start to lift her, slowing her descent. With a wide smile she called out in excitement. She had always wondered what it was like to soar like a bird, and now she knew. Working her arms and flapping the metal wings she found that she had great maneuverability, and started to glide from side to side, flipping and rolling in the air. For a minute she completely forgot that she was plummeting to the planet surface, or how she had been thrown from the shuttle by Aeria.

Coming back to her senses, she realized there was no time for games. If there was any hope of rescuing Kaya, Kira needed to focus. She was still high in the air, but she could start to make out the land below her. She could tell she was soaring over an enormous jungle that stretched as far as she could see. She remembered Master Yu-On talking about the wild lands of the other side of Tython but Kira had no idea they were so huge. Aeria must have thought this would be a good place to dump Kira's body, as no one was likely to ever come looking for her here.

Gliding lower and lower, Kira was able to make out the individual trees and could see an open field a few hundred yards ahead of her. She knew she was moving too quickly to land directly so she angled her arms in such a way that she started to circle around the field, losing altitude and speed as she did so. A few seconds later she was able to slowly land in the center of the field, her armor changing back to its original shape as she approached the ground.

She breathed a sigh of relief as her feet gently touched the ground, but now what? She was marooned on the opposite side of the planet, with no idea how to get back to Ishkur or the others. She looked around at her surroundings, noting that the dense jungle seemed to be brimming with life. Birds were calling, and there were bugs everywhere.

Swatting away some insects that resembled mosquitoes, she remembered something. She still had her holodisk!

Reaching into her armor she fished the device out, and readied herself to call her emergency pod, but stopped before she did. If she called for the pod then a distress beacon would be activated, and if Aeria was still up there she might see it. In fact she might very well be searching for one, just to be certain that Kira wasn't still alive. *Damnit!* Kira swore silently. She couldn't risk trying to communicate with any of the others either for the same reason. Her only option was to use the mapping system to find the right direction to go and make her way on foot.

Opening the map, she searched for the nearest settlement and was disheartened to find that it was nearly a thousand miles away. Even if she could maintain a full sprint, which she knew the jungle wouldn't allow, it would take her several days to cover that much ground. Time she couldn't afford to spend, but what other choice did she have?

Shaking her head in disappointment she found the right direction and started heading towards it. The armor gave her great speed, but even with all of its advantages, the terrain she was covering was unfriendly at best and downright perilous at worst. It would be a long trip.

* * *

Aeria watched the sensors, waiting for a beacon or a transmission from Kira's holodisk, but nothing came. With a satisfied smile she decided that her plan had worked. There was some worry that the girl would have found a way to survive the fall, but clearly she hadn't been so lucky. Turning to look at Kaya who was still sobbing, she said "Your sister wasn't as strong as I thought; it seems she died after all."

But Kaya refused to give her the satisfaction. She shook her head, wiping her tears away and shouting, "You don't know anything about her! She's not dead!"

Aeria scoffed and rolled her eyes. "If you say so, but the sensors don't lie. She didn't make it. But that's the last thing you should be worried about. I was just going to kill you like I did her, but after her impassioned plea to keep you alive, I've decided to take you to the prison planet, Draco. We'll find out what secrets the two of you have been keeping."

Kaya glared at her and with as much spite as she could muster, she spat at her, hitting her on the cheek. Aeria gritted her teeth and wiped the spit away. "So be it, I was going to leave you on the more hospitable side, but after that little indiscretion I've changed my mind. You'll get to spend your final days in the abyss, with the rest of the ingrates."

"It doesn't matter where you put me, Velion will find out what you've done and he'll come for me," Kaya retorted.

"I wouldn't be so sure about that. After he finds out about your treason he won't care what I've done with you. Now shut up, before I change my mind and flush you out the cargo bay too."

This time Kaya didn't respond, knowing that pushing her luck wouldn't be in her best interest. She didn't care what Aeria said, they would figure out what happened and they would come for her. As for her sister, she couldn't explain it but she somehow had an intense feeling that Kira was still alive. She didn't know how that could be, given what just happened, but she knew it, more deeply than she had ever known anything before.

Aeria, satisfied that Kaya wouldn't give her any more trouble, turned back to the control consoles and worked with the navigation computer. Before inputting the jump coordinates she sent a short message to Thanatos, telling him to find Aithos on Earth and take him into custody for questioning. A few seconds later the ship jumped to subspace and was making its long journey to the prison planet Draco. As she sat back in her seat a strange feeling filled Aeria's stomach and for the first time in as long as she could remember she felt guilt.

Had she done the right thing? It had been necessary, hadn't it? Velion and Pisus would have never taken the matter seriously, and together they would have doomed the kingdoms to fall right into the rebellion's plan. She was the only one who understood the danger they were in; the only one who saw the humans for what they were, a threat. Pushing the thoughts away, Aeria tried to suppress the feeling. She wouldn't allow her softer side to get the better of her, it was necessary and one day they would thank her for preserving their way of life.

CHAPTER 14

Kira had been running for hours, traversing the thick and unforgiving jungle as quickly as she could, but even the armor didn't save her from exhaustion and she found herself needing to stop. According to the map she had run nearly seventy-five miles, but this didn't make her feel better. At this rate it would take the better part of a week to make it to the nearest outpost, and even so, would she have enough time to save Kaya? Her sister was resilient, but would she be able to withstand torture?

Kira's thoughts were interrupted when her stomach growled with hunger. She realized that she hadn't eaten since the sweet roll Thanatos had brought to her room. Remembering what Velion said about the holodisk she pulled it out and pointed it towards a section of the tree she was sitting on. Kira pressed the symbol for 'rations' and the device came to life, shooting the tree trunk with a strange sort of laser. After a few seconds the laser shut off, revealing that the section of the tree had been converted into a sort of organic nutrient bar.

Picking it up, she sniffed it. It smelled a little like stinky feet, but appeared edible enough. Biting into it, she discovered that Velion hadn't lied about the bad taste, but she was so hungry she didn't care. Shoving the entire thing in her mouth she chewed in tranquility, wondering if she should find a place to take a nap. Before she could decide, a strange noise started coming from her left. At first it was a low humming noise, but as time passed it grew into a loud roar.

Recognizing the sound, Kira realized that it was a ship, and from the sound of it, it was circling the area around her. Realizing that the tree canopy would prevent anyone from being able to see her, she decided to knock down a few of the trees. Gulping down the disgusting nutrient bar, Kira started to amass energy. One after another she proceeded to blast the trees around her, opening a wide hole in the canopy as they crashed to the ground. As suspected, there was a ship circling the area and once the trees were down the person flying it seemed to notice her presence.

The ship moved over top of her, and hovered for a few moments until it lowered a small platform held by four long cables. Stepping onto the platform once it reached the ground, Kira grabbed on to the cables and waited for it to lift. As it started to move upwards towards the ship she prepared herself for a fight as she was unsure of who was piloting the ship. Several seconds later the platform was pulled up inside the cargo hold, and to Kira's surprise she found Thanatos standing by the platform's control console.

"How did you find me?" she called out as the cargo hold floor closed below her.

"Aithos tracked your holodisk here. What the hell are you doing way out here? How did you even get so far away from the palace?" He demanded, looking concerned.

"I don't know that you'd believe me if I told you. A lot has happened since I saw you last. You said Aithos tracked me. Is he on the ship?"

"Yes, he's piloting it, but you didn't answer my questions," Thanatos reprimanded, but Kira ignored him as she made her way towards the bridge.

As she entered the bridge, Aithos turned to her and said, "Oh thank heavens you're okay. After I was knocked out back on Earth I thought for certain the worst had happened."

"You were knocked out? That lunatic!" Kira shook her head trying to understand why Aeria had done this.

"Who are you talking about? What happened to you?" Aithos asked. Thanatos nodded and gave Kira an urgent look, also wanting the same answers.

"Aeria. She followed us to Earth and was spying on us when we met with my family. She seems to think that we are part of the rebellion and that we were having a secret meeting, or something," Kira fumed.

"Well that explains why she sent me to take Aithos into custody. She must have thought you were a traitor," Thanatos concluded, giving Aithos a worried look. "How did you end up with her anyways?"

"She showed up at the transport building; said that Aithos had something to do on Earth, so she was supposed to bring us back to the palace for him. I told her to take us to Velion but instead she made us get in a ship with her. I knew there was something wrong, but I didn't listen to my instincts!" Kira paused, shaking her head.

"What happened after that?" Aithos looked alarmed.

"That's when she flipped out on us. She said something about a note and then started calling me a traitor and asking what the rebellion was planning. I tried to tell her that we weren't traitors, but before she would let me explain she attacked me and tried to kill me. She locked me in the cargo bay and set it to decompress while I was in it," Kira finished. Aithos and Thanatos looked to each other in disbelief.

"But you are alive. How did you survive the decompression?" Aithos marveled.

"I don't know, I just used the armor like Thanatos trained me to do but that doesn't matter. The important thing is that Aeria still has Kaya! And she is taking her to Draco!" she shouted, growing weary from all their questions.

Aithos's eyes widened in surprise as he listened to Kira. Thanatos shook his head and said, "We need to take this back to Velion right away. He needs to know what Aeria's done and he needs to know about the information you discovered on Earth. Don't worry about your sister; she will be okay. We'll go get her after we talk to Velion."

"No! You don't understand, Aeria won't listen. She's convinced that we are traitors and she's taking Kaya to Draco to torture her for information. There is no way to know what she will do if she finds out I survived," Kira objected.

"Aithos, get us back to Ishkur. Kira, just try to remain calm, we are going to take care of this."

Kira wanted to protest more, but she knew it would do no good. Sitting down in one of the co-pilot seats she folded her arms and shook her head. *Kaya, just hold on, I'm coming for you!*

* * *

The trip back to Ishkur didn't take long, as Aithos kept the ship at full throttle the entire way. Even his landing in the hangar was faster than expected, but Kira appreciated the haste and was grateful that he was taking her seriously.

Much to her surprise and relief, finding Velion was quite easy as he was standing near the entrance of the hangar, flanked with nearly a dozen guards. She expected Velion to look pleased to see them, but was surprised to find that he looked quite angry. Thanatos and Aithos exchanged puzzled looks as the three of them disembarked and made their way towards Velion and the guards.

"Take the girl into custody. I want her stripped of her armor and imprisoned immediately. Leave the other two for now, I'll deal with them," Velion ordered his soldiers.

"What? Why are you taking her into custody?" Aithos protested, placing himself between Kira and the approaching guards. The guards paused, looking back to Velion for further instructions.

"I'd like to ask you the same question! What role have you played in this treachery, Aithos? Where have you been for the last 24 hours?" Velion demanded, ignoring the confused guards.

"Treachery? What treachery?!" Aithos exchanged worried looks with Thanatos.

Velion did not seem amused. "This morning I received a note that the human girls were responsible for the attack on Gaius 5, and that they had evidence stashed in their apartment. I went to question them, but found them missing from their room. Trying to disprove the note I took the liberty to search their quarters only to find that the tip was correct. I discovered several incriminating documents that indicate the girls played a role in the militant attack. So I ask you again, where have you been?"

"You can't honestly believe that this girl had anything to do with Gaius 5! She's been confined to the palace since she arrived and under supervision, no less! How could she have orchestrated such an attack without anyone knowing?" Aithos roared, the anger in his voice growing by the moment.

"Last chance, Son. Where have you been?" Velion looked livid.

Hoping to quiet the hostility Kira pushed past Aithos and intervened, "Velion, there is no time for this! I had nothing to do with Gaius 5 and you *know* that. Someone is clearly trying to make all of you think that my sister and I are traitors and I think I know who it is."

Velion did not respond immediately. He leveled a piercing gaze at Kira and stared at her for a long time before saying, "You have my attention, but I would advise you not to lie. You have one chance to prove your innocence."

"So be it. If you want to know where Aithos has been I can tell you. He was with me, on Earth. He agreed to arrange a meeting with me and my father, who was in possession of very important information." Kira could see that Velion was already dismissing what she had to say, but she pressed on, "I am not as distant of a relative as you think I am. My father on Earth wasn't my real father. Someone in the royal family is." She finished, hoping she caught his attention.

"What is this? Is what she says true, Aithos?" Velion asked, but he would never get the answer. Just as he finished his sentence a cargo container exploded, throwing everyone in the hangar to the ground and knocking Kira unconscious.

* * *

Coming to several minutes later, Kira looked around dazed. The room was hot and the air was thick with smoke. She couldn't make out any definitive sounds, as her ears were ringing so loudly that everything sounded like a dull roar. Trying to focus as her head swam, she was able to survey the damage of the hangar bay. Several of the guards nearest to the explosion were clearly wounded or dead, while the remaining people in the room were either unconscious or just now stirring. Kira searched for Aithos and was relieved to see that he appeared unscathed, despite being unconscious on the floor next to her.

Looking to her other side she noticed that Thanatos was also out cold, but looked no worse for the wear than Aithos did. Fighting a feeling of nausea, Kira tried to locate Velion, but regretted it instantly when she found him. He was conscious and was getting to his feet, but the fury in his eyes told her that he would not listen to her. He would not hear reason or believe what she had to tell him, even if it was true. Somehow the explosion just confirmed his suspicions of her, no matter how far off they were.

Kira stood up, trying not to topple over as she did so. Velion pointed at her and said something that she couldn't make out, but it didn't matter. She could tell by his expression that he fully intended to have her arrested and tried as a traitor, but she had no intention of letting that happen. Kaya was still at the mercy of Aeria, and there was no time to fix the mess here. Her only chance of getting to her sister in time was to escape.

Taking advantage of Velion's shaken state, Kira pulled in as much energy as she could, and with a scream unleashed the largest shockwave she had ever managed straight at Velion. The attack caught him off guard and sent him flying back through the hangar entrance into the corridor of the palace. Not wasting any time Kira dashed towards the auxiliary corridor that led to the royal hangar, where her ship was parked.

To her dismay there were four palace guards running in the opposite direction, most likely to investigate the source of the explosion. Again she amassed a wave of energy and unleashed it on the unwitting guards, blowing them back through the passage the way they had come. She tried to hold back so she didn't kill any of them, but there was no way to be certain she hadn't.

Making her way out of the long corridor, she spotted her ship at the other end of the hangar. Somehow the vessel was aware of her approach and was rotating to allow her aboard. Dashing up the ramp and rushing to the pilot controls, Kira frantically worked at the consoles. Trying to remember everything Thanatos showed her was impossible in such a rush, but there was no time to waste if she hoped to escape the palace. Deciding it might be best to just use the autopilot, Kira engaged it, hoping it would save her time.

As the ship powered up and began the lift off sequence, Kira felt a pang of regret at having left Thanatos and Aithos behind. There had been no time to raise them and even if she had, it would have only made things worse for them. At least by abandoning them, they would appear more innocent than she did, which might save them from whatever hell there was to pay for this incident. Someone was going to great lengths to make her look like a traitor, and after she rescued her sister, she had every intention of finding out who they were and who her real father was.

The ship's autopilot completed the lift off checks and was already guiding the vessel out of the hangar by the time anyone came after her. A few guards, followed by Velion, entered the bay just as the vessel engaged thrusters, propelling it up and into the atmosphere at blinding speed. She had managed to escape the palace, but her journey was far from over. She only hoped they didn't have enough time to scramble fighters from the Trident before she could make the jump to sub-space.

Deciding it might be best to get the navigation computer ready, Kira searched for the planet Draco on the stellar map. Thanatos hadn't lied when he said it was the furthest planet from the center of the galaxy. It was a small, dark planetoid about 25,000 light years away from her current position. The navigation computer estimated that it would take nearly two days to get there, even at full speed.

Kira input the jump coordinates just as the vessel broke through the upper atmosphere. By the looks of the scattered fighter formations around the Trident, Velion hadn't had enough time to alert them to her escape. At least something was going Kira's way. Breathing a sigh of relief, she initiated the jump sequence once the navigation computer finished plotting a safe course. In the blink of an eye, the silver ship disappeared from view, unnoticed by the fleet nearby.

* * *

The trip to Draco was long, but Kira was grateful for the time alone to think about the recent turn her life had taken. Digesting the news about her father took some time. She regretted the harshness of her response, realizing that revealing the truth must have been hard on him as well as her. She couldn't imagine having to tell her children that they were really the offspring of a stranger from a different world, especially if she couldn't tell them who it was or why they had been abandoned.

Was she really just the puppet in some stranger's scheme to overthrow a kingdom? How could that be? It seemed impossible, yet, she knew her father hadn't lied. It really did explain some things, if she thought about it. She always felt different growing up, somehow always knowing there was more to the world than her people had taught her. And her mysterious ability to use Tythonian royal technology suddenly made much more sense.

If she was the descendant of one of the council members then who was it? Could it have been Aithos? He did show a level of familiarity with her that the others hadn't, but if that were the case then why was he so surprised by the news? Surely it couldn't have been an act. What about Velion? He had appointed her to the council despite the protests of the others, was it because he knew she was his daughter? That didn't make sense either. He hadn't been any more aware of the location of Earth than the rest of them. If she really thought about it, none of the men on the council made sense. Did Kronus have another child that the others didn't know about?

Kira shook her head, dismissing the thoughts. The never-ending questions were giving her a headache, and she knew she should really be preparing for what was ahead. The navigation computer indicated that there was only an hour left before she arrived on Draco, and there was no telling what sort of resistance she would encounter when she got there. Would there be guards? It was a prison planet after all, so it was almost certain that there would be, and what of her sister? How would she know where to look for her? If only she had Aithos with her; then she could track her sister's holodisk, assuming Aeria hadn't taken it away from her.

Thinking of Aeria drove Kira nearly to madness. She had never particularly cared for the woman, but what she did was unforgivable. Trying to execute her and then kidnapping her sister was beyond recompense. She only hoped Aeria had left Draco already and wasn't waiting for her to show up. She felt comfortable enough in her armor, but Aeria was supposedly a remarkable warrior, undefeated and terrifying to behold.

That was the kind of trouble she hoped to avoid, although she wasn't certain how she would be able to do that forever. Even if she did manage to find Kaya, where would they go? Where could they hide? After the attack on the palace they would surely be hunted, and what of Earth? How would the accusation of her being a traitor affect her people and the way the council handled Earth? Would they change their decision, and end up enslaving them after all?

Kira sighed in exasperation. The situation was beyond repair, and thinking about it didn't seem to be helping. She needed to focus, she needed to calm her mind and plan her attack. Once the ship dropped from subspace she would scan the planet for life and determine the most likely place Kaya would be. Luckily she had taken Thanatos's advice by reading the owner's manual; otherwise she wouldn't have known she could do such a thing. In fact she had spent nearly four hours of the previous day poring over it, trying to learn as much as she could about the ship, in case she needed the knowledge. She discovered that the ship was equipped with several weapons arrays and about a dozen missiles, including one nuclear warhead.

She shuddered at the thought of such a destructive device being on board. Master Yu-On had taught her about them, showing footage of the devastation that they left behind. The kingdoms made an agreement that they would only ever be used as a last resort, and only by the authorization of one of the council members. Frankly, Kira was surprised Velion had entrusted her with one, but then again, she was supposed to be a council member. If things had gone according to plan, she would have been groomed to be just like the others, and would have been given dominion over a territory, and probably her own planet to rule. She couldn't lie that the thought was pleasing to her, but now it was just a dream. She doubted there was any way they would ever trust her again, even if they figured out that she was innocent.

Kira looked over at the navigation computer, which indicated she would be arriving at Draco in ten minutes. Breathing a nervous sigh, she stood to her feet and started stretching. If she was going to level a full-on assault on a prison, she would need to be limber. Luckily, she had managed to get some sleep the night before despite her anxiety, so she felt rested and ready to find her sister. She just hoped that she could avoid any unnecessary attention.

The final ten minutes of the trip seemed to drag on for an eternity, until the ship dropped from subspace and Kira was overwhelmed with the desire for more time to prepare. The first scans of the area indicated that there were no other ships in orbit above the planet, which alleviated some of her anxiety, but not all of it. Sitting in the pilot's seat and working at the control consoles, she scanned the surface and was surprised to find that the majority of the planet was completely barren. There were only two sections where any life was detected, and both appeared to be cities of sorts. *One of those must be the prison,* Kira thought, marveling at how minute both settlements were. One settlement was much smaller than the other and resided on the dark side of the planet, which was almost completely covered in ice. The other settlement was almost twice the size and resided on the bright side of the planet.

This made things easier for Kira. She had anticipated having more places to worry about, but if there were only two settlements, then that meant Kaya had to be at one of them. But which one should Kira start with? If she attacked the wrong one first, then the second one might have time to prepare for her arrival, reducing the chance she would find her sister before they called for help.

Kira closed her eyes and tried to think. Which one would Aeria have taken her to? If her ship dropped out of sub-space at the same place that Kira's ship had, then the closest and most logical settlement was on the bright side of the planet. It was the best rationale she could come up with, so she decided to just follow her gut. Taking a deep breath, Kira took control of the ship, beginning her descent to the planet.

The atmosphere of Draco was much thinner than the one on Tython, making the descent less jarring than her previous landing. As far as she could tell, the planet had minimal technology, which was surprising for a prison planet. She had expected there to be heavy security and a large military presence, but the council must have decided against such measures. As she approached the ground she started to understand why. The planet truly was primordial, filled with jagged mountains and volcanoes that were constantly erupting. It was a wonder that anything could survive on the planet, even with all the technology of the so-called Gods. Clearly this was a place where one was sent when they could think of no greater punishment.

Deciding that it would be best to land her ship away from the settlement, so as to hide her approach, Kira searched for a decent landing spot. This was no easy feat as the terrain around the settlement was anything but forgiving. She had to circle three times before she found an area large and smooth enough to set the ship down, and even that spot was precariously close to a nearby volcano. She would just have to be quick and hope that luck was on her side, because this would be a short trip if her ship was destroyed before they could escape.

As her ship touched the ground, Kira let out a long sigh as she readied herself for the task at hand. Pulling up the scans of the settlement, it looked like the entire thing was encompassed by a gargantuan wall that was several yards wide. The area inside the wall was nothing more than a few hundred small buildings, and a couple of large complexes. At the far end, there seemed to be some sort of mining operation as there were large industrial buildings and expansive underground tunnels. The scans also indicated that the ambient temperature of the settlement and outlying areas was far hotter than either Earth or Tython. For a planet with little to no atmosphere, that was impressive.

Deciding there was nothing more she could do to prepare, she walked to the back of the ship. Taking a deep breath, she opened the rear hatch and was instantly blasted by the hot air outside. Squinting in the extreme heat, Kira stepped out of her ship.

Humid. Hot. Suffocating heat and vapor. The smell of sulfur and fire. Kira looked around at her surroundings as her heart sank. How would she ever find what she was looking for in this place? All around her was a dark, burnt, jagged landscape with little light except for the orange glow of molten rock far below her. The heat was unbearable and the smoke stung her eyes. She walked a few feet and looked down into a crevasse to her right. A hundred feet below her she could see a wide river of molten rock splashing and gushing slowly down the mountain side. The heat rising from it was enough to make her eyes water. She looked away towards her left. Her eyes followed the rock wall up until she had to crane her neck to see the peak of the mountain she had landed on. The top of it was hollow and was emitting an ominous red glow. All along the face of it she could see more molten rock spewing out and running down conduits like rivers of fire. Occasionally she heard explosions as more molten rock tore through the nearby mountainsides, spraying ash and steam.

She could feel fear creeping into her mind. She had never been to a place like this nor had she ever imagined such an unforgiving landscape. It was no wonder the others were so afraid of it; but there was no choice. Something very precious was here and she needed to reclaim it. Kira tried to remind herself of the important task she had set out to accomplish, but the vaporous air and unbearable heat clouded her mind. She tried to search for a clear path towards the settlement, but there was no easy way to get there. She would have to put her jumping skills to work and hope that she didn't accidently fall into a river of lava or a hidden crevasse.

Shielding her face from the heat, she prepared to leap to the nearest flat area. Pushing off the ground she jumped high in the air, soaring nearly seventy feet to the nearby rock face. The humidity in the air skewed the image of the landing, and what had appeared to be a level plane, was actually a slanted and slippery rock face. When Kira's feet hit the glassy surface, she lost her balance and fell hard against the rock, propelling her into a downward slide towards a cliff.

Panic overtook her and without planning it, she closed her eyes and envisioned a rock wall. Immediately the slanted rock surface morphed its shape, forming a large wall at the end where the cliff had been. Kira slid hard into it, slamming her body against the unforgiving stone. Pain shot through her shoulder as she collided against the newly formed wall.

Heart racing and brow sweating, Kira's mind reeled from the close call. If she hadn't formed the wall in time, she would have fallen into a wide river of lava and her rescue attempt would be at an end. Why hadn't she thought of changing the stone earlier? She was able to mold rock to her will, so why was she risking dangerous leaps?

It had to be the heat. It was unbearable and was making it hard for her to concentrate. Closing her eyes again she envisioned a solid, level surface and before she knew it the slanted rock she was on shifted until it was level. Standing to her feet, Kira rubbed her shoulder. She would have a bruise there later, if she survived the day.

Employing her rediscovered resource, Kira focused on the jagged landscape before her. Closing her eyes she envisioned a long and flat pathway. Holding the vision, she moved her hands pushing and pulling the rock before her into a level pathway that she could walk on. Opening her eyes she was pleased to find that a long, level pathway had been molded before her. There were breaks here and there where the crevices were too wide, but leaping across those would be much easier than her previous attempt.

Relieved at the new path before her, Kira took off again. This time she moved a bit slower and gauged each jump with precision. With this tactic it took only a few minutes before she was close enough to see the outer wall of the complex.

To her surprise there didn't appear to be any guards patrolling the wall. As far as she could tell the entire area was unwatched, which gave her a moment of relief. She was afraid she'd have to fight her way into the settlement, but if there were no guards making her way inside wouldn't be a problem. From the look of the wall, it had been cut out of the surrounding rock, which meant that she'd be able to manipulate the stone and potentially walk straight through.

Grinning at her lucky break, she failed to notice a green object streaking across the sky that was headed directly for her. As she approached the wall the object came crashing to the ground right in front of her, kicking up dirt and rock, and knocking her to the ground.

Slowly recovering from the unexpected collision, Kira sat up. Blinking and coughing in the dust, she looked around to find the source of the impact. As the air cleared, it revealed a human-like figure crouching in a deep crater. Recognizing the figure immediately, Kira's heart sank in disbelief.

Standing up, Aeria let out a high pitched laugh, "So you managed to survive after all, half-breed? I should have known it was too easy. Oh well, killing you in a fight will be more fun anyways." Aeria grinned maliciously as she climbed out of the crater she had just made. Kira was at a loss for words. *Why was she still here? Did Aeria know she would be coming?* "Oh, what's wrong? Cat got your tongue? Or weren't you expecting me?" Aeria grinned maliciously.

The shock finally wore off and Kira got to her feet. Seeing the goddess again made the fury flow through her veins again. "What have you done with my sister?!" she shouted, leveling a spiteful gaze at Aeria.

"Oh she's in good hands, don't you worry. You really ought to be more concerned with yourself right about now," Aeria replied, clearly enjoying the exchange.

Deciding that a fight with Aeria right at the wall might accidently put her sister in danger, Kira took Aeria by surprise and turned to flee. Dashing back the way she came she tried to get some ground between her and the settlement. Aeria did not pursue at first, but merely watched in amusement as Kira fled.

Aeria called out, "Did I scare you away?! Was it something I said?!"

Kira stopped following the path and veered off to her right. She didn't want to be near the walls, but she had no desire for Aeria to destroy her ship either. Leaping from one ledge to another she was able to gain a good bit of distance from both the settlement and the ship. Finally landing on a wide and solid plateau, Kira stopped and waited for the goddess to follow after. She knew Aeria wanted a fight, and wouldn't be able to resist following after her, especially when she thought Kira was afraid of her.

Just as expected, Aeria came after her, but what Kira did not know was that Aeria had the ability to fly, a fact that became abundantly clear when she arrived at the plateau, only to hover a few feet in the air.

"You seem surprised; does that mean silly old Thanatos never taught you how to fly? What a pity, that will take some of the fun out of killing you," Aeria jeered, clearly reveling in the advantage she had over Kira.

"I wouldn't count on it, you psycho. I have no plans on dying at your hands," Kira spat back at her, readying herself to fight.

Aeria laughed and shook her head, "Silly little half-breed traitor thinks she's going to beat me, the goddess of war. If you insist on a fight, then I can oblige..." but Kira didn't allow her to finish. Launching herself directly at Aeria, Kira drove her knee into the goddess's midsection with as much might as she could muster. The attack was not expected and the force of it knocked Aeria out of the air, sending her flying into a nearby rock wall.

Despite her surprise, it didn't take Aeria long to recover from the attack. Standing, she glowered at Kira and said, "For that, I'll be sure to draw your death out." Letting out a scream of rage the goddess leapt forward, heading straight back at Kira, but she was ready. Waiting until the last possible second, Kira dodged Aeria's attack, countering by blasting her in the shoulder with a shockwave as she passed. The wave sent Aeria flying again, but this time she was able to recover before hitting another rock wall.

Landing hard several yards away, Aeria stood and laughed. "So you want to play with energy, do you? I thought we could spar for a while first, but if you insist." With that she twisted her face into a scowl and pulled her arms to her sides. Kira looked on in horror as the goddess pulled in the largest shockwave she had ever seen. With a wild look Aeria let out a roar, thrusting the enormous blast directly at Kira. There would be no dodging the attack, so Kira crossed her arms in front of her and ducked her head. Closing her eyes and gritting her teeth, she readied herself for the blast.

The wave hit like a freight train, knocking Kira back and throwing her to the ground. She slid nearly a hundred feet across the jagged mountainside before finally coming to a stop. Coughing in pain, Kira got back to her feet and tried to recover from the blow. Looking up just in time, she noticed Aeria starting to amass another attack. Without thinking, Kira pulled at the stone around her and flung a huge boulder straight at Aeria. The goddess failed to react in time and the boulder hit her in the chest, knocking her to the ground.

Kira tried to take advantage of her downed opponent by pulling at the ground again and sending two large boulders flying directly at Aeria; but neither would make it. With lightning speed, Aeria leapt to her feet and pulled out her twin blades, slicing through both boulders in a green blur.

Seeming to decide that the game was over, Aeria attacked again, this time with both of her swords. Moving at an alarming speed she closed the gap between her and Kira in a heartbeat, and started swinging the blades in a blind fury. Kira had no time to escape or counter so all she could do was dodge the attacks. Aeria's attacks were relentless, but Kira would not falter; each time Aeria swung her blade, Kira would move out of its path just in time.

Keeping this up was no easy feat as Aeria was much faster than Kira. Several times her blades came within a hair's breadth of hitting Kira, but none of them made contact. Finally one of her attacks overextended her reach, leaving an opening for Kira to counter. Kicking as hard and quickly as she could, Kira hit Aeria squarely in the chin, sending the goddess flying backwards.

Before hitting the ground, Aeria was able to flip herself over and land on her feet. Pausing for a moment, she stared back at Kira with more malice than Kira would have thought possible. Aeria tasted the inside of her lip and spit a large glob of blood on the ground. Kira could see that the blow had done more damage than expected, if only to the goddess's ego.

Recognizing the minor victory, Kira taunted her, "Seems you aren't immortal after all. You bleed like the rest of us."

Aeria didn't respond with words but instead did something completely unexpected. The goddess leapt into the air, flying up and away from Kira at breakneck speed. Once she had gained enough altitude she stopped and turned to look down at Kira. With an intense look of concentration Aeria started rotating with her swords extended to her sides, almost as if she were dancing in the air. Over and over she oscillated the blades in an elaborate fashion, gaining speed as she did so. Spinning faster and faster until the goddess became a blur of armor and swords.

To Kira's amazement Aeria started to glow brightly as she spun in the air. Without warning, massive green energy balls started shooting out from Aeria in all directions, spraying the mountainside around Kira. Each time a ball collided with the mountain an enormous, ground-shaking explosion sent debris flying in all directions.

Overcome with panic, Kira frantically tried to dodge the energy blasts, but she wasn't quick enough. Fleeing one green ball, she leapt into the path of another and collided with it. The explosion was bright and deafening, and the pain that came afterwards was beyond description. The collision sent her flying hard into the mountainside, causing her to black out.

A few moments later Kira came to. Her body screamed in agony, but she knew she had to keep fighting. Wearily she stood up, swaying in the extreme heat. Looking around at the blasted mountainside she realized that she had been thrown nearly a hundred feet, and was now surrounded by much more dangerous territory. There were rivers of lava on all sides of her and the ground under her feet was as sharp and jagged as glass.

The ash in the air burned her eyes as she searched the horizon for her enemy. Aeria was faster than expected and the steam rising from the lava made everything hazy. Squinting, Kira once again saw the green object she now knew to be Aeria streaking across the sky towards her. Aeria was screaming with fury and coming at full speed with her twin blades outstretched.

Clenching her teeth, Kira flexed her arms and with as much willpower as she could muster, she summoned two massive boulders from the jagged mountainside and flung them directly at Aeria. The look of fury on Aeria's face shifted to amusement as she dodged not one, but both of the boulders. Kira panicked and without thought, turned to her left creating a massive shockwave that propelled her backwards, out of Aeria's path.

Everything seemed to slow down as the adrenaline surged through Kira's veins. Flying backwards, she crossed both of her arms in front of her, envisioning a barrier. Immediately her armor responded and molded into a large metal shield that stretched from above her head, all the way down to her knees. She formed it just in time, because immediately after conjuring the shield, Aeria crashed into the mountainside with unfathomable momentum. The collision was so intense that the shockwave sent enormous chunks of debris hurtling in every direction.

Blocking the debris with the shield drove her

backwards even faster and hurtled her towards a slanted wall of jagged stone. Again, almost without thought, Kira used her momentum to flip her body gracefully through the air until her feet were pointed towards the wall. Landing hard against the stone surface, she clenched her leg muscles as tightly as she could and used the residual inertia to spring herself back towards Aeria.

Flying directly back at the goddess, Kira amassed a huge shockwave. Aeria turned to look half a second too late and Kira, with a scream of rage, unleashed the shockwave into the ground below. The mountainside exploded again, hurtling large boulders directly up at the goddess, who for once did not have time to react. With a look of terror, Aeria was thrown back in a blur of dirt and rock.

Kira landed next to the massive crater, and watched as the goddess disappeared beneath the spray of stone and rock. Panting and doing everything she could to stay on her feet, Kira stared at the massive pile of rubble before her, watching for any sign of blonde hair or silver armor. Everything seemed to go quiet as the rocks settled on what Kira hoped was Aeria's grave.

A few moments passed without incident, but before Kira could take comfort in her critical blow, bright green light started to shine through the cracks in the rubble and the ground began to tremble under her feet. Panicking, Kira swung her arms down and summoned a stone barrier from the ground before her, forming a wide wall of rock. As she did so the mound that Aeria was buried in exploded with green light, sending the dirt and rocks flying in all direction. With a scream of rage Aeria shot towards Kira's barrier. Lowering her shoulder the goddess crashed through it, colliding with Kira on the other side. The unexpected blow knocked the wind out of Kira and sent her flying several yards back, landing hard against the rocky mountainside.

Gasping for air, Kira tried to stand, but her damaged body screamed in protest. She had been thrown against the mountain too many times, and even her armor wouldn't give her the strength to stand. Only managing to prop herself up, she watched in terror as a dirt- and blood-covered Aeria marched towards her in fury. Her hair was caked with mud and the orange gleam in her eyes from the nearby lava made it look as though she was about to breathe fire. Kira tried to move away, but couldn't find the strength.

Frantically, she tried to remember back to her training. *What would Thanatos do in this situation?* Kira searched her mind as Aeria closed the gap between them, panting heavily as she marched. *Never forget your surroundings and use them to your advantage,* she could hear him say. *But I'm surrounded by lava and ash! What good is that?* she protested, but she didn't have to think about it for long before remembering that lava was just molten rock.

As Aeria quickened her pace and prepared to kick Kira in the stomach, Kira desperately pulled at the nearby lava stream. Immediately the orange liquid swelled and gushed over the nearby rock, rushing directly towards Aeria. Kira grinned, impressed with her quick thinking, until she realized that the lava was heading straight for her as well.

Aeria stopped mid kick, and with a look of horror, leaped away from the incoming lava. Kira gritted her teeth and tried to move again, but she still couldn't muster the strength. She knew there was only one thing left to do, so with closed eyes she amassed another shockwave and pointed it towards the ground beneath her. With an explosion of rock, Kira was sent flying up and away from the lava. This time she was able to swing her body around and land on her feet, although doing so made her realize just how damaged her body was. She knew she wouldn't be able to keep fighting for much longer.

Staggering to her feet, Kira looked around for Aeria. Through the steam and vapor Kira could see her standing several yards away and was surprised to find her cupping her hands over her left cheek. Squinting to make out the details Kira noticed that Aeria's armor was scorched in several spots from where the last shockwave had sprayed lava at her.

"What have you done to my face?!" Aeria roared as she pulled her hands away from her cheek. Through the steam Kira could make out several circular burns speckled across the left side of Aeria's face where the lava had melted her skin. With a look that was beyond fury, Aeria screamed, "You will suffer for this, half-breed! I was going to just kill you, but now I've decided to make you watch your sister die first!" With a wild look, Aeria turned away from Kira and prepared to leap into the air.

Kira knew that if she didn't stop her there would be no catching her. Mustering all of her strength she bent her knees and shot towards Aeria. Like a rocket she soared across the lava pool and before Aeria was able to take off, she readied her attack. With a scream of rage and pain, Kira bent her elbow and drove it as hard as she could into Aeria's shoulder, managing to take the goddess by surprise once again. The two of them crashed to the ground in a jumbled mess of dirt, metal and blood.

Kira's body screamed in protest yet again but she wouldn't listen. She had to protect Kaya if it was the last thing she did and there was *no way* she was going to let this clearly deranged woman get anywhere near her again. With a groan of effort she got to her feet and reached down to grab Aeria's ankle. With a great exertion of strength, Kira pulled hard on Aeria's leg and flung her into the nearby rock face. The already-stunned Aeria crashed into the stone wall, causing it to crumble on top of her. This time Kira would not hesitate to see if the goddess recovered. Amassing one shockwave after another, Kira unleashed a frantic barrage on the rock pile before her. The stone crumbled again and again as shockwave after shockwave hit it, until enough had been blown away that she could see Aeria again. With renewed fury, Kira hastened the speed of her blasts, blowing the stunned Aeria further and further into the rock wall behind her until she could no long muster the strength to stand.

Dropping to one knee a few feet from Aeria, Kira's head swam with exhaustion. She stared at the crumpled body of the goddess before her as she panted with fatigue. To her surprise the goddess started to stir. With a groan of pain, Aeria opened her eyes to look at Kira. With a wicked grin and a labored laugh Aeria whispered, "Is that... all you've got? How does it feel" –Aeria coughed and spat another glob of blood onto the ground- "to know you've failed your sister again?"

This time the wrath was too much to quell. Reaching out, Kira grabbed one of the goddess's twin blades by the hilt and turned it against her. Aeria's eyes widened in terror, but it was too late. With a scream of indignation Kira drove the sword into Aeria's chest, slicing through the armor and cutting through to the other side.

The goddess coughed and gagged as blood oozed out of her body. She tried to say something but it was no use. Kira let go of the sword and stood over her as she took in one last breath. Aeria's head slumped over and her eyes went lifeless. It was finished.

Kira stood there in the sweltering heat and humidity for a long time, staring at the lifeless body of the goddess before her. She felt strange, never having killed another person before. She felt a pang of guilt, wishing it hadn't come to this, but there had been no other choice. If she hadn't finished her, there was no telling what she might have done to Kaya.

A tear rolled down Kira's cheek as she bent down to close Aeria's eyes. In a quiet voice that was nearly drowned out by the erupting of a nearby volcano, Kira whispered, "I'm sorry it had to be like this. It wasn't that long ago that you saved my life, and now I've taken yours. I hope one day I can repay the debt." With that Kira turned and limped away.

* * *

The walk back to the settlement took quite some time as Kira's legs protested with each step. She wanted nothing more than to lie down and rest, but her task wasn't completed yet. Somewhere inside that settlement her sister was waiting for her, hopefully still alive. She had to be alive, there was no other option. All of this couldn't have been for nothing.

As she approached the exterior wall, everything started to go fuzzy. She tried to blink it away but as she did, stars appeared in front of her eyes. Swinging her hands at them she tried to swat them away, but they wouldn't leave. Stumbling over a rock, she collapsed to the ground with a thud. Everything went dark for a moment, and with great satisfaction she embraced the sweet nothingness. Just as she started to slip away something called to her.

"Kira!"

She was imagining things; she had to be. The exhaustion had finally gotten to her and she could no longer focus.

"Kira!!"

Clenching her teeth she fought the darkness. She fought the fatigue. Opening her eyes, she moved her arm under her and pushed herself off of the ground. Picking herself up took all of her strength but she knew she had to press on.

"Kira!" a voice called out from her left. Kira turned her head, causing everything to swim again. She had to be imagining things; had to be hallucinating. Running towards her was the image of a young girl with long blonde hair, dressed in a white and green gown. The gown was no longer as pristine as it had once been, now that it was covered in soot and ash.

"Kaya?" Kira managed, swaying as she tried to focus on the image before her.

"I knew you were alive! I knew you'd come for me!" the girl before her cried out, running up to her and embracing her in a tight hug.

"How? Where did you come from?" Kira asked vaguely, certain that this was a hallucination.

"I found her." Another, taller figure approached behind the blonde girl. Kira tried to look up at the figure but could no longer keep her balance. Crumpling to the ground she closed her eyes and gave in to the nothingness.

* * *

Kira opened her eyes and was confused to find herself lying on a bed inside of a small, dimly lit room. She tried to move but her body screamed in protest, nearly causing her to pass out again from the pain.

"Don't move, you've been badly injured," a somewhat familiar voice said over the roaring inside her head. Turning her head towards the source of the voice Kira was alarmed to find Pisus sitting next to her. He had a concerned look on his face as he gave a soft smile. "I suppose I'm the last person you expected to see, aren't I?"

"Where is my sister?" Kira suddenly remembered what she had been doing before passing out. Again she tried to sit up and again her body protested.

Pisus seemed amused at her attempts to get up. "Don't you remember?"

"Remember what?" Kira had no idea what he was talking about.

"I suppose you were pretty out of it when we found you. Your sister is just fine. She is on the bridge with Aithos, where I asked her to stay so I could talk to you alone." Pisus's smile faded.

"Talk to me? About what?" Kira asked curtly. Her head was throbbing and the conversation was only making it worse.

"It's important that you answer honestly. Did you kill Aeria?" Pisus asked, looking grim.

"She tried to murder me and was going to kill Kaya. I had no choice," Kira replied, unsure of what Pisus would do.

"Then it is as I thought. I cannot say I blame you for what you've done, but I'm afraid her death will only make things worse. There is no need to discuss this now, though, so try to get some rest. I'll do what I can to heal your wounds," Pisus finished, gently touching her arm to reassure her. Kira wanted to know what he meant, but the desire for sleep was too great to ignore. Closing her eyes again she drifted back into the nothingness.

Pisus sat back in his seat and watched as Kira

drifted back to sleep. A deep look of concern moved across his face as he did so and just as Kira's breath became rhythmic, a figure appeared at the door. Aithos crept into the room, trying not to disturb Kira's sleep.

In a quiet whisper he asked, "Is she going to make it?"

Nodding, Pisus responded, "She has unbelievable strength. I doubt anyone else could have survived the beating she took."

Aithos grinned with pride. "She is something else, isn't she? And to think she's half human."

Pisus fixed Aithos with a penetrating gaze and said, "I believe it is because she is half human that she was able to defeat Aeria. Their potential seems... limitless."

Aithos smiled again, "I was beginning to think the same thing myself. So what are we going to do with her and her sister? We can't take them back to Tython."

Pisus looked back at Kira and thought to himself for a moment. "I'll bring them to Thalon with me; I can keep them hidden there. They'll be safe until we decide how to proceed."

Aithos frowned, "Are you certain that's a good idea? You'd be risking everything by taking them in."

Pisus nodded, "I'm aware of the risks, but there is no other way. We are going to need them before the end and Velion will never think to look for them on Thalon. You are positive that you're the only one who can track the holodisks?"

"Yes. No one else knows how to read the frequency," Aithos assured him.

"For her sake, you better hope you are right. Set a course for Thalon, we will just have to hope fate is on our side," Pisus concluded.

"As you wish," Aithos bowed politely and left the room.

Pisus turned his gaze back to Kira and whispered, "I hope you're the savior we need, because you're all we've got."

EPILOGUE:

A tall figure appeared as if from thin air and looked down at the crumpled body of the blonde woman. His dark eyes fixated on the blade that was protruding from her chest and he shook his head in disappointment. Two smaller figures appeared in the same fashion, seeming to walk out of nothingness to stand by his side. They looked down at the body before them and seemed confused.

"My lord, what do you want us to do with the corpse?"

The taller figure laughed, and said, "Is that what you see? A corpse? *Tsk tsk.*" The two smaller figures glanced at each other, looking for some sort of explanation. Shaking his head again the taller figure said, "No, my foolish servants. She isn't dead, at least not yet."

Kneeling down beside the crumpled body, the taller figure pulled the sword from her chest and started to make a strange hissing noise. All around the body, black smoke oozed out of the ground and enveloped the woman. It hovered around her like fog, spinning and churning as the he continued to make the sound. Then, without warning, the smoke shot inside the woman's mouth and up her nostrils, filling her lungs with its essence.

Her body stirred, and jolted. Her eyes flew open and with a gasp of air she sat up. It took several seconds for her to regain her senses, but as she did she noticed the figures standing above her. Looking up at the tall figure she realized that she recognized him. With a confused look, she asked, "What... what happened?"

The man smiled down at her and said, "I'll explain later. For now, come. There is much to be done."

ABOUT THE AUTHOR

R.T. Edwins is a self-published author who lives in Minnesota with his wife and their dog and cat.

Additional Acknowledgements:

I'd like to thank the following people for their support. Without your pledges and belief in this story, this book would not have been possible:

Brad Carlson
Kevin K.
John Thrumston
Tina-Marie Ledom
Lisa Beise
Jacob Pangburn
John Heine
Greg Marshall
Travis Clarke
Jennifer Pederson
Jillian Dressel
Sabrina Cooke
Jason Schmidt

53295096R00181

Made in the USA
Middletown, DE
26 November 2017